THE AMSTERDAM LAWYER

René Appel

Translated from the Dutch by Josh Pachter

Genius
Book Publishing

Milwaukee Wisconsin USA

Published by:
Genius Book Publishing
PO Box 250380
Milwaukee Wisconsin 53225 USA
GeniusBookPublishing.com

ISBN:

230220 Trade

Chapter 1

"I'd like to make sure the defendant fully understands his situation," Judge Vreeland said.

He peered at Barry Wesseling, David Driessen's client, who sat slouched in his chair despite David's express instructions to maintain an engaged and interested posture. So far, the only indication that the teenager was following the proceedings at all was an occasional shake of the head at the prosecution's accusations.

The judge turned his attention to David, who nodded to show that *he* at least was hanging on Vreeland's every word. This, David knew, was what Vreeland wanted and expected. A good relationship with the presiding judge was always a step in the right direction.

"Mr. Wesseling," Vreeland resumed, "according to your case file, at approximately ten thirty on the evening of Thursday the 27th, you entered

Mr. Van Wijngaarden's home." Barry had repeatedly denied this—during his original questioning by the police, again before the investigating magistrate at his pre-trial hearing, and yet again here in the courtroom. "According to Mr. Van Wijngaarden's statement, his doorbell rang, and he opened the door to find a young man on his front steps. That man roughly pushed him aside, hard enough that he fell against the wardrobe in the foyer and was knocked temporarily unconscious."

David swiveled to look at Van Wijngaarden, who was sitting in the dead center of the courtroom's first row of benches.

"When Mr. Van Wijngaarden regained consciousness, the intruder was gone—along with his laptop, which had been sitting on a side table in the foyer. Meanwhile, Mrs. Tienaert, who lives across the street from Mr. Van Wijngaarden and was at that moment leaving her home for the purpose of walking her dog, saw a young man rush out of the Van Wijngaarden house and run off down the street with an object approximately the size and shape of a laptop computer clutched in his arms. She immediately called 112. There was a patrol car in the vicinity, and the officers were able to apprehend a suspect. Mrs. Tienaert identified that suspect—you, Mr. Wesseling—as the young man she had seen fleeing the Van Wijngaarden home. The case seems quite clear to me, but I understand that your attorney has another version of the events to offer—as defense attorneys are often wont to do."

Several spectators, including Van Wijngaarden himself, chuckled at this remark. David looked around the courtroom, and only now noticed the well-dressed man sitting about halfway back, motionless, staring straight ahead. There was no one on either side of him, and that seemed not to be coincidental. The man occupied not just his own seat but somehow seemed in control of the space around him as well. From a distance, he resembled David to a noticeable extent, though his hair was shorter and he wasn't wearing glasses.

"He has listed Mrs. Tienaert as a witness for the defense," Vreeland continued, "although she has already given testimony for the prosecution to the investigating magistrate. So, Mr. Driessen, you're up."

David stood and cleared his throat. "Your Honor, my client has been the victim of a series of coincidences, which unfortunately have conspired to make him seem guilty of a crime he did not in fact commit. Neither he nor I will deny that he was on the evening in question found in possession of a laptop belonging to Mr. Van Wijngaarden, and that he for that reason was arrested and charged by the police. But his explanation of how the laptop came into his possession differs significantly from the interpretation which appears in the case file you've referred to."

He felt a pair of eyes boring through his legal robes and into his back and had to resist the urge to turn away from the judge. There was no need to check, though. He knew it was his almost-*doppelganger* who was staring at him.

He went on with his defense. According to his own statement, Van Wijngaarden hadn't gotten a good look at his attacker. The light in the foyer had burnt out, and everything had happened so quickly. No evidence of Barry Wesseling's presence in the house had been found. No fingerprints, nothing whatsoever.

"Now, of course you ask yourself, if my client didn't steal the laptop, then how did it come into his possession? I refer you back to his original statement to the police. He happened to be walking down Mr. Van Wijngaarden's street when a stranger ran up to him and thrust the stolen computer into his hands."

David could feel the incredulity in the courtroom. But he was holding his strongest card in reserve. All he was doing now was attempting to sow the seeds of doubt.

Under Dutch law, the prosecution had to establish guilt "beyond a reasonable doubt." But how much doubt was "reasonable"? That depended on the case, and especially on the judges. It would be easier in the U.S., where jury trials were standard. Here in Holland, though, a panel of three experienced judges heard criminal cases, and their standard of "reasonableness" was perhaps more stringent than would be expected from a dozen average citizens. Still, there were times when a one-percent doubt was doubt enough. And the creation of doubt was David's forte.

"When the police arrested my client," David went on, "he immediately turned the laptop over to them. 'Here,' he said, 'this isn't mine, and I don't want it.'"

Judge Vreeland, his voice dripping irony, interrupted: "In your opinion, then, Mr. Driessen, your client was simply acting like a responsible member of society. It's a shame that the arresting officers don't remember his having used those words."

"With your permission, Your Honor, I'll remind you that neither officer *denies* that he said them, either. Quoting from the testimony given to the investigating magistrate, 'Yes, he might have said that.'"

Behind him, David heard someone in the courtroom clap his hands together, twice.

Judge Vreeland scowled. This was his courtroom, and his case. "Order," he demanded.

"Now I come to the crucial point." David paused to glance around the room. Even Barry was finally sitting up straight. "And with this point in mind I have taken the admittedly unorthodox step of calling Mrs. Tienaert as a witness."

Judge Vreeland and his two colleagues seemed annoyed by this turn of events. A delay in transporting Barry from the House of Detention to the courthouse had caused the proceedings to begin almost an hour later than planned, and the judges were clearly concerned that their entire day had been thrown off schedule.

Mrs. Tienaert was a small, pudgy woman, her gray hair pulled back in an old-fashioned bun. She shot a quick glance at the defendant, then turned her attention to the judges. She seemed afraid that Barry might attack her, right here in the courtroom. David could understand her nervousness, given his jailhouse conversation with his client. "If I could get my hands on that bitch," Barry had growled, "I'd—"

Once the introductory formalities were concluded, David began his questioning. He was reasonably sure of himself. This would be a nice little performance. If only Mirjam could be here to see it, but it was at least two years since the last time she had accompanied him to court at his invitation to watch him argue a case he'd been confident he would win. She no longer seemed interested in his work. She was always busy with the children, her girlfriends, shopping, the housework…

David walked the witness through the events of the evening in question, as if they were rehearsing their lines for a TV show, from the moment she snapped the leash to her dog's collar to the moment she'd called 112 from her cell phone. David didn't get the impression she knew that Emiel, who did occasional legwork for him, had oh-so-casually asked around the neighborhood about her, and had learned that she was apparently rather short-sighted, especially after dusk.

"Mrs. Tienaert, you say that you saw the defendant leave Mr. Van Wijngaarden's house with a laptop computer in his arms."

"That's right."

"And you told the police that you could identify the defendant as the man you saw."

"Yes."

"How exactly were you able to recognize him?"

"By his face and his clothing."

"And what was he wearing?"

"A sort of jacket, a jogger's jacket or whatever they call it, with a hood."

"Was he wearing the hood up or down?"

"Up, but I could still see his face."

"What color was it?"

"The jacket? Dark. Dark blue, I think."

"You *think*, but you're not *certain*?"

"Well, no, not really." Mrs. Tienaert seemed to shrink in on herself.

"And you say you were also able to identify his face." David knew that the police had only shown her a photograph of Barry. There hadn't been a lineup, with half a dozen men, all of roughly the same type, standing in a row and the witness hidden away behind a one-way mirror. They hadn't seen the need in such an apparently cut-and-dried case.

"That's right." She glared at Barry. "You don't forget a face like that."

"A face like that. You know, it looks like a perfectly normal face to me, the face of a pleasant young man, but never mind that. How far away from him were you, when he came out of Mr. Van Wijngaarden's house?"

"I don't know. He was on the other side of the street."

"That's fine. With your permission"—David turned to the judges—"I'd like to try a little experiment." He slid four large photographs from a portfolio that leaned against the defense table. Each picture showed a young man in an athletic jacket with the hood up over his head, and all four of the men were similar in appearance. David stood about twenty-five feet from Mrs. Tienaert, held up the first photo, and asked her if the person in the picture was the defendant. As he expected, she was visibly uncertain.

"I can't really tell. The picture's too dark."

"Yes, but it was *after* dark when you claim to have seen my client come out of Mr. Van Wijngaarden's house carrying a laptop. I've been there myself and checked, and there's no streetlight near the house."

He held up the second photo. "What about this one?"

"Well, I… I don't… yes, that's him."

"Are you certain?"

"Yes, I recognize him."

"But this is a picture I found on the internet," said David, "and had enlarged. I have no idea who the man is, but he's got nothing whatsoever to do with this case."

ↀ

Mirjam stretched luxuriantly, like Sally the cat, arms and legs fully extended. If only she, like Sally, had someplace to dig her claws.

She rolled onto her side and ran her gaze down the length of Steven's body. Why was sex so much better in the middle of the afternoon? Was it the excitement of having stolen an hour from Steven's busy workday?

Whatever the reason, it was delicious to have this time together, to deliver herself so completely to her lover while the world outside ceased to exist.

Stolen moments. Fairy-tale moments.

She'd met Steven seven months ago when she'd interviewed for a job at his company, a successful advertising agency. She hadn't gotten the job—but she'd gotten Steven. Had she seduced him, or had it been the other way around? No, they'd seduced each other.

Once, she'd teasingly wondered if the walls of his apartment were soundproof.

"Ask the neighbors," he'd said.

Now, he turned toward her and held up the bottle of Pouilly-Fumé. "Another glass?"

She saw that he was still hard and smiled mischievously.

He repeated his question.

"No," she said, "better not. I have to get the kids from school."

"You think they'd notice? You've got mints in the car."

"All right, fine, then." A glass of wine after sex was like the cherry on an ice-cream sundae, a crowning touch now that they'd done everything they could think to do in bed.

Well, really, everything *Steven* could think of.

For just a moment, an image of David flickered through her mind, an unwelcome intrusion that almost spoiled her pleasure.

Steven sat up beside her. It had taken her a while to get used to his waterbed, to the way it magnified every movement. Now, though, it was perfect. With him, at least.

They clinked glasses and drank.

Mirjam held the wine in her mouth, letting its full flavor accumulate before she swallowed. "I'd better get in the shower."

"It's only a quarter to three," Steven protested.

"I have to be there by three thirty. Last week, I was almost fifteen minutes late."

He stroked her arm, her breast, drew a tender circle around the nipple. "Don't you want to come before you go?"

"Eeuw," she said, and shook her head sharply, as if to shake off the bad pun.

"I've got the whole afternoon," Steven whispered. He licked her earlobe hungrily.

With difficulty, she pulled away from him. "I don't," she said. "Unfortunately."

"Can't your husband fetch the kids for once? You're not his servant, are you?"

"No, but I'm not *yours*, either."

He laughed, got out of bed and drank some wine. "Are you sure?"

☙

As David approached his Alfa Romeo, a figure appeared out of nowhere, blocking his way. *Like a special effect in a movie*, he thought. The man was an inch taller than him, but otherwise similar in body type, maybe just a bit broader in the shoulders.

"Nice car. A little old." The voice had a trace of an Amsterdam accent.

David recognized him at once. It was the man from the courtroom, the man with the penetrating eyes. "Still rides great," he said.

The man stepped aside, as if granting David permission to continue on his way. "Well done in there," he said.

"Thanks." David took a business card from his wallet and handed it over.

Without even glancing at it, the man tucked it away in the inside pocket of his expensively tailored suit jacket. "I know who you are," he said. "David Driessen, from Starrebeek & Starrebeek. I should introduce myself, but I don't have a card. Hein Wesseling." He extended a hand.

The name startled David for a second. "Wesseling?" he said. The man's grip was strong. "Any relation?"

"Yes."

"I don't see a family resemblance," said David. Hein Wesseling was still shaking his hand, and it seemed certain that the physical contact would continue until the man was ready for it to end.

"Same father, different mothers. He's my half-brother. He's also an idiot—all this trouble for a cheap laptop. By the time he's twenty, he'll have a record and have ruined his future."

David shrugged.

"You don't agree?" the man said.

"I do, but—"

David checked his watch. He was already running late for a meeting, but he'd texted the office before leaving the courtroom.

Hein Wesseling seemed not to notice that he was in a hurry. "You saved his ass, as they'd say in the States. The old lady completely caved, and there wasn't anything the cops could do about it. I could see it on the judges' faces: Barry'll walk."

"I hope so."

Finally David was given his hand back. He nodded a formal goodbye, got in his car, and drove off. In the rear-view mirror, he could see Hein Wesseling watch him go.

Naturally, he'd recognized the name. Wesseling had been arrested a couple of times for major drug-trafficking offenses. Nowadays he seemed to be involved in an assortment of shady real-estate deals in Amsterdam. Not exactly a hoodlum, perhaps, but definitely playing on that side of the fence, pulling strings from somewhere in the background. Two arrests, David thought, but no convictions.

⌘

"How was your day?" he asked after Bas and Romy were snuggled away in their beds. He'd read Romy her usual bedtime story—she was probably too old to be read to, but she wasn't ready to let go of that part of her nighttime ritual just yet. Sally lay in his lap, purring contentedly.

"Oh, fine. Went to my parents'. Nothing new with them." Mirjam barely looked up from her book.

She'd seemed distant lately. Maybe that's why she didn't ask him about *his* day, or maybe she wasn't really interested. Maybe *he* ought to show more interest in her, instead of relying on his usual clichéd question. A few weeks ago, he'd read an article in one of the women's magazines she occasionally bought. "Ten Sure-Fire Ways to Keep the Home Fires Burning," it was called. The title had caught his attention. The article talked about marriages that had lost their spark. No major problems, no irreconcilable differences, no conflict, just entropy, the inevitable dwindling of passion. Eventually, what was once new and exciting becomes ordinary—that was the article's basic premise. Three women were interviewed. They talked frankly about the decline of their marriages. David remembered one of them saying, "He's become my friend, my best friend—and who wants to go to bed with their best friend?"

Mirjam turned a page. When she read, she always wore a serious expression, her brow furrowed, as if she was thinking, "Say *what* now?" He watched her read. Maybe, if he paid enough attention, he'd be able to figure out what was bothering her. He could imagine the conversation if he just came out and *asked* her:

Is something wrong?

No, what could possibly be wrong?

I don't know. I just thought maybe you had something on your mind.

No, it's nothing. I'm just wondering if Romy's really ready for ballet lessons.

Sure, he could ask, but he knew she'd only avoid the real issue, whatever it was.

He opened his newspaper but continued watching his wife over the top of the page.

The women in that article weren't having affairs and didn't seem to *want* them—at least, that's what they said. But what about Mirjam?

He suddenly felt less sure of himself, less sure of her. She hadn't been keeping up with her household responsibilities lately. Yesterday, he'd wanted to make himself a cup of coffee, but they were out of pods.

And at that moment the thought popped into his mind, as suddenly and unexpectedly as Hein Wesseling's appearance this afternoon. A clear and unavoidable suspicion, ripe with frightening implications.

What if Mirjam…

What if Mirjam had… found someone else?

More and more, it seemed to him that her mind was elsewhere. What if it wasn't simply that their marriage had grown stale, worth preserving only for the sake of the children? What if she'd taken a lover, someone who'd found a way to reignite Mirjam's fire?

Shit.

She turned another page, and a faint smile danced across her lips.

He began to formulate his opening statement.

Mirjam, I think we need to talk about…

It seems to me that you…

Do you think our sex life has gotten less…

No, even if there *was* anything to his suspicions, she'd just deny it. It was pointless to even raise the question. She'd simply accuse him of mistrusting her.

All he had was the vaguest suspicion, fed by his perception that the intensity of their relationship had begun to fade.

Perhaps he could ask Emiel to do a bit of discrete investigation, to lay his fears to rest. This was, after all, the same type of situation he faced almost daily in his law practice, and in the final analysis it was *facts*, not guesswork, that mattered.

Chapter 2

The woman, perhaps forty years old, her color unhealthy, her hair wispy, her drab clothing hanging loosely on her rail-thin body, gave the impression that she was nothing but skin and bones. Unlikely that she was capable of the level of violence she was accused of.

He was on call this weekend and had gotten the assignment from the Public Defenders Bureau at eleven fifteen. On Sunday morning! When he told Mirjam, she'd first just glared at him, then huffed off into their bedroom and lay down.

"It's part of the job," he reminded her. "I have to go. I'd much rather do something with you and the kids. Just the four of us, go someplace fun."

No reaction. He sat on the edge of the bed and laid a calming hand on her thigh, but she gave no acknowledgment of his presence. At least she didn't push him away. Even the smallest victories were still victories.

"It's my on-call weekend, you know that."

He suddenly felt queasy, as if he'd eaten something well past its expiration date and might need to puke. Without another word exchanged between them, he went out to his car.

∞

"Mrs. Rijkhof, we need to talk."

She nodded, whispered a few inaudible words.

David waited several long moments, his eyes fixed on the woman who sat across from him, cringing in her chair.

He knew little more than that she'd been taken into custody this morning after one of her neighbors had called the police. Her husband had apparently been seriously wounded. Aggravated assault, or possibly attempted murder? To look at her, she didn't seem dangerous enough to hurt the proverbial fly.

"What happened?" asked David.

All at once, a torrent of words gushed out of her. "I couldn't take it anymore. It was too much, too awful. He was always complaining, always mad, I never did anything right. We've been married for eight years. He wanted children, but it just didn't happen, and he blamed me. He blamed me for everything. It was crazy, the things he accused me of. If the hot water heater broke down, I must have done something to it. If a trash bag split open, I filled it too full, or put something sharp in there…"

There was more. Bad weather when they took a vacation? She must have picked the wrong place to go, or the wrong time of year. No cold beer in the house? It was her job to see they didn't run out. If a road crew had the street torn up and he couldn't find a place to park, *she* was the automatic target for his uncontrollable rage.

David tried to get a word in, but her litany continued. Being given the opportunity to talk about it was probably therapeutic for her. You saw that in this kind of case. Ordinary people driven by circumstance to extraordinary action were often happy to have done what they'd dreamed of, what they'd visualized as the only possible solution to their problems. As she went on, he jotted a few words on his legal pad: "provocation… psychological abuse… straw/camel's back."

In each of his cases, he made notes from the very beginning. They often turned out to be useful later, when he structured his defense.

"And then this morning I just couldn't take it anymore," said Mrs. Rijkhof, her voice louder now, giving her words an extra measure of importance. "It was so silly… he said his coffee was too weak, but I made it exactly the same as always. I was standing there in the kitchen, and then he said that, about the coffee being weak, and I'm too stupid to even make a decent cup of coffee. And then I—"

She looked at him for the first time. There was neither sadness nor regret in her eyes, only anger, burning anger, a fire her actions hadn't quenched. She took several deep breaths and released them, calming herself, but never finished her sentence.

David waited. In his experience, this was the best course of action to take. Prime the pump, then let them unburden themselves at their own pace. Sometimes it all came out in a minute, sometimes it took an hour—and some of them never told their stories at all. Of course, he was never entirely certain whether or not they were telling the truth. But that wasn't really important. He wasn't after "the" truth, just a part of it, the part that would be of most service to his client. Like in Barry Wesseling's case.

Sometimes David heard the cautious, critical voice of what—for want of a better word—he called his conscience, but he was usually able to convince it to hush. Obviously Barry was guilty as hell, but David loved the challenge of getting them off, innocent or not. It was all a game, defense versus prosecution, and all that mattered was who came out on top.

The woman asked an unexpected question: "How long will I have to stay here?"

David explained the procedure. The preliminary hearing before the investigating magistrate, the waiting period in the House of Detention, how long it was likely to take before the case was called, what would happen if she were eventually found guilty. "You can pick your own counsel. That can be me, if you'd like, but you're free to get someone else. It's entirely your decision."

Honest citizens like Mrs. Rijkhof generally didn't know any attorneys, other than the superstars who showed up on the television news, so in fact there really wasn't much of a decision for them to make.

She shrugged.

"Fine, then. With your agreement, I'll continue to represent you."

"I guess."

"Do you feel up to finishing your account of what happened?" he asked carefully, as if afraid that too straightforward a request might bowl her over.

"Well, he said that, about the coffee." She picked up her tale of the events that had brought her to this place. "And then everything just went sort of red…"

"Red," David wrote on his pad.

"We were in the kitchen, and there was a frying pan on the stove, a big iron one. There wasn't anything in it. I made meatballs in it last night. Of course, he didn't like them. 'Crap,' he said. So I picked up the pan, by the handle, you know, and I—I hit him in the side of his head." She lifted an imaginary pan, cocked her arm and swung. "Just once, with everything I had. I didn't know what I was doing. It wasn't really me. I wouldn't have thought I'd have the courage, but I couldn't stop myself. I didn't have a choice."

"I understand." David wondered how this meek, frightened little woman could have managed such an act of violence, but apparently the years of frustration had finally given her a strength he wouldn't have suspected her of possessing. Still, he noticed something odd about her story, but he couldn't quite put his finger on it, let alone figure out how to use it, whatever it was.

"He fell to the floor, screaming. I didn't even hear him, but that's what Maaike told me. She was just outside our door."

"And who is Maaike?"

"My neighbor. She called the police." Mrs. Rijkhof looked around her. "And now I'm here. It's all his fault."

"How's he doing?"

"Concussion, a possible skull fracture."

"That's pretty serious," said David.

"I'm sorry he's not dead."

❧

She'd parked Bas and Romy in front of the TV, then called Steven from David's study. Somehow, that made it all more exciting. First she looked through a few of her husband's files. Nothing unusual. The standard legal mumbo-jumbo. Cases she knew nothing about. There was a yellow Post-It stuck to the desk lamp. All it said was "Emiel." She'd met Emiel once. A lowlife, stank of cigarettes.

"Can't you get rid of the kids?" asked Steven. "Drop them with friends, a girlfriend? My calendar's clear. You're more than welcome. I've got a bottle of prosecco in the fridge."

"I can't just dump the kids, not on a Sunday. Anyway, David'll be home in an hour, two at the most. It'll freak him out if we're all gone."

It was foolish of her to have called Steven. She should have known this was what he'd suggest.

"You can't make it work?" He sighed. She could almost feel his breath in her ear. "I want you," he said. "I want you *now*. I can't wait." He kept on, as if his words, his vision of their future together, the castles he built for them in the air, would change her mind.

"It's impossible, Steven. Not today." She did her best to ignore the stirrings of passion that flickered inside her.

"Then why did you call me?"

"I wanted to hear your voice."

"You want me just as much as I want you, Mirjam, but when it comes down to it, you back away."

"I'm not trying to tease you."

There was silence on the other end of the line.

"You still there?" she asked.

"Of course." Steven paused. "Come on, Mirjam. Figure something out. Make up an excuse. I'm longing for you. I haven't seen you for three days."

"I miss you, too. I wish we could—"

She heard a scream from downstairs. There was a pregnant silence, and then one of the children—probably Romy—began to wail. "I think somebody's being murdered," she said. "I have to go."

✿

David brought her a huge bouquet from the flower shop in the Beethovenstraat.

"I hope this makes up a little for leaving you alone again with the kids," he said. He wrapped his arms around her.

Mirjam wriggled free from his embrace. "They're beautiful. Let me put them in water."

For the rest of the day, David tried to be as agreeable as possible. Fortunately, there wasn't another callout—one more would have meant all out war. He played board games with Bas and Romy, set the table, cleared up after dinner, loaded the dishwasher, carried the empty bottles and old newspapers out to the bins on the corner, helped the kids put away their toys—what with birthdays, Sinterklaas, Christmas, surprises from the grandparents, sometimes it looked like a tornado had raged through the house—and tucked them in bed.

Mirjam was watching a reality show about a group of spoiled Dutch youngsters who were left without adult supervision in a Third World country. Cold water showers huddled beneath a bucket with pinholes punched through its bottom. Strange meals cooked over campfires, maybe snakes or grasshoppers. The toilet nothing more than a hole in the floor of a rotting shack. A cup of brackish water in place of toilet paper.

He retreated to his study, turned on his computer, and checked his e-mail. Emiel had written from Crete, where he was vacationing for a couple of weeks. He hadn't had time before he left to launch a preliminary investigation into Mirjam's possible misconduct, but he enclosed an estimate of what it would cost. David couldn't write this expense off to the firm. Approximately four thousand Euros—a good deal more than he earned in a month. Maybe Emiel would give him some sort of frequent-flyer discount. *Come on, Emiel, I throw a ton of work your way.* He pulled the Post-It from his desk lamp, balled it up, and tossed it in the trash.

David logged into his online banking and checked his balances, but he already knew what he would find. He was two months behind on the mortgage—thank God Mirjam's parents had been willing and able to loan them enough cash, interest-free, to keep them afloat. They were going to need a new furnace before winter. And Mirjam was agitating to install radiant floor heating throughout the house. "These are the original, first-generation radiators," the HVAC guy had said. Then, doing his best to sound encouraging, he'd added, "Top of the line. They'll last forever, if you want them to." The old ones also had those damn sharp edges. Not long ago, Bas had banged into one of them during a play fight with a friend, and they'd had to take him to the hospital. Four stitches in his forehead, and he might wind up with a scar. "Those stupid radiators," Mirjam had said.

Of course, upgrading their heating would be ridiculously expensive. You'd have to take up the floors, go through the walls. "But Thera has it," Mirjam had said. "It's wonderful." He'd barely managed to avoid quoting one of his father's favorite old chestnuts: "Yes, and if Thera jumped into the canal, would you jump in after her?"

When they'd bought the house, David had assumed that Mirjam would go back to work as soon as both kids were in school. In fact, she'd committed to doing so—but after applying first for a sales position at an antique shop in the Nieuwe Spiegelstraat and then at an advertising agency in Zuid and failing to be hired for either job, she didn't want to be reminded of her promise. Whenever he tried to discuss their financial situation with her, she made some excuse to delay the conversation. And he didn't dare force the issue, since it would be immediately obvious where the problems lay and who was responsible for them. Their mortgage—and the additional loans he'd taken out, which Mirjam knew nothing about—hung like albatrosses around his neck. Soon, he'd have to hit Maarten Starrebeek up for a raise. Why hadn't he been made a partner? He'd been of counsel for almost seven years now, yet Maarten insinuated at regular intervals that he still considered David a rookie who hadn't yet mastered the intricacies of the practice. Meanwhile, his son Paul—the second Starrebeek in Starrebeek & Starrebeek—had only been with the firm for five years. David had checked the vacancy listings in the *Advocatenblad* from time to time, but so far he hadn't taken the step of actually applying for a position elsewhere.

He pushed the folder aside with a muttered "Fuck!"

It was quiet in the house, deathly quiet. As still as the grave. At this moment, Mrs. Rijkhof was probably stretched out on the bunk in her cell, kept awake by the cries of the stumblebums who'd been locked up to sleep off their drunks someplace where they wouldn't disturb polite society. Maybe she was feeling free at last and saw her cell as preferable to the mental prison she'd been confined to by her husband's unceasing rage.

David listened to the stillness. Something had to change, to get him in gear. He needed *something* to happen. Without any conscious thought on his part, his fingers tapped out the URL of a poker site on the keyboard. He stared at the log-in screen for a long time, his body vibrating with excitement. Then he got up and went to the bathroom. But he returned to his desk and typed in his username and password. Maybe tonight he'd have better luck. A hundred Euros. If he lost that much, he'd call it a night.

Shit, how many times had he made that exact same promise and failed to keep it?

He'd been doing so well, had stayed away from the seductive sites for almost a year—without the crutch of therapy. He'd actually shown up for an intake appointment at the Jellinik addiction clinic, but had ultimately decided not to undergo their treatment, convinced he could defeat his demon on his own. And he was *doing* it, damn it!

He shut down the computer.

He thought he could hear it heave a sigh of relief.

Chapter 3

Barry walked. Excellent. David hadn't expected anything less, but he still took pride in the ruling. This was the way things were supposed to happen. Almost ninety percent of the cases that came before a judge resulted in convictions, a grim statistic. In his summation, he'd asked to have the arrest expunged from Barry's record, and that request had been granted. But now he couldn't reach his client to deliver the good news. Barry seemed to have moved from his address of record, and his cell number, at which David had previously been able to contact him, was now out of service. He couldn't even leave a voice mail.

Hein Wesseling, he thought. Why not get in touch with Barry's half-brother? Continued efforts to reach Barry directly seemed pointless, but the idea of calling Hein was... intriguing. Sitting at his desk with his eyes closed,

David could visualize Hein Wesseling as he'd seen him in his rearview mirror when he'd driven away from the Palace of Justice parking lot. Was his desire to talk to Barry really just an excuse to get in touch with Hein? Was he hungry for more of the older brother's praise?

After placing calls to several of his colleagues, David finally came up with a listing, but he didn't dial it right away. He opened another case file but found that he couldn't concentrate on it. He looked absently out the window for a time, then punched the number he'd tracked down. The phone was answered instantly, as if someone at the other end of the line had been waiting for his call. "Hello?" In the background, he could hear the sounds of a busy café.

"Is this Mr. Wesseling?"

"Would you state the nature of your business with him, please?"

"I have some important information for his brother Barry," said David, "but I can't seem to reach him. I thought maybe—"

"Oh, it's you, D Squared." And then, apparently directed at a waiter: "Is that coffee coming, or are you still picking the beans?"

David wasn't sure he'd heard him right. "D Squared?"

"Sure, David Driessen, two Ds."

"So this *is* Hein Wesseling then?"

"Who else?"

David shrugged, and realized the gesture was meaningless over the phone. Wesseling asked about David's important information.

"Two words," David said. "Case dismissed."

"Well done, then. Congratulations."

"Thanks."

"I won't forget this."

David wasn't sure what importance to attach to those words. Could they be the onramp to a position with Wesseling's usual attorneys, the best-known firm of criminal advocates in The Netherlands? He could just imagine himself fielding Matthijs van Nieuwkerk's probing questions on *De Wereld Draait Door*. It seemed advisable to respond as modestly as possible. "I just did my job," he said. "I was hired to provide my client with the best possible defense."

"Where'd you get this number?" Wesseling asked.

"From an acquaintance."

"What acquaintance?" Wesseling demanded. When David didn't reply at once, he asked again, "Who was it?"

"I promised I wouldn't identify him."

"Bullshit. Obviously I need to know who has my private number. This is not a good time to fuck with me."

"But I—"

Wesseling interrupted him. "There are places where I draw a line, David, and you can believe me when I tell you that those are lines you don't want to cross." His voice had taken on a sharp edge.

David considered what he already knew about Wesseling, added in the man's appearance and voice, and came to the same conclusion. It wouldn't be a good idea to get on Hein Wesseling's bad side.

"It was one of my colleagues," he acknowledged.

"Ah, then I think I probably have an idea."

David wanted to ask who Wesseling suspected, but decided to keep his mouth shut.

☙

Lucas and Selma, Selma and Lucas. They'd emerged from the womb almost simultaneously and had been inseparable—their names often pronounced as a single word, Lucas-and-Selma, Selma-and-Lucas—until, in the third grade, their teacher worried that they were becoming too isolated from the other children and moved them into different classes.

As fraternal twins, they were seen as two halves of a larger whole and, at first, that was more or less the case. As they grew older, though, they grew more independent, developed their own very different personalities, but the connection between them, forged *in utero*, remained unbreakable and unshakable. As toddlers, they developed a private language that no one else understood. As far back as Lucas could remember, Selma had always been the weaker of them, and he'd always had to back her up, support her, help her. Sometimes it seemed as if they'd only been issued a set amount of mental ability, of which he'd been blessed with the lion's share.

When they turned fourteen, there came a period when Lucas' love for his sister was no longer enough to protect her from a world she saw as increasingly threatening. Excessively insecure, Selma began to cut herself. No one knew it at first, since she was able to keep the wounds and scars hidden from view. When it finally came out, Lucas couldn't understand what she was going through and felt powerless to help. It took more than two years of therapy before Selma finally mastered her self-destructive impulses, but her fragility never left her.

In Lucas' opinion, all twins were Siamese twins. If Selma developed a crush on some boy, Lucas felt betrayed and hurt. It wasn't the pain of watching the object of your desire reject you for someone else. No, not that, it wasn't jealousy. But he always felt that Selma's boyfriends weren't good enough for her.

And he knew that she felt the same way about him and his romances. She was overly critical of Annefleur, with whom he'd gone to Spain on a brief vacation. During that trip, he'd realized that they really weren't right for each other, after all. "The only person who could ever live up to your standards," Annefleur spat during their breakup fight, "is your sister."

His sister, who now huddled pitiably on her bed. The last few months—ever since what he thought of as "the fatal event"—had been hard on her. Lucas had proposed a visit to Finland, where their parents lived—their father worked at the Dutch embassy in Helsinki—but she'd refused. She didn't want them to know what had happened, and told them she had to stay in Amsterdam for summer school. Lucas, who played on his college baseball team, wouldn't be traveling north this year, either; he didn't want to miss even a practice, let alone a game. Besides, he needed to be there for Selma.

At first he hoped, maybe even expected, that she'd pull herself together, that the psychic wounds would slowly mend—like the cuts of six years earlier. But it didn't seem to be happening. Maybe after the court case and the inevitable conviction, maybe then the healing would begin. But that was still a long way off. Tomorrow was the pretrial hearing before the investigating magistrate. He wanted to be there for Selma to lean on, but his presence was not permitted. The accused's attorney, a Mr. D. Driessen, had requested the hearing. Lucas had googled Driessen's name and found nothing out of the ordinary.

He flipped open his folder and scanned the brief newspaper stories for the hundredth time. None was more than a few lines long. They trivialized the importance of the case, but the true impact of what was described in such cold, businesslike prose was enormous. Since it had happened, Selma had completely abandoned her studies. All she did was watch television, though Lucas had the impression she wasn't paying any real attention to the images on the screen. He hoped that a sufficiently heavy sentence would set her on the road to recovery.

∾

"I didn't know we were having a party. Did you order this?"

Mirjam held up the magnum of Moët & Chandon she'd just unpacked. "What are we supposed to do with this much expensive bubbly? It's not like we have anything to celebrate, not if you look at our bank balance."

"Crazy, that much champagne," David said. "Of course I didn't order it."

"Well, who, then? Bas, stop! If Romy wants to watch that, she can watch it. It's none of your business. Just put down the remote. It's Romy's turn to pick, you know that."

"You didn't buy it?" It struck David that *someone* must have ordered the champagne in their name, and eventually they'd get billed for it. Not too long ago, he'd had a case where some guy had charged a ton of stuff to his ex's credit card, everything from pizzas to dresses. Maybe this was some dissatisfied client's mean-hearted way of getting back at him? He remembered Robert De Niro in *Cape Fear*, playing an ex-con terrorizing the family of the attorney—Nick Nolte?—who'd defended him.

"You stop that right this minute, Bas! What did I tell you? If you can't behave, you're going to get a timeout."

"Bas, you listen to your mother," David backed her up.

"I don't need any help," Mirjam snapped. "I handle them by myself every day when you're not home."

David swallowed an objection. The corner of an envelope peeked through the packing peanuts. Mirjam apparently hadn't noticed it. He fished it out, a plain white envelope, nothing written on it. Inside, a simple note, which he read and understood in the blink of an eye. He passed it over to Mirjam.

"'To D Squared from HW,'" she read. "Is this some sort of code? What's it supposed to mean?"

๛

"Beer for you, David?"

"Sounds good." They'd briefly considered bringing the bottle of Moët & Chandon along but decided that'd be too showoffy. *Look at us, we've brought enough champagne for everyone, aren't we special?*

David had considered calling Hein Wesseling to thank him for the generous gift, but he had the impression Wesseling didn't appreciate unsolicited contact, certainly not for something like this. Should he bring the bottle to the office? Why bother? Why should they get to share in his good fortune? After all, *he'd* done the work for which the pricey champagne was a thank you.

Uncle Bastiaan handed him a bottle and a glass. This was an old-fashioned birthday party, the kind David rarely attended anymore, with all the adults sitting in two circles, the women in one and the men in the other, only one dissident woman daring to join the menfolk.

The conversation skipped from the latest political crisis to the Euro to the economic belt-tightening called for by these troubling times to the prime minister's cabinet to the upcoming European Union meeting in Brussels. David nodded from time to time, made occasional comments of the "on the other hand" variety, innocent enough that no one would be likely to take offense. A year and a half ago, at Uncle Bastiaan's own last birthday but one, two of the guests lit into each other over Geert Wilders' anti-Islamic ravings. The argument had gotten completely out of hand, and the combatants had wound up in a nose-to-nose screaming match which had almost degenerated into a fistfight before someone finally managed to break it up.

David couldn't hold his peace, though, when one of the neighbors started in on the two Moroccan boys who'd run down and killed a pedestrian in a zebra crossing while fleeing from the police after a bungled supermarket robbery. It wasn't clear which of them had been driving the moped and which had been a passenger. Each accused the other of being the driver.

In the absence of an eyewitness, the judge had no way to determine who was lying, and so he'd ultimately convicted both of them on a significantly lesser charge. Reckless operation of a vehicle, if David remembered the news reports correctly. They'd each gotten a couple of months' prison time, which under the circumstances seemed completely proper. With credit for time served awaiting trial, both boys went straight from the courtroom back out onto the streets.

It turned into one of those conversations everyone at the office bitched about, thanks to the unavoidable conventional wisdom that transformed perfectly reasonable judicial decisions into fuel for irrational layman's head-butting. A few years ago, a cousin of Mirjam's had attacked his defense of an alleged pedophile who'd been charged with abusing two children in his neighborhood. There was little actual evidence, and the testimony supported a contention that the detectives had put words in the kids' mouths. But all of David's usual arguments—which boiled down to the simple fact that, in a democracy, everyone has the right to the best possible defense—were scoffed at.

"But it's scandalous," said the neighbor, looking pointedly at David. "They did it, they're guilty, so they ought to be punished. It's a question of justice."

David knew that he was now expected to respond, but he also knew it didn't matter what he said; they'd all gang up against him.

He heard the chatter from the women's circle, caught the words "Botox" and "injectables" and "stretch marks." He would have much rather involved himself in that trivial conversation, although it probably wasn't trivial to the women, certainly not to the over-forties. Not long ago, he'd watched Mirjam stand naked in front of their bedroom mirror. She'd cupped her breasts in her hands and pushed them up. "Think I should have them lifted?" she'd asked. He'd said he thought they were as lovely as ever. "Not after two kids," she'd said, turning to examine herself from behind. "My ass is starting to sag, too." He'd remembered a line from an old crime movie. "Mir," he'd smiled, "I love that ass. Now get it into bed before it hits the floor."

"What do you think, David? You're an insider."

"Ah, sorry, I drifted off. Think about what?"

"They should be found equally guilty since they were in it together."

"No such thing as 'group guilt' under Dutch law," he replied. "Only individuals can be tried, and only individuals can be punished for their individual actions. So there's no such thing as 'you're equally guilty, since you were in it together.' Only one of them was driving, so only one of them can be held responsible. And that's the one who can be punished."

"Okay, but each of them's blaming the other, so you don't know which is responsible. Doesn't that make them *both* responsible?'"

There were murmurs of agreement. "Both responsible… put 'em both away… both of them."

David shook his head. He knew he'd never be able to explain it to them, but he couldn't stop himself from trying at least to clarify the principles of his profession. "Say the perpetrator is sentenced to eight years. If the two of them share the responsibility, then they obviously have to share the sentence, and each of them gets four years. That means that the one who's innocent spends four years behind bars for something he didn't do. We can't allow that to happen. It goes against our sense of justice."

"Maybe *your* sense of justice, but not mine," said the neighbor. "They should just tell the truth about which one was driving."

"But a suspect has the right to remain silent," David said. "No one can be forced to testify against himself. That's just the way the law *works*."

"Yeah, but—"

"—and if you don't like the law, you suddenly want to ignore it, at the same time you think we ought to crack down harder on crime!"

"Defense lawyers always find a way to weasel around the real issues," said a man David hadn't met before tonight. They'd been introduced and shaken hands, but David couldn't remember his name. "You've always got your escape routes handy, your little excuses and exceptions and technicalities. You get hard evidence thrown out because the cops shouldn't have been listening in on some crook's phone calls, or you get a killer off with that 'diminished capacity' bullshit, or—"

"Every defendant has the right to the best possible defense."

"And it doesn't matter whether he's guilty or not?"

David felt the tension building in the room, but he wasn't about to back down. "It matters to the court, but not to me. I have to do the best I can for my client, use every legal maneuver that's available to me, expose every weak link in the chain of evidence. My clients have the right to expect that—from me, and from the system."

"And if you *know* they're guilty? At least *then* you'll agree they deserve to be punished?"

"It doesn't matter whether I agree or not." He thought of Barry Wesseling. "The only thing that matters is that the evidence against them has to be one hundred percent watertight. And even if it is, I'm obliged to try my best to discredit it. That's my *job*. If I don't want to do it, I shouldn't be a defense attorney."

"So you'll help a criminal get away with it, even though you *know* he did it."

"In principle, yes," said David. "What I know is irrelevant. What's relevant is what the court believes. If the court has any doubts, who am I to say they should convict the man anyway?"

"If you did, you'd be a good citizen," said Thomas, Bastiaan and Josje's son.

"Maybe so, but I'd be a lousy lawyer."

"That's more bullshit."

Uncle Bastiaan made a placating gesture and asked David if he was ready for another beer.

"No, thanks, I'm driving."

"And if you get pulled over for drinking and driving, you're in for it," said Thomas. Then added, laughing, "Unless you've got a good lawyer."

That lightened the mood for a moment, until the neighbor resumed his attack. "Say you know someone's committed a murder—"

"I see mortgage rates are going up again," Uncle Bastiaan tried to head him off.

But the neighbor stood his ground. "—but you manage to get him acquitted, and then he kills someone else. *Now* what do you say?"

∽

David tried not to keep looking at the clock, but his eyes the and he saw that it was only two twenty. At six forty-five, his merche would ring. So, no more than five hours of sleep, tops. When they'd gotten home, he'd suggested a nightcap, but Mirjam said she'd already had too much for a weeknight and would rather go straight to bed.

"Just a quick one?" he'd insisted.

"Are we celebrating something?"

"Yes: love," he'd wanted to say, but he wasn't sure she'd find that worth drinking to.

He had some vacation time coming up in a couple of weeks. Jesus, he was ready for it. The office was running him ragged. They'd booked three weeks at a resort near St. Tropez and had paid half in advance. The complex, with its pleasant swimming pool, lay only half a mile from the coast. With a little luck, there'd be some Dutch kids there for Bas and Romy to play with.

Even when he tried not to think about it, he found himself thinking how hard it was not to think about anything. He tensed and relaxed his muscles in an attempt to distract himself, starting with his toes and working his way up. He concentrated on each individual muscle group, tightening, releasing, determined not to let himself cramp up from the effort.

He slipped out of bed as quietly as he could. When he was almost to the door, Mirjam groggily asked him where he was going.

"Can't sleep," he said.

"Take a pill."

"That's my plan."

Chapter 4

At least in part thanks to Investigating Magistrate Houtkoop's sonorous, gentle baritone, Selma Groothuis felt comfortable enough to describe the events of

the night of June 7-8. From time to time her emotions overwhelmed her, and she had to pause to recover. Her lawyer, Heleen ter Bruggen, obligingly offered her a handkerchief.

"So, when you left the café, you got on your bike, intending to head straight home?"

"Yes, it was after one in the morning and I… um, I had to get up early to study for an exam." A tentative smile flickered across her pale face. She didn't seem to have gotten much in the way of sleep in recent weeks.

Not the toughest of cookies, David thought. *Shouldn't be hard to break her.*

She was a decent girl. He almost felt sorry for her, but as Patrick Hamilton's attorney he couldn't permit himself that luxury. He'd have to do what he had to do in his client's interest.

Selma Groothuis came across as the good little student. On Saturday night, when her classmates were getting their crazy on, she reined herself in, knowing she'd need to spend the next day at her books. Heleen ter Bruggen—with whom David had crossed swords more than once—had probably coached her to bring up that exam. Heleen had a soft spot for society's weaker members, especially women, and *especially* women who'd apparently been victimized by a representative of that malicious species known as the male sex, who she saw as having one and only one mission in life, i.e., making women suffer. If the defendant was in fact found guilty, she'd immediately file a civil suit seeking substantial damages.

"And according to the statement you gave to the police, Patrick Hamilton suddenly appeared beside you."

She nodded.

"And then?" asked the investigating magistrate.

"I already told the police."

"But I'd like to hear it directly from you, please. And then Mr. Driessen will be given the opportunity to ask you some questions."

"Questions?" Her head jerked up, her eyes confused. "Why? What about?"

"To gather information regarding the offense for which his client has been accused. So if you would please just tell us what happened when Mr. Hamilton suddenly appeared."

"He asked if he could ride a bit with me." She fell silent and looked around doubtfully.

"Go on."

"And then we got to my building. I rent a little room in a house. And then he asked me if he could come up for a cup of coffee."

"And what was your reaction?"

"I said no, I was going to bed."

"And then?"

"He grabbed my hand and asked again. He was almost begging. I can tell you exactly what he said. He said, 'Come on, Selma, we're both alone in the world.' So then he came upstairs with me."

"You didn't find that strange, that he said 'we're both alone'?"

"No."

David made a note. If Selma Groothuis went on in this vein, she'd be making it easy for him. Pity. She seemed like a nice enough girl—but fragile, and her fragility would not protect her. *Au contraire.*

"And then?"

"It was okay, at first. We talked about a few courses both of us had taken, and how far along he was in his program. What he was planning to do over the summer…"

They'd talked about her summer plans, too, she said, though of course now she'd had to cancel them. Her voice was a drowsy monotone. After his practically sleepless night, David had trouble keeping his eyes open. He balled his hands into fists, digging his nails into his palms hard enough to hurt.

According to Selma, Patrick had sat on the edge of her bed, she on a chair a few feet away. He asked her to come sit beside him. At first, she demurred, but, when he insisted, she moved to the bed and sat. He asked if she had a boyfriend. No, she didn't. He didn't have anyone either. Then he said, "So, what's stopping us?"

"Did you understand what he meant by that?"

"Of course."

"And what happened then?"

"He tried to kiss me."

"And what did you do?"

Selma glanced at David for a moment, then looked away.

"Can you tell us what you did?" Houtkoop repeated.

"At first I could, um, hold him off, but he was stronger than me, and so… then I couldn't." She sighed, as if this part of the story was hard for her to admit. "He… he kissed me, and then he tried to put his tongue in my mouth, and he was tearing at my clothes." There was a silence that lasted for several seconds. "He unzipped my jeans and—"

"You didn't tell him to stop?"

"I *did*, but it was like he didn't hear me. He kept on, I couldn't stop him. And then, finally—"

Selma began to cry.

The investigating magistrate called a brief recess and had a glass of water brought for the witness. David had spent about an hour talking with Patrick. A sympathetic kid. It would ruin him if he were convicted. According to him, Selma *had* put up some token resistance when he'd kissed her. "But it wasn't like she really didn't want to, more like she was just playing hard to get, like she didn't want to give in right away but wanted me to work for it."

After the recess, Selma picked up her story. Patrick had ripped off most of her clothing and forced himself onto her and into her, although she'd tried to fight him off. But she wasn't strong enough to get away from him, and finally she'd stopped struggling, terrified he might start to hit her. Once he came, he got out of there almost immediately. Selma lay awake half the night. The next day, she told her twin brother Lucas what had happened. He wanted to find Patrick and tear him apart, but Selma dissuaded him. That afternoon, though, he brought her to the police station to file a complaint.

Then it was David's turn.

"When Patrick Hamilton told you he wanted to go up to your room with you, did you have any idea what he had in mind?"

Selma shook her head.

"That's hard to believe, Ms. Groothuis." David spoke so that his disbelief was clearly audible. "A girl of fifteen would have understood the situation. You must have been aware of Mr. Hamilton's intentions. Yet you *did* permit him to accompany you up to your lonely student lodging. Were you perhaps looking for company, for a bit of male companionship?"

"No," Selma said softly.

"But you agreed to allow him upstairs. We can only speculate as to your reasoning, but it would have seemed obvious to Patrick Hamilton." David paused. On the one hand, he hated to drag the girl deeper into a swamp of sorrow, but on the other hand he took great pride in his work. He saw an opportunity here, and he took it on behalf of his client. "And that's why he behaved as he did. Your invitation didn't give him explicit permission, but it did at least grant him *im*plicit permission to pursue your, ah, favors." David knew that Selma hadn't invited Patrick up; she'd simply *allowed* his visit, and there was a world of difference between invitation and permission. He was delighted when the investigating magistrate allowed his suggestive remark to pass without comment.

"Another point, which has unfortunately not yet been mentioned. I'm sorry to have to raise it now, but I'm afraid I have no choice." David wasn't the least bit sorry. In fact, he was enjoying himself, but he knew better than to seem too eager. "Ms. Groothuis, you were involved in a relationship for about a year, a relationship which ended not long ago. Is that correct?"

"I don't see the relevance," Ter Bruggen began, but Houtkoop cut her off with an abrupt gesture. This was between the victim and the accused's counsel, and her interference was inappropriate.

"Is that correct?" David repeated.

Selma nodded.

"Since the end of that relationship, have you had other relationships? Sexual relationships, I mean?"

"What does that—?"

"Answer the question, please," said Houtkoop.

"Yes, a few."

"Were they long or short involvements?"

"Short."

"One evening? One night?"

"Yes, that's right."

"One-night stands?"

"Yes," Selma whispered.

David saw Heleen fidgeting uncomfortably in her chair. From a straightforward rape, the case was devolving into an instance of consensual sex to which one of the participants in hindsight regretted consenting.

"The boys or men you had sex with—were they also students?"

"Yes."

"They attended the same school as you, I assume, as did Patrick Hamilton. And he perhaps learned of your, ah, 'availability' from them. That *is* the sort of thing boys will talk about, I remember that from my own university days. So Patrick might well have expected you to be as open to his advances as you were to theirs?"

"Stick to the facts, please, counselor," warned Houtkoop. "We're not here to deal in expectations."

"My point is that, given Ms. Groothuis' recent history, Patrick Hamilton could reasonably conclude that she would have no moral objection to another in her series of one-night stands."

David observed the slightest of nods from the investigating magistrate.

"And now a third point," he said. "Did Ms. Groothuis scream, or make any other attempt to call for assistance from the other students in the building? I note that she shares a kitchenette and bathroom with two other young women who have rooms on her floor."

Selma was silent.

"Did you scream, Ms. Groothuis?"

"It wouldn't have done any good."

"Why is that?"

"It wouldn't have stopped him."

"Another question," said David. "Why didn't you go to the police immediately, that very night or perhaps the next morning?"

She shrugged.

"You're an intelligent young woman, twenty-one years of age, so you must realize the importance of filing a complaint at the earliest possible opportunity. Why did you fail to do so?"

"I don't know."

David played his final trump. "Was it perhaps that it wasn't until after you'd talked with your brother—your twin brother, so I assume this was someone with whom you have the closest of connections—was it only after your conversation with your brother that you decided to interpret your sexual escapade with Patrick Hamilton as a sort of rape?"

❧

Mirjam was dozing, but she came awake when Steven asked her when exactly they were leaving for the south of France.

"You know when." She nestled up closer against him.

"And you'll really be gone for three weeks?"

"Yeah," she sighed.

"Three weeks," said Steven. "That's too long. I don't know if I can handle missing you for three weeks."

Mirjam leaned on one elbow and gave him a long, lingering kiss. "You'll be fine."

"Will you?"

"I'll have to be." Three weeks of playing happy family, three weeks of being the doting mother, and—most challenging—three weeks of pretending to be the devoted wife. It made her sick just to think of it. Her throat went dry, her stomach cramped.

"What is it?" asked Steven.

"Nothing. Never mind."

He rubbed her back and shoulders so tenderly a shiver ran up her spine. "Maybe I could drop by?"

"What?"

"I could take a long weekend, Friday to Monday. Get a flight to Marseilles—or is Nice closer? Rent a car, get a hotel room somewhere nearby."

"And then what?"

"And then you come to my hotel, obviously."

"No way," she said, but the idea had already lodged itself in her mind. It was barely possible, but it *was* possible, if she wanted it badly enough, if she was prepared to take the risk. "Don't be ridiculous. It's impossible." She could already feel the excitement. She and David and the kids in their little apartment and, not far away, in a hotel room, her own personal mystery guest.

"There's always a way. Make up some excuse, a girlfriend there in the area."

"David knows my girlfriends. He'd never believe it."

"Then pick a fight with him," Steven proposed. "A knock-down, drag-out fight, so bad you need a couple of days to get over it. You hear about that happening when people go off on vacation."

"He'd stop me."

"He'd try, but you wouldn't let him." Steven allowed a moment to go by, then whispered in her ear, "Because you'd know I was waiting for you."

❧

Mrs. Rijkhof had gotten some color in her face, which was odd, because the sun rarely penetrated into the House of Detention. She'd also begun to recover from the shock of her experience. Sometimes, life behind bars can actually do a body good.

The latest medical reports on Mr. Rijkhof's condition, though, weren't encouraging. He was getting worse, not better. It seemed probable that he'd suffered a brain hemorrhage, but further testing would be required before that diagnosis could be confirmed. The hope was that his decline would eventually reverse. If not, the Public Prosecution Service might decide to charge her with murder. In that case, mitigating circumstances would have less of an impact at sentencing.

"So," said David, "let's talk."

"Okay." She didn't seem especially eager to escape the solitude of her cell. Or perhaps it was just *his* company that wasn't welcome. If that was it, then why not?

"Your husband's not doing well, I hear."

She stared straight ahead, as if he was referring to an ordinary illness that had nothing at all to do with her.

"Let's hope he pulls through. It'll be worse for you in court if he doesn't."

No reaction.

David plunged into his rote speech. He had to know as much as possible about the background of the case and what exactly had transpired. This information would help him to present the best possible defense. He particularly needed to know the ways in which she'd been emotionally abused—"actually, 'terrorized' would be a better word"—by her husband, what exactly he'd said and done. Those details were of the utmost importance. "It's my intention to demonstrate that he provoked you, that in fact he forced you to attack him. His behavior trapped you inside a pressure cooker that sooner or later *had* to explode into violence. I'm going to tell the court something I'm actually not allowed to say but won't be able to avoid, which is that he basically *asked* for what he got."

Suddenly Mrs. Rijkhof began to talk. "That's true. Maaike always said she didn't know how I could stand it, why I didn't leave him, but, you know…. I knew he'd come after me and bring me back. I was so afraid of him."

"Right, right, Maaike, the neighbor. Did you have much contact with her?"

"Oh, yes. She knew exactly what was going on. If it hadn't been for her, then…" The sentence trailed off.

"Then what?"

Mrs. Rijkhof turned away from David. "I never would have had the courage."

A vague idea began to take shape in David's mind, an idea he didn't want to pursue, since it would pull the rug out from under the defense strategy he was planning. "The neighbor lady sympathized with you," he said. "You could unburden yourself to her."

"Yes."

"Now tell me exactly what happened on the morning you knocked your husband down."

Mrs. Rijkhof went back over her story again, her husband's mistreatment, the red mist before her eyes.

"And he screamed when you hit him?"

"Yes. It was so loud that Maaike, who was just coming up the steps, heard it."

"Right, that's what you told the police. A coincidence, that she was right there at the time."

Mrs. Rijkhof nodded.

"And when exactly did he scream? At the moment you hit him? After he hit the floor? When?"

"I'm not sure. I was all upset. It was lucky she was there."

Clear as daylight: Maaike had been Mrs. Rijkhof's guardian angel, but in what way specifically? David wanted an answer to that question, although he couldn't see how it could affect the case one way or the other.

∽

"This Is Hein Wesseling."

David didn't react.

"Is that David Driessen? Yes? Okay, listen up."

"I'm listening," said David. He found himself trembling with anticipation. Hein Wesseling was calling *him*? He couldn't imagine why, but it had to be something important.

"For some stupid reason, the cops have picked me up. I'm in custody. I figure you can be here in half an hour, and I don't want to spend a minute more in this hole than I have to."

David looked at his watch. Almost five thirty. If he wasn't home by six, Mirjam would be pissed—especially tonight, since she had yoga.

"I'll be there in fifteen minutes," he said. "Where are you? The Elandsgracht Detention Center?"

Chapter 5

Lucas strode across the room and back, again and again and again. He found it absolutely impossible to sit still.

He wanted to smash something to smithereens with his baseball bat, but there wasn't anything handy, so he settled for pounding his right fist into his open left palm hard enough to hurt. It was probably best there was nothing breakable within reach. But something would *have* to break, soon. A *lot* of things were going to have to break. Maybe everything.

Selma had cried for a long time. Well, it wasn't crying, really, at least not at first. It was more a sort of moaning. But then the dam burst and the tears came, an endless stream, a river, a flood. He remembered a line from an old song: "I cried my heart out." That was what it was. She was crying her heart right out of her body.

It was worse than before she'd gone into therapy. He tried his best to comfort her, but she screamed "Don't touch me!" and pushed him away with strength he hadn't realized she possessed.

"But I—"

"Stay away from me!"

When at last she'd cried herself out, she sat there motionless, staring straight ahead, as if the world around her was an alien place and not *her* world. She looked past Lucas, through him, ignoring his presence. He knew she hadn't eaten anything all day. The chocolate croissant he'd brought her—he brought her one every morning, and there had been a time when she wolfed them down greedily—sat there untouched. The croissant was a reminder of the days when things were going fine for Selma. When she was busy with her studies, when she was happy, when she talked and laughed with her girlfriends and the cutting problem had been vanquished. Maybe he ought to let their parents in Helsinki know what was going on, though Selma had made him swear he wouldn't. He didn't understand why she didn't want them informed, but she'd made her objection fiercely clear.

He poured her a glass of water, and she sipped at it until it was gone. Then she stretched out on the bed. Quiet, motionless. Like a corpse. *Except she isn't dead*, thought Lucas. *She isn't dead, but she's not really alive, either.*

On the night of the rape, he'd *known* that something was wrong. He'd awakened in the middle of the night from a terrifying dream of his sister. He wondered if he should go over and check on her. His intuition when it came to Selma was usually right. The connection between them, forged in the womb, was undeniable.

The ticking of the clock on the wall beside her bookcase grew louder, accentuating the silence. Here at the back of the house, on the second floor, you couldn't hear the slightest sound from the street.

Finally, she sat up and told him what had happened with the investigating magistrate.

"So that lawyer, Driessen, tried to make *you* look bad," said Lucas. "Like the whole thing was your own fault."

"Yes, that's what it came down to. As if I"—Selma took a tissue from the box beside the bed and blew her nose—"as if I was lying."

"What happened then? What did he say?" Lucas hated making her relive the traumatic hearing, but he had to know. In his own mind, there was no doubt: Patrick had brutally overpowered his sister, a textbook case of rape, that was a hundred percent certain. He knew Selma better than anyone. If that's how she said it had happened, then that was how it had happened.

"He acted like I brought it on myself, like I invited Patrick upstairs because *I* was the one who wanted to have sex, like I'm some kind of slut who just goes to bed with everyone." She'd gotten past her reticence and rattled on about how Patrick's lawyer had twisted her words and gotten her to paint herself into a corner. "He made me feel dirty, like I *was* a slut."

It had all seemed so simple to Lucas. Patrick would be convicted. Selma might even have a right to punitive damages. It wasn't about the money, of course, but about making the son of a bitch *pay* for what he'd done. Lucas had talked the case through with a law student on his baseball team. The facts were clear, and Patrick was dead meat. But now everything had changed. "I want to talk with that lawyer," Lucas said angrily. "But first Patrick. We're gonna have a nice little chat."

❧

"They haven't got a thing on me," said Hein. "Absolutely nothing."

"So why are they holding you?"

"Well, you never know, you know? The police have gone all gay-friendly in their recruiting. One of the guards has been looking me over. I think he's interested."

Some of the clients David interviewed in the House of Detention seemed already beaten by the system. Others raged against whatever injustice they believed was being done to them. *How stupid can these cocksuckers be?* That sort of thing.

But Hein's response to his arrest was different. He was neither forlorn nor furious. In fact, he was practically glowing with energy. It emanated from his pores and reflected off his skin. David could feel it. Hein had a sense of *joie de vivre* that David wished he could capture in his own life. All the everyday annoyances, the slings and arrows of outrageous fortune—gone.

Life, enjoyment, squeezing every last molecule of pleasure out of the time allotted to us, that was the whole point, wasn't it?

David wasn't that fully evolved. Which was why he finally had to say something about that magnum of Moët & Chandon. "About the champagne, Hein. We appreciated it, but it really wasn't necessary. I get paid to—"

Hein cut him off. "You don't mind a special treat, do you? A taste of the good stuff, every once in a while, instead of the cheap supermarket crap you usually swill? Something to save for a special occasion, Saturday night, the kids in bed, your wife lounging in a bubble bath, smoked salmon on toast, maybe caviar—I don't like it, myself, it's overrated—but whatever, a nice bubble bath and a glass of bubbly. Then a little hot sex. You wouldn't turn that down, would you?" Hein gave him a friendly shot in the arm.

He licked his lips. "Yeah, but a gift like that could get me into trouble at work. If they find out—" He could hear the way he sounded, like a pompous ass, but he kept on talking. "We operate on the principle that—"

"Oh, fuck your principle, David. *My* principle is, you handled Barry's case like a star, and a star's entitled to a little something extra, a bonus. What's wrong with that?"

David shrugged.

"Can we forget the damn champagne," Hein said, "and get back to business?"

"Sure, of course." David pulled out a notepad.

"You don't need to write anything down. This doesn't even really have anything to do with me. It's about Theo Wildschut. You probably know who he is."

David nodded. Theo Wildschut had started out as a vendor in one of Amsterdam's open-air markets and clawed his way to the top of the real estate world. David wasn't up to speed on the details of his career, but he knew the man's dealings in property had ultimately enabled him to build a small empire of stalls in the Dappermarkt, one of the busiest street markets in the city, not to mention a number of cafés. Although Wildschut was also suspected of running a thriving trade in soft drugs, he'd never been arrested, let alone convicted. There were so many smokescreens swirling around his various activities that no one could be quite sure *what* exactly he was responsible for.

"Theo's a friend of mine," Hein continued, "a real pal. He'd do anything for me. And he's had some trouble with John van Bremen over the delivery of a couple of properties in the Rivierenbuurt. Now there's an issue with one of John's flunkies, some Turkish asshole, Halil, a nobody. He's in the hospital, had a little accident. Apparently got run off the road, cops haven't picked anyone up for it but they figure Theo must have been behind it. It's total bullshit, but there it is."

David understood how these connections and inter-relationships worked. In Amsterdam, everyone pretty much knew everyone else in the kinds of circles in which Hein Wesseling and Theo Wildschut traveled. "So why were *you* arrested?"

"They're hoping I know something about it," said Hein, and you could tell from his tone that anything he *might* know would never be revealed to the police. "They think they can get to Theo through me—they know they'll never get him on their own."

"Why you?"

"I don't know. Maybe because John and I have had some conversations lately. Nothing serious, just a misunderstanding we had to clear up about a couple of properties. Small potatoes."

"Were you some kind of liaison between Theo and John?" asked David.

"Me, a liaison? Absolutely not. Just because I had a chat with the guy, doesn't make me a liaison." Hein sounded irritated, as if he were offended by the thought. "I don't need to help these guys make their deals or whatever. They're grownups, they don't need my help."

David doubted that Hein was telling him the whole truth about his involvement in the conflict between Theo Wildschut and John van Bremen, but that wasn't important now. Sometimes it was best *not* to know all the details. That gave him more room to maneuver.

"We don't need to worry about that, anyway," Hein said. "There are two things we *do* need to talk about. First, I have to get word to Theo that I've been arrested."

"Not gonna happen," said David. "While you're in custody, the only outsider you can talk to is your attorney. Me. You know that."

"But you can call him for me."

"No way. Totally out of the question. You have no idea how much trouble I'd get into." David knew he had to draw a line in the sand. He could go so far for Hein, but no further. Lawyers who delivered messages for arrested clients were known as "carrier pigeons." It was usually impossible to prove anything against them, but there were those in the world of defense law who were gossiped about. And, before you knew it, you had a stain on your reputation that would never fade. On the other hand, the concerned parties were guaranteed to keep it on the down-low, so who would ever know?

"I'm sorry to hear you say that." There was indeed disappointment in Hein's voice. He scooted his chair closer and eyed David sharply, as if he wanted to hypnotize him with his gaze. "One little phone call to Theo would do it. You'll get paid more money than you can believe, David, just for doing me a quick favor, take you less than a minute. It'll be just between you and me, off the books, nothing you need to report to anybody, nothing to worry about. I'll give you Theo's cell number. It's a hundred percent secure, definitely not being tapped. If there was *any* risk at all, I wouldn't ask you. You know that, don't you?"

David couldn't hold back a sigh, but he tried not to let it sound overly dramatic.

"Don't you?" Hein leaned in even closer.

"Yes, of course. And I *want* to help," said David, "but, really, this is too much."

"Come on, D Squared." Hein said "D Squared" as if it were a pet name. "I swear, there won't be any trouble. It'll just be between you and me. One simple phone call."

David hesitated. He looked around the small interview room, but there was no sign of a camera or microphone. No, they wouldn't record a conversation between attorney and client in the House of Detention. If that ever came out, the Minister of Justice would be in deep shit.

"I thought you'd be a little more flexible." Hein smiled. "This is not that unreasonable for me to ask, is it? All you have to do is tell Theo I'm in here, and he needs to move the stuff out of Boomtown."

"Boomtown? What's that?"

"A little holding company, but it doesn't matter. Theo just has to know what to do."

"What's the second thing you wanted to talk about?" asked David.

"Well, obviously, I want you to get me out of here as soon as possible. They're only trying to scare my, ah, associates. They haven't got anything on me. They'll ask me a lot of questions, but it's just one big fishing expedition."

"Questions about Boomtown?"

"Exactly. See, I can really *talk* with you. You understand me." Hein grinned broadly, and David automatically returned the smile. "They'll tell the investigating magistrate they need to hold me while they investigate. But they know they can only keep me locked up if they actually *have* something, and they don't, which makes this whole thing bullshit. They have no legal right to keep me here. You agree, don't you?"

⌘

It was a mystery to David why Bas had insisted on fencing, when most of his friends played hockey. As a boy, David himself had played soccer, but maybe his proletarian genes were recessive, and it was Mirjam's upper-middle-class makeup that had been passed down to their son. Whatever the explanation, the fact remained that fencing was an absurdly expensive sport. Why couldn't anything in his family ever be reasonably priced?

According to Bas, today was the last practice session before summer vacation. David drove him to the facility in the IJsbaanpaad. It was all sports in this neighborhood, with tennis courts and several soccer fields nearby.

David was always uncomfortable when he watched Bas fence. Despite the protective clothing and precautionary safety measures, he worried that his son would get hurt. He could imagine bright red blood staining the white jacket. His mood improved, though, whenever Bas won a match or earned a compliment from his coach.

There were plenty of free spaces in the parking lot. Only a few of the kids Bas usually trained with were there with their chauffeur parents. The coach was among the missing, and no one had a clue where he was. After a wasted fifteen-minute wait, it became clear that there would be no session today. It turned out that, last week, the trainer had cancelled this week's practice, but apparently Bas and a few of the others hadn't heard the announcement.

"I wish you'd pay more attention," said David. "This isn't the first time something like this has happened."

"Philip and Dan didn't hear it, either."

"Just because they're not listening, that doesn't mean you…"

David swallowed the rest of the sentence. At least this would get them home sooner. Then, after dealing with the obligatory household chores—an obligation he'd volunteered for, he reminded himself—he could get some work done. Starrebeek had dumped a couple of extra cases on him.

℘

Of course she could have thought of it earlier, but the idea only came to her after David and Bas had already left the house. It took three phone calls to make the arrangements. Romy could play at Ariane's house for a couple of hours, and Mirjam would pick her up at two. After David dropped Bas at home, he'd go back out and do the grocery shopping.

Mirjam hated to use the clichéd expression, but there was no way around it. She had butterflies in her stomach. She tried to distract herself by freshening her makeup. Did what they were doing make the least bit of sense? Probably not, but who said everything always has to be sensible?

She hoisted Romy into her bicycle's kiddie seat. Romy complained that she wanted to ride her own bike, but that would take too long, and every minute mattered.

Ariane's mother invited her in for coffee.

"Thanks," Mirjam said, "but I'm in a bit of a rush."

She could read the question in Ariane's mother's eyes. *A rush? What's that all about?*

Mirjam smiled. How shocked would she be if she told her she was on her way to steal an hour with her lover? She gave Romy a kiss. "See you, sweetie."

℘

The house was empty, except for Sally, who rubbed her head affectionately against his leg. No Mirjam, no Romy. Did she decide to do the shopping herself? Then why hadn't she called him? He checked his cell. No, no missed call, no message, no text. He looked outside. Mirjam's bike wasn't there. "Where are they?" he asked the cat. "You don't know?"

Maybe *he* should have called when he'd realized today's fencing practice was off. Bas had gone home with Philip, a classmate. David had promised to pick him up in a couple of hours.

He fixed himself a cup of Nespresso, settled in with the paper and read an article headlined "American cook cooks wife."

"Los Angeles (Reuters)—A jury of six men and six women found American chef David Viens, 49, guilty of second-degree murder on Thursday. According to courtroom testimony, Viens cooked his wife in a vat of boiling water in order to get rid of the evidence of his crime." No mitigating circumstances *there*. "Viens testified that he bound and gagged his wife, Dawn Marie Viens, 39, to prevent her from leaving their home while he slept. When he awoke, Dawn was dead. He cooked her for four days." Four days! "'I let the water cool and poured it off,' the chef testified, and went on to admit that he then disposed of the body in a dumpster. The remains have never been found. According to Viens' testimony, this was not the first time he bound his wife with duct tape to prevent her from slipping out at night and coming home drunk and in a cocaine-induced stupor."

The article failed to address a key question: How big a pot do you need to cook a human being? Or had this other David first chopped his wife into more manageable pieces? He probably had experience butchering animals.

When he turned to an interview with the head of the Public Prosecution Service, David's interest waned. He found himself with an unexpected free afternoon, but something was bothering him. He couldn't decide what it was. He called Mirjam's cell but got her voice mail. He left a message.

Mirjam…

David could see her sitting across from him at breakfast that morning. She'd seemed perfectly normal. Not in the best of moods, but she never *was* a morning person, least of all with the kids sitting there pestering each other. He'd suggested they give themselves a date night sometime soon, arrange sleepovers for Bas and Romy, have dinner someplace nice, take in a movie, grab a nightcap in a café, and have a meeting of the minds, so to speak, back home in bed.

"Maybe we should," she'd said, but she hadn't seemed enthusiastic.

Emiel would be back next week. Maybe he'd come up with something. That would mean more expense, though. The phrase "professional courtesy" wasn't in Emiel's vocabulary. How sick would that be, paying to have his own wife shadowed?

When he came home from work, David sometimes remembered to ask with a show of interest how her day had gone, what she'd been up to. She always had plenty to report, but it was never all that interesting, except when she'd been to see her parents. He considered calling them now to see if she was there but decided against it. What if she wasn't? His in-laws flew into panic mode at the slightest sign of anything wrong. He could already hear Mirjam's father's reaction: "My God, she's not home? Where could she have disappeared to?"

What did she *do* on an ordinary weekday? Take the kids to school, shop, cook supper, drop in on a girlfriend for coffee, read the paper, more shopping, read a book…

She'd been working her way through the same book for weeks now, Sylvia Helmoed's *Eyeshadow*, with an illustration of a huge, wide-open, heavily made-up eye on the front cover and a photo of a thirty-something blonde on the back. Didn't really seem like Mirjam's cup of tea, but there it was on the end table beside the sofa.

David stared at the eye. It seemed to want to tell him something, but he had no idea what.

It was a quarter to one. David fixed himself two cheese sandwiches and drank a glass of milk. It didn't often happen that he was home alone for this long. He could stretch out and go through a couple of case files, but instead he wandered aimlessly around the house.

What if something had happened? He could imagine Mirjam pedaling along the Willemsparkweg with Romy in the child seat. A driver roars out of a side street and—no, anything like that and he'd have gotten a call.

He went up to his study. Calling Theo Wildschut turned out to be no big deal. He picked up the phone without even thinking about it. Wildschut was grateful for the call. "I won't forget this," he said. "What goes around, comes around. You'll see."

He slid a folder from his briefcase. Simple matter: A woman who'd been arrested for shoplifting. Already scheduled for court. Noteworthy that the woman's husband was a bigwig at the ABN Amro Bank. He had an impressive name, probably in and of itself enough to earn him a hefty annual salary: Van Middelheim thoe Harchem. They lived in the Prinses Margrietstraat. Not too shabby, Amsterdam's Gold Coast. You wouldn't think this was a woman who needed to steal, but she'd been caught with ten pairs of panties in her purse. And she had a record. Eighteen months ago, she'd gotten a stiff fine for stealing five bras. She always helped herself to a nice assortment of colors and sizes. Next year, fifteen or twenty teddies?

David hadn't shut the study door. From downstairs, he heard Romy's excited voice, rattling on about Ariane's collection of My Little Ponies.

He headed for the stairs, and Mirjam spotted him when he was only halfway down. She seemed surprised.

"You're here," she said.

"Didn't you see the car? Practice was cancelled. Bas is at Philip's."

She hesitated. "Nice. You been home long?"

"Almost two hours. Where've you two been?"

"Romy was at Ariane's, and I went into town."

"Stores crowded? Did you buy anything?" He tried to keep it as light as possible.

"No, just did a little window shopping."

"You want me to cook?" he offered. "It's been a while."

In the early days of their marriage, he'd done his fair share of the cooking. Once Mirjam stopped working, though, she'd taken full command of the kitchen.

"Sure. What's on the menu?"

"I'll surprise you."

Mirjam smiled. "That means Indonesian."

He kissed her. "How'd you guess?" Bami goreng was his specialty, and it was easy to prepare: cut up some chicken and pan fry it with vegetables, boil the noodles, mix it all together with a packet of Indonesian seasoning. And, wonder of wonders, Bas and Romy both actually *liked* it.

"I'll have to pick up a few things," he said.

Chapter 6

Hein had said that his office was "everywhere and nowhere." That meant, David figured, that wherever Hein happened to be at a given moment served as his office for the time he was there.

They agreed to meet at Hein's favorite café and arrived simultaneously. Hein didn't look like a man who'd just spent several days in jail. He pointed to the far corner of the room. "That's my favorite table. Nice and quiet, you're not in the way, and there's nobody behind your back."

The table was occupied by a couple in their seventies. Hein approached them. "What are you drinking?" he asked politely.

The man looked at him, confused.

Hein repeated his question.

"Ah, coffee?" the man replied, turning the word into a question of his own.

David considered how he would tell the story later on. *You have to hear what happened today....*

Hein slipped a ten-Euro note from his wallet and laid it on the table. "This should cover it. Would you sit somewhere else, please?"

"Hein," David said, "we can—"

Hein took a step closer, so he loomed menacingly over the couple. "Please," he said.

The woman adjusted her glasses with a trembling hand and murmured something inaudible.

Hein grinned. He knew he had already won.

That's Hein, David thought, *always a winner.*

"Two free coffees," Hein said. "That's an offer you can't refuse, eh?"

It was impressive to see how quickly Hein's mood shifted from intimidating to friendly.

"Thank you," the man said. He grasped his cane, which David hadn't previously noticed, and struggled to his feet. Hein put a hand under his elbow and helped him up.

"My pleasure. It's lovely out. Have a nice day."

A pretty waitress came over. "What can I do for you gentlemen?"

Hein smiled. "How far are you prepared to go?"

She laughed. "Not that far." She handed them each a menu. "Can I start you out with something to drink?"

"Something white," Hein said, running his eye down the wine list. "I'll try a glass of the Domaine des Rosiers."

"Sounds good," said David.

When she returned with their drinks, they each ordered a caprese salad. They clinked glasses.

"To our collaboration," Hein said.

"Collaboration?"

"Sure. We understand each other, David. You feel it, don't you?"

David knew he was right. He couldn't have explained it, but it was the simple, undeniable truth.

Without saying a word, they would indeed understand each other.

Hein asked a string of innocent questions about David's children, their vacation plans, his workload at the office.

David wondered how Hein knew he had children. He didn't think he'd ever mentioned Bas and Romy.

Their conversation meandered on. Over the phone, Hein had expressed his appreciation for David's getting him released from custody. The court had been receptive to his argument, which boiled down to the contention that there was no concrete evidence against his client, just a cloud of vague suspicions based on gossip.

For the time being, David kept his talk with Theo Wildschut to himself. "You going on vacation this summer?" he asked.

"My whole life is a vacation," said Hein. "Another glass of wine?"

"Better not. I'm meeting a client in the Havenstraat."

Hein knew from his own experience that the House of Detention was in the Havenstraat.

"Better you than me. I get within three blocks of that fucking place and I'm as depressed as a blind man who's lost his seeing-eye dog. But one more won't hurt, will it? It'll fortify you."

Hein ordered another round from the chipper waitress, who told them their salads were on the way.

"Nice girl," said Hein. "She's new, I haven't seen her before. I might just have to initiate her."

"Initiate?"

"You know what I mean."

"Ah, yeah, sure. You're not married?"

"What difference would it make?" said Hein, with obviously put-on indignation.

David knew that, in Hein's eyes, he must look like a petty bourgeois little man. "Well, probably none to you."

"Hey, by the way, thanks for calling Theo. You really came through for me. I knew I could count on you." Again he lightly punched David's upper arm. "That's what I mean by collaboration. We don't need a signed contract for that."

"I hope no one ever—"

"My lips are sealed." Hein touched an index finger to his lips and winked.

It seemed clear that, though Hein held meetings in this café and perhaps others, *important* business would not be conducted in such a setting, since you never knew who might be listening—even way back here in the corner. David had often laughed at movies and television shows where all sorts of complex legal issues were discussed in crowded bars or walking along busy city streets. Hein would never take that kind of risk. Beyond a casual mention of David's call to Theo, he went no further.

The server brought their salads and wine.

"Thanks, hon," said Hein.

They ate their lunch in silence. After his last sip of wine, Hein took a thick envelope from his inside jacket pocket and laid it on the table. "I'll leave first. You just sit here for a couple more minutes. This is for you. There's no name on it. A little something for your trouble. When I need you again, I know how to reach you."

David had to force himself not to pick up the envelope and stash it out of sight. Instead, he pushed it back across the table. "I can't accept this," he said. He wondered how much cash was in there. "The office will bill you."

"Seriously? When did *you* get all holier than the Pope? Come on, D Squared, I swear, there won't be any trouble about this. It's just between you and me." He pushed the envelope back towards David.

"You can't buy me, Hein."

"I'm not trying to. I'm just showing you my appreciation. And I bet you can use the money. There's five grand there. With that fancy house of yours and that fancy wife who doesn't work, I know you can put it to good use."

David was silent. Hein was apparently well aware of his troubled finances. He still owed for their vacation apartment, and his summer bonus was already spent. The next humiliating payment to Mirjam's father was coming closer. And there sat five thousand Euros for the taking.

"I'm trying to help out a friend here, David. What's wrong with that?"

"I just can't."

"Fine." Hein returned the envelope to his jacket pocket. Then he dropped a fifty and a twenty on the table. "For lunch. You'll let me cover *that*, right?" He smiled ironically. "I'll see you around."

David could hear the disappointment in his voice.

A few minutes after he left, the waitress came back. "Everything okay, sir?"

"Yes, fine, thanks."

"And your brother?"

"He's not my brother."

"Oh, I'm sorry, I thought—"

David handed her the seventy Euros. "Keep the change."

Back on the street, he looked around, but Hein was nowhere to be seen. Maybe it had been stupid to turn down the money. He'd earned it, hadn't he? He'd gone out on a limb for Hein, because Hein had trusted him. What if Hein interpreted his refusal to take the gift as an insult, when all David had meant to do was abide by his professional code of ethics? He didn't want to—couldn't afford to—embarrass the man.

Maybe he'd been *scared* to pick up the envelope? But what was he afraid of? Cowards are losers, he realized. He knew Hein was afraid of nothing and no one.

It began to rain. David jogged to his car as if he was on the run from an enemy.

∽

Mirjam was sitting at an outdoor café in the Vondelpark, drinking tea with her girlfriend Thera. A pale summer sun struggled to peek out from behind dark clouds that threatened rain. A sudden sprinkling almost forced them inside, but it vanished as quickly as it had begun.

She'd told Thera about Steven, unable to keep the secret from her friend.

"You practically *glow* when you talk about him," Thera said.

Yes, she glowed—she knew it, though she tried to deny it.

She biked home. Several pedestrians looked up in surprise at the sound of a cackling chicken, her ringtone. Steering around a slower bike with one hand, she fished her phone from her pocket and saw Steven's name on the screen.

She pressed ignore. She couldn't handle Steven right now. It was too much, it was getting too serious, it was beginning to interfere with her family life. Until recently, Steven had occupied a place on the edge of her existence— an important place, yes, but very definitely on the outer edge of the world she lived in. Lately, though, he seemed to be moving closer to the center. At first, she could forget all about him when she was home with David and the kids, but that was getting harder.

Despite her misgivings, she decided to listen to the voicemail he'd surely just left.

She pulled over, propped a foot on the curb, and reached again for her phone.

No, don't. This was getting crazy. No way could she even *think* of letting Steven come to France. And she really had to start treating David better. Their marriage was becoming hollow, infected by some deadly virus.

Why did David seem so annoying, lately? He hadn't really changed. She was the one who was changing. She wanted more than the sweet little family with the two kids and the tastefully decorated home in Oud-Zuid. The best years of her life were behind her… ten years ago, she'd had a job she liked, was building a career and meeting interesting people. Now, she'd be competing with young women fresh out of school who hung out on café terraces twittering and tweeting their way through a maze of social networks. By the time she could put herself back out on the job market—when Bas and Romy were both in all-day school—she'd be in her late thirties. Too old, too little experience, too expensive to hire. No, she was finished… and she hadn't really ever gotten started.

Her life was as predictable as the TV schedule: news at six, eight, and ten, but the same old stories every time.

Tonight, after she put the kids to bed, David would spend some time working upstairs, then come down to the living room, stretch out in his favorite chair, page through the paper, drink some wine, offer her a glass. They'd go upstairs around eleven thirty. They'd brush their teeth, undress, crawl beneath the comforter.

'Night, dear. Sleep tight.

She stood there by the side of the road, staring dreamily out into nothing.

"Hey, you forget how to pedal?"

She snapped back to reality and saw that she was blocking the crosswalk.

☙

David's visit to his client in the House of Detention in the Havenstraat produced nothing he could use in court. The man had gotten into a fight in a café with another man who in his opinion had become a little too friendly with his girlfriend. In the resulting brawl, Mr. Client had knocked Mr. Other Guy unconscious. He was now under arrest because this was not his first violent offense but his third. The man was apparently pathologically jealous, which led in turn to aggressive outbursts. "They mess with my girlfriend," he'd told David, "they're messing with *me*."

David had tried to come up with some mitigating factors, but there were none to be found. His client had been raised in a perfectly ordinary home. A nuclear family: mother, father, two sons. No divorce, no developmental issues. He'd been a good student, then spent a couple of years in the Army, no difficulty there, even given his three months in Afghanistan.

Maybe Afghanistan was worth pursuing? Could he plead post-traumatic stress? Probably not, since there'd been no signs of it during the debriefing all soldiers went through on their return.

He'd worked at a small insurance agency for several years, and both he and his boss were fully satisfied with his performance. But his peaceful existence had now been stained by violence on three separate occasions. David warned him that his future depended on his conduct before the judge. "You need to make it clear not only that you regret your actions but that you're more than willing to go through anger-management counseling. That'll make the right impression."

Now he was on his way to the Parnassusweg for Mrs. Rijkhof's hearing before the investigating magistrate. Two cars had collided head-on in the Minervaplein, blocking traffic in both directions. An ambulance and a patrol car were parked by the side of the road. He saw a young couple stroll arm in arm across the square and onto the sidewalk, oblivious to the accident. They came to a stop and faced each other and fell into a passionate kiss, as if this were the perfect time and place to celebrate their love.

He and Mirjam had been like that once. The world disappeared when he took her in his arms. He remembered one time, much like this, when they'd been wrapped around each other in the middle of a crowded street and a passerby had snarled, "Get a room!"

Mirjam…

How jealously would *he* react if another man approached her with obviously inappropriate intentions? Was he strong enough to take such an intruder? Back in his university days, some aggressive asshole had picked a fight with him in his neighborhood pub. David had accidentally bumped into him, spilling beer on the guy's shirt. He couldn't remember who'd thrown the first punch, only that a bartender had tossed his opponent out the door.

The line of cars in front of him inched forward. As he crawled through the intersection, he got a glimpse of a woman on a gurney being loaded into the ambulance. She was bleeding heavily.

He was five minutes late for his appearance before the investigating magistrate, who began with a quick summary of the medical report on Mr. Rijkhof's condition. The man remained in a coma, and—"I'm sorry to have to say this"—the doctors had little hope that he would awaken. Then he took Mrs. Rijkhof through the story David had already heard. It was a clear-cut case: attacker, victim, weapon, motive. But something kept nibbling at the corners of David's mind. Something about the victim's scream and the neighbor lady who just happened to be in the right place at the right time to hear it.

He racked his brains, groping for a possible alternate scenario, but the answer eluded him. He needed one more link in his chain of reasoning, but he had no idea where to find it. How do you search for something when you're not sure what it is you're after?

When the case came to court in a couple of months, David's job would be simple. Keep hammering away at the idea of psychological abuse, keep insisting there'd been no premeditation—and certainly no intent to do grievous bodily harm, as the prosecution would surely claim. And then of course he'd have to introduce every imaginable mitigating circumstance. He'd probably be able to use the psychologist's report. With luck, he could get her off with a couple of months—which, given time served, would put her right back out on the street.

So far, she'd shown no interest whatsoever in her husband's condition. But nothing else seemed to get through to her, either.

He decided to pick up some flowers for Mirjam on the way home. When they were first living together, he brought her flowers at least once a week. Maybe he should go back to that old habit. Their relationship needed *something*, some regular boost.

❧

It had been easy for Lucas to get Patrick's address. He'd stopped by twice and rung the doorbell, but Patrick, who lived on the third floor, had been out both times. The second time, Lucas had rung another student's bell and, when admitted to the building, climbed the two flights of steps and pounded on Patrick's door. But there was no response, and the door was locked.

"Can I help you?" the guy in the next room had asked. "You want to leave a message?" No, that wouldn't be necessary.

Now he was trying again. Third time's the charm? And, yes, indeed, Patrick opened the lobby door himself.

Lucas had prepared a whole speech, but now that the moment had come, the words deserted him.

"Yeah?" Patrick said. "You looking for me or somebody else?"

"You're Patrick Hamilton?"

"Yeah, you?"

"Lucas."

"Do I know you?" Patrick eyed him as if he recognized the face but couldn't match it to a name.

"I don't think so."

"What do you want? I'm on my way to the library… got a paper to research. You selling something?"

Lucas shook his head. And then he said her name: "Selma."

"Selma?"

"Yeah, I want to talk to you about Selma, what you did to her."

"What's she to you?"

"She's my sister, my twin sister." Lucas took a step forward and pushed past Patrick into the building. "Let's go up to your room."

"Why?"

"So we can talk."

"We can talk right here."

"We're gonna need privacy." Lucas latched onto Patrick's arm and steered him toward the stairs. "Your room."

"Hey, fuck you!" Patrick shook off Lucas' hold. "I don't have anything to say to you. What happened happened, and the judge'll decide if I did anything wrong."

"Right, now that you've told your lies."

"Lies? That was your sister, man. She made it all up."

Lucas grabbed Patrick's shirtfront in both fists. "One more word like that and I'll beat the shit out of you."

A bulky kid with a shaved head came down the stairs and saw them.

"Trouble, Pat?" he said.

Chapter 7

Explaining his suspicions to Emiel was for David a small victory over his own hesitation. Emiel had been a police detective until a couple of years ago, when he had left the force to set up his own investigative agency. "Nothin' beats bein' your own boss," he'd said. David couldn't argue with that. Sometimes he imagined it in his own future: *The Driessen Practice, Attorneys at Law*. A nice building on one of the main canals, a couple of ambitious young partners, a good secretary. They'd handle big cases, newsworthy cases for interesting clients—like Hein, for example.

He knew the look in Emiel's eyes. Getting the goods on errant spouses was the man's bread and butter. And here David was, cutting him off another slice. It was embarrassing. It seemed so old fashioned. Even the phrase "errant spouse" was old fashioned, like a scene from an American film noir: *When a man's wife cheats on him, he's supposed to do something about it. It doesn't make any difference what you thought of her. She is your wife, and you're supposed to do something about it.*

"Any concrete evidence?" asked Emiel.

"No. She's just been acting strangely. It's like I'm married to a different woman."

"*Vive la difference?*"

"It's not funny," said David. "Do you see me laughing?"

"Sorry." Emiel lifted his hands in apologetic surrender. "What about the sex? I hate to ask, but I need to get a feel for the big picture."

David wanted to say it was none of Emiel's business, but he decided not to ruffle the man's feathers. When you need somebody's help—even if it's help you're paying for—it's generally advisable to give the helper a little leeway. "Not a lot to talk about, lately. Two or three times a month, tops, but it's been like that for a while. That's, ah, normal wear and tear in a marriage, I think. Two kids and all sorts of responsibilities, you know how it goes."

"I do?"

"Don't you?" David wondered how good Emiel was at interrogating suspects and witnesses. His cynical remarks would put most people off. Or maybe that was a conscious strategy. You rub them the wrong way, maybe they say more than they ought to? Truth was, he used that tactic himself from time to time.

Emiel made a few notes. "Anything else? Unexplained absences, unusual appointments, like that?"

"Once in a while, but that's not really new, either. Mirjam's always been pretty casual about time. When we first started dating, sometimes I had to wait for her for hours. If I wanted to take her to a nine forty-five movie, I'd tell her it started at nine. That way there was at least a chance we wouldn't miss the beginning."

"Why don't you just ask her if there's somebody else? Straight out, face to face, *ask* her. See how she reacts."

David shook his head. "No, I need proof—or at least more than just suspicion. Otherwise, she'll just bluff it out. I don't want that." He left out the fact that he simply didn't have the guts to confront her without solid ground under his feet. At work, he needed hard facts. Intuition and vague indications weren't enough. He could already hear Mirjam throwing it back in his face: *Don't you trust me?*

Any answer he gave to that question would be wrong. If he said yes, she'd say, *Then why are you asking?* But if he said no, she'd blame him for not trusting her after so many years of marriage.

Emiel smiled at him patronizingly, which made David feel even more like a loser. "You got a landline, right? I can tap that. But can you get me her cell for a couple hours? If she's got a boy toy—or a girl toy, for that matter, hey, who knows anymore?—they more likely use that. Even if they're careful to erase the call logs, I got a guy who can recover the data."

Jesus, a "girl toy," was that possible? David hadn't even considered it. He made a mental list of Mirjam's girlfriends, tried to remember if she'd ever dropped a hint that she might be attracted to one of them. Sure, she talked about other women's looks, but there was never anything that suggested desire—criticism, usually, maybe occasional jealousy, but that was all. Or had he just never noticed, because the possibility had never even occurred to him?

Mirjam with another woman. What would the kids think? First a divorce, and then "Romy has two mommies." David recalled a case in which two women married and had a child, then divorced—and the nonbiological mother sued the birth mother for visitation rights.

"Yo!" Emiel waved a hand in front of his face. "You still with me?"

David knew he spent too much time fantasizing. He'd get an idea in his head and run with it until it ran away with him.

"Her cell phone," Emiel repeated. "You checked her contacts?"

David nodded. "Yeah, there are dozens of names in there, probably more than a hundred."

"Well, if he's in there, she probably gave him some kinda code name. You can't expect her to list him under L for Lover." Emiel guffawed. "Anyway, they probably spend a lot of time on the phone."

"How do we check that?"

"Like I said, I got a tech guy. Two, three hours with her phone is usually all he needs. Beats the hell out of followin' her around for weeks on end, sneakin' photos of every dude she sees. And the phone records don't lie. If he's in there, he's *in* there."

David sighed. So it had come to this. He was going to steal his wife's phone. How far would he have to go to back up his suspicions with evidence? "I'll try, but I don't know if I can swing it. She's practically glued to the damn thing." In fact, he'd given her the smartphone for her birthday, two years ago. "And we're leaving town next weekend, be gone for three weeks."

The south of France, a little apartment in a complex with eighty units, what could be safer? The kids could play on the beach, everyone would relax, eat great food, have a glass of wine here and there; a chance to breathe new life into their relationship.

He could see them lying in a big bed after a stress-free day in the sun. Her smooth skin baked a golden brown, except for the white patches her bikini covered. That excited him, the contrast, the bronzed arms and legs and belly, the pale white breasts with their dark-brown nipples…

He could feel himself getting hard.

"Okay," said Emiel, "so you'll try for her cell, and we'll see what happens."

❧

David's client listened to the judge, his head bowed. David had tried without success to bolster the man's confidence, but the facts were inescapable: He had accepted under-the-table cash payments for an assortment of painting and construction jobs, all the while collecting unemployment benefits from the government.

Last night, David had felt just as defeated, sitting at his computer until he couldn't keep his eyes open a moment longer. It had been stupid, stupid, colossally stupid, but he hadn't been able to stop.

After his meeting with Emiel, he had to do *something* to distract himself from his unease and fear. So he sat behind his desk, flipping through a stack of case folders, not really seeing them through his daydreams and fantasies.

And it had been so simple to let himself drift back into it. It wasn't that he'd chosen to go back to the dangerous old routine, but more that the old routine had chosen him again—and, goddammit, he was entitled to a little R and R every once in a while, wasn't he?

He'd opened an account at *888casino.com*. It was a site he hadn't previously visited, and that meant he had no history there, no past. He gave himself permission to play this one time only, and then that would be the end of it. He'd dragged himself free from the addiction before, and this time he'd be smart enough not to get in over his head in the first place.

At first, it seemed like they'd rolled out the red carpet for him at the online roulette wheel. They clearly knew he was visiting the site for the first time, and they wanted him to feel at home. So, his head burning with excitement, he sat there at his computer and played.

And, for once, everything went his way. It was one of those glorious nights when he just couldn't lose. In his mind, he paid off all their bills, wiped out his debt, ordered a new furnace, booked a weekend trip to Paris— Grandma and Grandpa would take the kids?—popped the cork on a bottle of the best champagne...

But then it all went south, and, like a total rookie, he grabbed on to the insane belief that the pendulum would swing back his way, that his beginner's luck would return. It had to. It *had* to!

He maxed out his Visa. If he'd only taken the money Hein had offered him, he wouldn't be in this mess. He'd have to take out yet another loan, there was no way around it. He couldn't go back to Hein and ask him to fork over the five thousand Euros after all.

"Mr. Driessen!"

David snapped to attention. He'd only let his thoughts drift out of the courtroom for a couple of seconds, but the judge was glaring at him, as if he knew precisely what he'd been thinking about. "Mr. Driessen, you're up. Is there anything you'd care to share with the court, or would you prefer to resume your daydreaming?"

"I apologize, Your Honor. I was gathering my thoughts."

"Well, I hope you've put them in a productive order. This is your final call."

❧

It was funny how you could wrestle with a problem for days on end, run through the gamut of possibilities and arguments without productive result, and then, completely out of the blue, hit on the perfect solution.

This time, it had come to him while he was squeezing his car into a narrow parking space. The wheels must just keep spinning in your head, ideas working themselves out on a sort of automatic pilot, even when you're preoccupied with something else. He almost yelled "Eureka!"

Obviously he'd explain his thoughts to Mrs. Rijkhof. The question was: How would she react? First to the office, where he had to take care of a few administrative details, bring his time sheets up to date. He instructed Hanna, his secretary, regarding several requests for extra compensation that had to be submitted to the Legal Aid Board in connection with cases that had required more of his time than was officially sanctioned. Later this afternoon, he had a meeting with a client who'd failed to pay five speeding tickets. He was sick of these petty little cases, these crumbs the firm kept throwing him. Scofflaws like this loser wasted his time with their foolish explanations and excuses, when the truth was they'd just fucked up, nothing more.

Enough crumbs, and you could cobble together a slice of bread—but it would be a stale and tasteless slice.

He checked his watch and saw that it was three thirty. Just enough time to get to the House of Detention and back.

❧

"This afternoon," Steven suggested. "I can reschedule a couple of things."

"No, doesn't work." Mirjam had promised herself to stand fast. The idea of a stolen hour was seductive, but she had to be strong. Giving in would be a defeat. Steven's calls always came without warning, but that was a consequence of the nature of his work. On the one hand, the uncertainty was exciting. All day long she could lose herself in the possibility that, at any moment, she might find herself in his arms. But on the other hand, the passive waiting was a constant strain.

"What about tomorrow? I can break away for a few hours, fake an off-site meeting or something. They can get along without me. You have anything planned? During the day, while the kids are at school?"

"I'm supposed to stop by my parents' and—"

"That can wait, can't it?"

She sighed. "I promised them."

"Come on, sweetheart, I'm aching for you. All day long, from the moment I open my eyes. God, I'd love that, just once, to wake up with you in the morning. Well, not just once. Often… always."

She held her breath for a moment. How did he know her desires so exactly? Waking up in his arms, their faces pressed together as his eyes flickered open.

"What's wrong?" Steven asked.

"You know I want it, too, but—"

It was hard to hold back the tears.

Apparently someone had knocked at his office door. "Come in," she heard him say, and then caught snatches of a conversation which ended when he said, "Sorry, I've got an important client on the phone." A door closed, and then, "I'm back. Tomorrow, Mirjam, please. You can't just keep me hanging like this. I have to see you before you leave for France."

"Well, maybe in the morning…"

∾

"You didn't do it." It seemed best to David to come right out and say it.

She stared at him.

"You didn't hit your husband."

"I did," she said, her voice a whisper.

David felt like a brute, but he needed to be sure. It wouldn't really matter, but he had to know. "No," he said, "you didn't. You haven't got it in you."

Mrs. Rijkhof stood up. "I want to go back to my cell," she said dully.

"Sit down. I'm not going to do anything that isn't in your best interest." He got to his feet, walked around the interview table, and put a hand on her shoulder. He could feel the bones beneath the skin. "I don't care what really happened. I'm not the police. I'm here to help you. But I'd like to know the truth. Please, sit down."

She nodded, but David wondered if she really understood what he was saying.

"I don't believe you struck your husband," he said again. "Maaike Vlietstra, your neighbor—she did it, didn't she?"

No reaction. She was still staring straight at him, but her eyes were dead. David laid it all out for her.

"You and Maaike are friends, close friends. She's the one person you can count on." He saw an almost imperceptible nod. "She knew all about your husband, the way he treated you. She's already testified to that, you heard her. That morning, she was visiting you. The idea that she just happened to be on the stairs outside your door when your husband screamed, that's just too big a coincidence. Besides, how could he scream when he was lying there unconscious on the floor? No, Mrs. Vlietstra was right there in the apartment, and your husband started in on you again, the coffee or whatever it was set him off. Maybe she was in the living room while your husband was yelling at you out in the kitchen."

He wanted to look Mrs. Rijkhof in the eyes, but she turned away from him.

"Anyway," David continued, "either she came into the kitchen or she was already there. And *she* couldn't take it anymore." He watched the woman closely as he came to the critical part of his theory. "*She* picked up the frying pan and hit him with everything she had."

She nodded again, but David wanted more than that. He wanted a confession—a confession of innocence.

"Was that the way it happened, Mrs. Rijkhof?"

She shrugged.

"Look, I have to make this clear: If you want to stick to your original story, I will back you up a hundred percent. Do you understand that?"

"Yes, I understand."

David interpreted this as a half admission. "You and Mrs. Vlietstra agreed to say that *you* hit him, not her. Is that right? That's the way it happened?"

"Yes." A whisper.

"Can you tell me why?" When she remained silent, he answered the question himself. "The two of you agreed that you'd take the blame. A lot of people know how your husband terrorized you. Your doctor, he testified to that effect before the IM—sorry, the investigating magistrate. You had a boatload of mitigating factors. I could maybe even argue that your husband brought the attack on himself. It was completely logical that you'd eventually break under the pressure, and that made it probable that you'd get off lightly. With time served, you might even get off altogether. But if Mrs. Vlietstra was arrested, *she'd* probably wind up doing serious time."

They both were silent. Again David tried to read the expression in her eyes, but again she refused to meet his gaze.

"Am I right or not?" said David.

"Yes, you're right."

He didn't know why, but he felt like hugging her. He settled for clasping her hand in both of his and holding it tightly.

"I told you. If you want to stick to your version of what happened, I won't say a word."

"That's what I want."

David saw her fail to hide the smallest of smiles.

It wasn't until he was back behind the wheel of his car that he realized it was possible to take his hypothesis a step further. Perhaps it was no coincidence that Maaike Vlietstra had chosen that morning for her visit. Perhaps it had all been carefully planned. She'd popped in that morning specifically in order to put her friend's husband down like a vicious dog. The argument over the coffee might well have been an invention.

Clever.

David had to admire them.

Chapter 8

Half a day. He needed the damn smartphone for half a day, possibly less. He could drop it off with Emiel's tech guy this morning, he had the address, a phone shop somewhere in the Indische Buurt. Pick it up this afternoon, no worries.

But how do you sneak a cell phone away from a woman who is attached to it by an umbilical cord? If they ever figured out how to implant a chip in your brain so all you had to do was think of a number and it would connect you, Mirjam would be first on line to volunteer as a beta tester.

As they sat at the counter that separated the kitchen from the living room, eating breakfast, he cast sidelong glances at the phone, which was on the table beside the front door where Mirjam had set it when she came downstairs, practically inviting him to take it.

Look, it's right over there, see? I could have put it next to my plate, where it usually is, but I made it easy for you. Don't miss your big chance!

He couldn't stop looking at it, as if his gaze could teleport it from the table to his pocket.

"Something wrong?" she asked.

"Like what?"

"You look weird. Romy, slow down and chew!"

"Do I look weird, Bas?"

"Yeah, weird." Bas had learned how to cross his eyes, and, now that he'd been given an opportunity to demonstrate, he did so happily. Romy laughed so hard she sprayed bits of bread all over the counter.

"Romy, don't be such a messy Bessie—and, Bas, you stop it right now or your eyes'll stick that way. You want to be cross-eyed for the rest of your life? Just stop laughing and eat. Come on, you'll be late for school."

David knew her threats were empty, at least where the kids were concerned. If they were late for school, it was the parents who got the dressing down, not the children. The principal had already sent around a letter complaining about the recent epidemic of tardiness. He was considering making latecomers and their parents wait for half an hour before the children would be admitted, which had led to considerable protest from the moms and dads. A half-hour timeout for *parents*? Is that what the inflated tuition they were paying was buying them? You want to provide your kids with the finest possible education, not be punished like a recalcitrant seven-year-old when life gets in the way.

David dawdled over his toast and jam. Mirjam's cell phone sat there for the taking. A sip of tea, a bite of toast, a little staring out the window, another sip of tea. He got to his feet and walked down the hall, slowed as he approached the table where the phone lay.

Mirjam asked where he was going.

"Bathroom. I don't have to announce that over the PA, do I?"

"You do," said Bas, "with a great big fart!" He put the heel of his hand to his mouth and, to Romy's delight, produced a perfect ass flapper.

"That's disgusting," said David.

When he returned to his stool, Mirjam poured them both more tea. "Won't you be late for work?"

"No," he said, "I've got a ten o'clock meeting in Noord. I need to check a few things upstairs."

"Can you drop the kids at school for once?"

He considered it. If Mirjam took them, she'd pick up her phone on her way out the door, and that would be that. So her request might provide exactly the chance he needed. When she wasn't looking, he'd snatch it from the table.

He went up to his study to fetch his briefcase. By the time he got back downstairs, the kids were in their bathroom, brushing their teeth. He didn't see Mirjam—she was probably also upstairs. He slipped her phone into the inside pocket of his suit coat. His heart was pounding.

When Bas and Romy clattered downstairs, he hurried them along.

"You've got lots of time," Mirjam called. "It's not even eight thirty."

The kids thundered back up to kiss their mother goodbye. Bas was now old enough to find the ritual embarrassing; he wiped the kiss off his lips with the back of his hand.

As they walked out the front door, David heard Mirjam yell, "Hey, anybody see my phone?"

❧

Looking forward to their trip, David had programmed the French national anthem as his cell's ring tone, and he was about to step into the phone shop to see Emiel's tech guy, an extremely fat Hindu from Suriname, when the opening bars of "La Marseillaise" rang out from his pocket.

"You got some time for me tomorrow?" asked Hein.

"Actually, I'm booked pretty solid. You know what it's like, the last couple workdays before vacation."

"You'll have a great time—you've earned it. But this is important."

"When I get to the office, I'll check my book and see if I can squeeze you in."

"Come on, David. You know I'm not the kind of guy you just 'squeeze in.'"

"Sure, but—"

"You *are* my lawyer, aren't you? Or not?" Hein's voice remained friendly. "And, remember, I'd rather not come to your office. People asking me what I was doing there, I don't need that."

"I understand."

"Anyway, I'm not asking you as a client." Hein paused for a moment. "I'm asking as a friend."

"Sure, I'll work it out."

"Tomorrow morning, then. There'll be three of us."

"But I—"

"Meet us at the Van der Valk Hotel in Breukelen. You know, the big Chinese-looking place, right off the A2. We'll be waiting for you in the parking lot at nine. If it all goes right, there'll be something in it for you."

This was no request, David knew. It was a straight-out command. "What do you want me to do?" he asked. He did *not* ask what might be "in it" for him. He could always refuse another envelope.

"You'll see. Leave it at that for now, keep it exciting."

David had more than enough excitement in his life already, but he held his tongue. "All right, I'll be there. Breukelen, nine o'clock."

When he was back in his car, *"Allons enfants de la patrie"* rang out again from his phone. Mirjam. Had he seen *her* phone anywhere? No, sorry, he had no idea. He felt hot, as if his brains had caught fire.

∽

He was back at the phone shop just before five.

Emiel's tech guy pushed two sheets of paper into his hand. "Page one's her outgoing calls, page two's incoming. Got it?"

David thanked him, but the man's mind was already elsewhere. Emiel would take care of paying him.

He hadn't seen a café anywhere in the neighborhood, but there was a Turkish coffee shop a few doors up the street. A bare space, Formica tables and wooden chairs, nothing to write home about. They apparently hadn't gotten the memo about the no-smoking law. The smell of tobacco hung heavily in the room. Whiny Turkish music played in the background.

A boy of no more than fourteen asked him in perfect Dutch what he'd have to drink. In a corner, four men sat playing cards. One of them looked David over curiously, maybe mistaking him for someone from Social Services or a tax inspector or some other unwelcome functionary. David wondered if he looked like a civil servant. His suit and briefcase certainly worked against him.

The television was on, its volume muted. David didn't recognize the station logo in the bottom corner of the screen; probably a Turkish channel. A man with a squarish head and a walrus mustache was reading the news. An inset above his shoulder showed pictures of military vehicles on parade, marching soldiers, and a woman weeping in the front yard of the ruins of a house. An earthquake, a military action, or both? Whatever it was, the card players paid no attention.

David sat and studied the two sheets of paper he'd gotten from Emiel's tech guy. The more he looked, the more he had to acknowledge that perhaps Mirjam *was* cheating on him. And the more he acknowledged the possibility, the more convinced he became that it was true.

The boy set a glass of coffee in front of David, who handed him a two-Euro coin.

"That's too much," the boy said. "Would you like a piece of baklava? It's really good."

"No, thanks, this is fine. Keep the change."

David sipped the strong coffee. Two packets of sugar failed to camouflage its bitter taste. He picked up the pages and was about to tear them in half when he saw the boy who'd brought him the coffee watching him from the open doorway that led, David assumed, back to the bathrooms and kitchen. He set the papers down and took another sip, not wanting to hurt the kid's feelings.

What he really ought to do now was go home and take Mirjam in his arms and forget his suspicions and fears.

What he did was look down again at the lists of phone numbers. They were mostly cell numbers. Three he didn't recognize showed up again and again on both pages. Girlfriends?

He dialed the first of the three from his own phone. As soon as Thera picked up and said her name, he broke the connection.

He tried the second number.

"Hello?" A man's voice.

David had counted on the person at the other end of the line answering the phone by saying his name, as Thera had done, as was usual in Holland. He wasn't sure what to do with a simple hello.

"Who's calling?" the man said impatiently.

"Ah, this is Joost Mouthuis. Is this Gerard Ketelaar?"

"Ketelaar? No, you've got the wrong number."

"I'm sorry," said David. "Who *is* this, then?"

"Not Gerard Ketelaar."

ᴇᴐ

Steven sketched out his idea of their future. His apartment was too small to take in Mirjam and the children, each of whom had the right to a private bedroom. "I'll sell this place, and we'll buy something bigger."

Mirjam snuggled in closer behind him, wrapped her arms around him and tickled his chest hairs. "Still here in this neighborhood, though, so the kids don't have to change schools. It'll be hard enough for them."

"Absolutely." He squirmed around to face her, kissed her neck softly, nibbled gently at her earlobe. "We'll furnish it together. Everything new, just the way we want it. Our house, our style. And we can—"

His cell phone rang.

"Must be the office," he said. "They're supposed to check in about a new account I've been trying to land. I'd better take it, sorry."

He answered the call.

"Hello?… Who's calling?"

Mirjam could hear a voice come faintly through the little speaker, but she couldn't make out what it said.

"Ketelaar?" Steven frowned. "No, you've got the wrong number."

Again the inaudible voice.

Steven looked annoyed. "Not Gerard Ketelaar."

"Who was it?" Mirjam asked.

He set the phone back on the night table. "I don't know. Joost something. Moutheim, or whatever. He dialed a wrong number."

"Joost Mouthuis?"

"That was it."

"That's funny. David's got an old friend named Joost Mouthuis. They're in the same firm."

"Coincidence," said Steven.

"Pretty strange coincidence."

"Don't worry about it, sweetheart. Relax. It's just a coincidence. It's not like David's checking up on you."

She always hated it when Steven used David's name. In a way, it brought her husband into the room with them, and David was the *last* person she wanted in the room with them. "What did he want?" she asked.

"I told you, it was a wrong number. He was trying to reach somebody named Ketelaar, Gerard Ketelaar. You know that name, too? No? See, just a wrong number."

"It's still really weird that he just so happened to dial *your* number."

"Why are you so nervous, all of a sudden? Come on, cheer up." He propped himself on an elbow. "There must be lots of Joost Mouthuises around."

The sense that there was something wrong spread through her body. She sat up on the edge of the bed. He rubbed her back, but she found his touch irritating. "Stop that. Give me a second. I don't know. I don't like this."

"I know what's bothering you. This is the last chance we'll have to see each other before you leave."

"I couldn't find my cell this morning. That never happens."

She stood up.

"Where are you going?"

"To take a shower."

"Come back to bed."

"If it rings again, don't answer it," she said tightly.

Steven got up.

She came to him, embraced him, felt the warmth of his body against her.

"I'm sorry, Steven. I just—"

"It doesn't matter," he whispered, and led her back to the bed.

⁓

"You're late," Mirjam said. "Why didn't you call? Oh, and I still can't find my cell. You sure you haven't seen it?"

David bent over to retie a shoelace.

"I called it from the landline, but I couldn't hear it ring. It must not be in the house."

Shit, of course she'd try that. Why hadn't he thought of it? Stupid. He was so preoccupied with the idea of her having an affair that he wasn't thinking straight.

"I'm ordering in pizza for dinner," she said.

"Sounds good. Mushrooms and pepperoni for me. I've got to take care of a couple things upstairs. Oh, and I have to go out for a few hours in the morning. It's a pain, but there's a case I have to deal with before we leave."

He was halfway up the stairs before he finished talking.

In his office, he fiddled with two or three of the case files on his desk. The sound of the television wafted up from below. *Sesame Street*?

He crept down the hall to the bathroom and set Mirjam's phone on the edge of the sink, covered it with a wadded-up washcloth and left it there. It would be suspicious if he "found" it himself.

⁓

Naturally Lucas could have accosted Patrick the moment he stepped out of his building, but he decided to hold off until they were further from the rapist's home turf. He followed along behind him, keeping fifty feet between them.

This morning, he'd talked with Heleen ter Bruggen, Selma's lawyer. She'd told him it didn't look good. Then he'd gone to see Selma. At first, she'd refused to buzz him in. "I don't want you to see me like this," she'd called down from her second-floor window. Finally, though, she'd admitted him, and he saw why she'd wanted to keep him out. She looked awful.

He did his best to cheer her up. *Go back to school, Sel, that'll take your mind off it. Go out with a girlfriend. I'll go with you. I won't let you out of my sight, I swear.*

All she said was that she felt worthless, dirty, disgusted by her own body.

Lucas had done some research online, and had learned that these reactions were common amongst victims of rape. It was hard for him to believe, but Selma was living proof—if you could still call the state she was in "living."

He remembered that the cutting had begun at another time when she'd felt herself worthless.

Patrick's intended destination quickly became clear: the library. If he was borrowing new books or returning old ones, he might not be in there for long. If his plan was to spread out in a study carrel and read, though, he could be hours.

Lucas waited outside the main entrance for fifteen minutes, then went in.

He spotted Patrick in the main reading room, leaning back in a chair with a laptop and a pile of books on the table before him. He settled in across the room, with a view of Patrick's back, and watched him page through his books, pausing from time to time to type something on his computer. His attitude was casual, not studious.

The minutes passed slowly. At last Patrick showed signs of preparing to leave. Lucas bent over a book he'd picked at random from the stacks, hiding his face. Out of the corner of his eye, he saw Patrick walk away from his table, leaving his laptop open. So he wasn't done for the day. Maybe a bathroom or cigarette break? To the best of Lucas' knowledge, Patrick didn't smoke.

He was soon back at his keyboard. Lucas had no plan of attack. He wanted to catch Patrick alone, just the two of them. When the time came, he'd know how to handle the situation. He drifted off into a daydream in which he ran into Patrick on a lonely country road. Nobody around, no one to see or hear them. He confronted Patrick, told him what his actions had led to, how Selma was suffering. Patrick had to make things right. But how? There was no way to undo what had happened. Well, for starters he could acknowledge his guilt, fall on his knees, and beg Selma for forgiveness. But then what? Would that be enough?

Patrick got up and left the room, again without his laptop. This time, Lucas followed him. In the canteen, Patrick bought a paper cup of coffee from one vending machine and a plastic-wrapped pastry from another. He took a seat at a vacant table. As he sipped his coffee, Lucas approached him.

"Getting some study time in?" he said, his voice low.

Patrick attempted to rise, but Lucas held him down with a hand on his shoulder. "You stay right there!" he commanded.

"What do you want?"

"You know what I want."

Patrick shook his head.

"I want you to admit what you did. Man the fuck up. This is tearing Selma apart, do you understand that?"

Patrick kept silent. He looked around the room, as if he hoped a policeman would be handy.

There were a couple of other students in the canteen, but they were paying no attention.

"She's a wreck. If you own up to it, maybe she can move on with her life."

Again, Patrick shook his head.

"I get it," said Lucas. "You confess, you go to jail. But my sister's going to spend the rest of her life in jail if you don't. You think that's fair? You want to have it on your conscience?"

"I can't confess to something I didn't do, man."

Lucas had to restrain himself from snatching up the cup of hot coffee and throwing it in Patrick's face.

Patrick seemed to read his mind. He grabbed the cup himself, emptied it in one long swallow and crushed it in his fist. Then he pushed the wrapped pastry into Lucas' hands. "This is on me, you stupid shit," he said. "I hope you choke on it."

❧

"Let me introduce you," said Hein. "Ben Heuvelink, David Driessen, my legal eagle."

They sat in the back seat of a brand new Mercedes GL, which David figured had to have cost at least fifty thousand Euros. The aroma of expensive leather hung in the air. Funny how a smell could suggest money and put you at ease. David knew that *he* deserved to be driving a car like this. Was there one in his future? Who knew?

The driver was taking a walk in the Chinese garden spread out to the south of the hotel. David could see him in the distance, standing atop an arched Oriental bridge, leaning against the railing, smoking a cigarette.

Legal eagle?

David had no idea what Hein had in mind, no idea what he was doing here in the parking lot of this suburban hotel, half an hour south of Amsterdam. Why was his presence needed? His specialty was criminal defense. He had little experience with civil cases.

"You work for John, too?" Heuvelink said, sticking out a gnarled hand.

David shook it, but, before he could reply, Hein said, "Let's not go into that. Anyway, John's old news."

Heuvelink chuckled. "And you're new news?"

"We'll see." Hein seemed completely sure of himself, whatever it was he was getting David into. "Cell phones are powered down, right?"

David checked his to be sure. Mirjam hadn't found her smartphone until just before they'd gone to bed last night. She'd carried it into the bedroom and showed it to David. "What was it doing in the *bathroom*?" she'd said. "I didn't leave it there."

"Maybe one of the kids was playing with it."

Luckily, she'd let the matter drop, pleased to have finally found the thing, and she hadn't said a word about it this morning.

Hein was telling Heuvelink that the money would be transferred from a bank account in Cyprus to Curaçao. "And then Boomtown can be liquidated. Right, David?"

David understood what was expected of him. "Yes," he said, "no problem."

The conversation moved on to buildings, investments, renovations, and the financing all that would require. This was worlds beyond the trivial pursuits Starrebeek dealt with: some loser caught with an ounce of heroin or a hundred caps of oxycontin and no prescription, or a welfare recipient with a hundred and fifty pot plants in his basement. This was high finance and, for David, until now *terra incognita*.

Heuvelink reached into the back of the SUV and came up with a bulky leather case. He opened it, revealing three crystal glasses and a bottle of scotch. Glenfiddich 18, way out of David's league. They toasted.

"A small formality," Hein said, handing Heuvelink a thin sheaf of documents. After a brief inspection, Heuvelink signed the last page.

"What are you going to do with this?"

Hein grinned. "Send it straight to the Public Prosecution Service."

"No, seriously," said Heuvelink. "I hope they're not, ah, interested in us?"

"Mr. Driessen is more reliable than the Nederlandsche Bank."

David drew a deep breath. So he was supposed to do something with these documents. But what? What did Hein expect?

After another five minutes of small talk, they shook hands all around. Heuvelink's seemed to have grown even knottier in the half hour they'd spent together.

Hein and David got out of the SUV. The driver slid in behind the wheel, and they watched the Mercedes drive off.

"Well, he walked right into that," said Hein, "with his eyes wide open." He threw an arm around David's shoulder. "How 'bout a drink, pal? We've got something to celebrate."

David eyed the hotel's grand entrance.

"No," Hein laughed, "not there. I know a much better place."

"Where?"

"You don't like surprises?"

"Sure, but I should probably be getting home."

"Home'll wait," said Hein. "You've got the right to be a little selfish, every once in a while. Now, for instance."

"Fine, then."

"Let's take your car."

"What about yours?"

"I took a cab."

David swallowed the observation that he could have easily given Hein a lift from the city.

"When you get back to the office," Hein said, handing over the sheaf of documents, "just lock all this in your safe."

David saw that Hein was simply assuming his cooperation.

As they approached David's car, Hein shook his head sadly. "Alfa, huh? Eight or nine years old?"

"Seven." David didn't add that he'd bought it used.

"It's like driving a trash can." Hein gathered up a collection of candy wrappers from the passenger seat, got in, cranked open the window, and tossed the paper out of the car.

"Where to?"

"Take the A2 north, then the N201 west to Vinkeveen."

On the highway, David noticed that his gas tank was almost empty. He pulled into a service station, and they both went inside. Hein insisted on paying. A muscular man with tattooed forearms stood behind them in line, talking loudly on a cell phone. After Hein paid, the man went right on talking into his phone while the young woman behind the counter rang him up.

"Excuse me," Hein said. "You don't think you should put your phone away until you're finished here?"

The man turned his head and looked Hein up and down. "What makes it your business, jackoff?"

"We're in a public place, I can express my opinion if I want to."

David watched Hein's smile stretch into a rigid grin.

"Some schmuck wants me to hang up," the man said into his phone, handing a credit card to the woman behind the counter.

"Correct," said Hein. "This young lady is a human being, made of flesh and blood, not an ATM. If I were you, I'd treat her with a little common courtesy."

There were half a dozen other people in the shop, and David saw they were riveted to the altercation, hoping for a sensational *denouement*. He didn't understand why Hein was making such a big deal out of it, apparently not even remotely concerned that the illustrated man might turn violent. He didn't really think the two of them were going to come to a pleasant meeting of the minds, did he?

The man stared at Hein venomously. "Get the fuck out of my face," he rumbled, and threw a roundhouse punch at Hein's jaw.

Hein reacted so quickly that David couldn't see exactly how he did it, but suddenly the other man was lying on the floor, writhing in pain.

Hein bent over him, picked up the phone from beside him, and offered it back to him.

"Here," he said. "Call an ambulance."

The man opened his mouth to respond, but, before he could say a word, Hein rammed the cell phone between his teeth.

Chapter 9

Floating on his back on an inflatable raft in the swimming pool, his eyes shut tight against the Mediterranean sun, David let his hand dabble in the water and shook sparkling droplets onto his chest. Mirjam was in a lounge chair beside the pool, reading in the shade of an umbrella. The family tensions were fading, and the soul-sucking weariness that had afflicted them was slowly evolving into a lazy, languid sense of peace—at least for him.

He couldn't really explain it, but he'd felt instantly at home the moment he and Hein had walked through the door of that nightclub in Vinkeveen. The soft jazz, the murmur of a dozen intimate conversations, the booze, the luxury. He'd returned home much later than he should have, but he hadn't wanted Hein to see him as some pussy-whipped little house husband who had to account to wifey for every move he made. By the time he even thought about calling home to check in, it was after eleven, and that was too late: Mirjam would undoubtedly be sound asleep.

He yawned noisily and turned his head. She was still working her way through *Eyeshadow*. Romy was busy with a new friend, a girl she'd met on their first day here. They'd futzed together a makeshift playhouse for their dolls and My Little Ponies, auditioning for their grown-up lives. He knew exactly where Bas was hiding but pretended to be searching the pool area for him. That was part of the game.

That nightclub…

David had known such places existed, but it was a world he'd never seen for himself outside of a film. Once upon a time, he'd paid a couple of visits to an illegal betting parlor in Amsterdam, before he'd started at Starrebeek. After he'd joined the firm, though, he didn't dare show his face there again, not even at the perfectly legal Holland Casino in the Leidseplein. People would talk. He remembered Starrebeek's warning words: *your behavior must be beyond reproach, do nothing that could be used against the firm, respect the ethical standards of the profession.* The internet was always alluring, but he'd never gone back to *888casino.com* after that single slip. Mirjam was counting on him to resist temptation. He'd promised her, and the one time he'd broken that promise haunted him.

When they'd stepped inside, after a brief exchange with an imposing doorman, Hein had said, "Tony makes a truly amazing cocktail. His Fizzling Dance is fantastic. Yeah, yeah, I know, you're driving. You wind up having a couple too many, though, I'll get you a driver." And that's the way it had unfolded. Around 1 o'clock in the morning, a young stranger in a nice suit had appeared. "I'm your designated driver," he'd said, and Hein had cracked up: "A DD for D Squared!" The young man had driven David's car home, with David sacked out in the back seat.

Two lovely eighteen-year-olds in skimpy bikinis paraded past the swimming pool, and David watched them swivel by. Two firm asses, two gorgeous pairs of ripe young tits… every man in and around the pool was drooling. *Check out the merchandise*, the girls seemed to be saying. *Buy one, get one free.*

It had been like that in the nightclub. No cheap, ordinary hookers, but beautiful women, dressed to the nines, women you could actually *talk* with.

Maybe students, picking up a little extra spending money? He hadn't gone any further than chatting with a pretty blonde who'd introduced herself as Nicole. She'd casually asked if he felt like going upstairs, but he'd turned her down without a second thought. How could he object to Mirjam fooling around if he himself jumped into bed with the first pretty girl who offered herself to him? So they just sat there, side by side at the bar, and Nicole launched into a long story about some crazy experience she'd had in the Australian outback.

David slicked back his short-cropped hair. It was easy to keep it looking decent at this length. That, he'd explained to Mirjam, was why he'd had it cut so short before they'd left for France.

Bas was certainly milking it for all it was worth, this time. David gazed across the pool, the lawn, the terrace. The drive down had been a nightmare. The roadside restaurants were worse than ever, the service-area restrooms dirtier, the traffic jams longer, and the heat unbearable with the Alfa's air-conditioning barely functional. At one point, when Bas and Romy were bored with their DVDs and games and had resorted to squabbling, he'd threatened to turn the car around and go right back to Amsterdam.

Next year, they'd fly down and rent a car. More expensive, sure, but maybe by then he'd be bringing home a better income, thanks to Hein. For what he thought of as their "Van der Valk venture," Hein had slipped him a thick envelope as DD was helping him out to his car, and, in his condition, David hadn't even thought of refusing to take it. Hein had also paid for their drinks, and for the designated driver. When David had tried to run his own tab at the bar, Hein had treated the offer as an insult.

"Since when do guests pay their own way? You're my guest, D Squared, you know that."

Hein had hinted that he was even prepared to pay for the services of one of the hostesses, if David was so inclined.

Bas broke the surface of the water and shoved up against one side of the raft, and David, spluttering exaggeratedly, sank out of sight. Bas swam off like an otter, and David chased after him, faking fury. He let Bas beat him to the side of the pool, then hoisted himself out of the water and caught up with him. He scooped the happily screaming boy up in his arms.

"No, no, don't! Don't, dad!"

He tossed his son back into the pool and jumped in after him.

☙

This was good, it was fun—but there was something missing. No, why kid herself. It wasn't some*thing* missing, it was some*one.*

She had intended to throw herself fully into the spirit of a carefree family holiday in the sun. The drive down to Sainte-Maxime had been a descent through at least five of Dante's nine circles of Hell, but now they were here, and all she had to do was enjoy herself. They alternated between cooking in and eating out. David was playing the exemplary dad. Last night, she'd even had sex with him, and she had to admit that it hadn't been bad. Actually, it had been pretty good. Slow, relaxing, satisfying. After, as she lay beside her husband, catching her breath, it struck her that she hadn't once thought of Steven.

But now he was back in her head and impossible to ignore. Steven gave her the strength to face her daily routine. She needed him.

She set her book aside, sipped her diet Coke, and gazed off into the distance, past the pool, past the lovely vacation complex, past Sainte-Maxime. She could handle the ups and downs of her ordinary life with David, but it was just *so* damned ordinary. With Steven, she was a different woman, more attractive, more adventurous, more eager to give freely and fully of herself. More and more, her imagination carried her off to a better life. A more glamorous, more exciting life, rich with unexpected, unpredictable adventures.

David and Bas were romping around in the pool. She tried to convince herself that David wouldn't suffer because of her taking a lover, as long as he didn't know about it. A lover, she thought. Such a nice word. A man to love, a man with whom she could *make* love.

Her family life and her life with Steven existed side by side, each in its own compartment. Somewhere along the line, she'd read an interview in one of her magazines with a woman who was having an affair. "You don't need love to have a family," she'd said. "Running a family is like running a business."

It sounded so cold, but there was more than a little truth to it: the grocery shopping, the laundry, taking the kids to school, picking them up, ferrying them to and from their various activities, mealtimes, waiting around for the plumber to fix a leaky faucet, buying new clothes for Bas and Romy. There was always something. If you worked a "normal" job, you could leave it at the office when quitting time came, but taking care of a family meant *living* at the office.

She'd read the article more than once. To keep David from seeing it, she'd hidden it beneath a pile of old newspapers.

The nervous excitement she felt now came from Steven's suggestion. He'd offered to come to Sainte-Maxime, said he couldn't stand to be without her for a whole three weeks. And he was the sort of man who meant what he said. She knew that a watched pot never boils, yet she kept checking her cell phone's screen anyway. At the same time, she was scared to death he *would* show up. That would turn everything upside down, fracture their pleasant vacation—and it would all be her fault.

Fracture their vacation? No, Steven's presence would *shatter* it, *destroy* it.

They'd been here a little more than a week now, and there'd been nothing from Holland. Not a phone call, not an email, not a single text. Of course, with Steven you never knew. He might simply turn up, unannounced, by the side of the pool.

Or, more dramatically, he might rise from the water like Botticelli's Venus.

৶

"Not so far this time, okay, Dad?" Romy was using her exaggerated petulant voice, patent pending. "It's *so* boring!"

"When you whine like that," he said, "*you're* boring. We haven't been on the road ten minutes yet. Don't kick my seat, Bas, it hurts my back. Look, you see that man on the big rock? Maybe he's going to dive into the sea. Would you do that? Not me. It looks really dangerous."

They shot past the rock before the man could launch his really dangerous dive.

The coast road was crowded. Past Saint-Raphaël, the scenery was even more beautiful. To one side the improbably blue sea—he'd convinced Romy that the French tourist board had dumped hundreds of cans of blue paint into the water to get that precise shade for the enjoyment of the summer visitors—and to the other side a charming landscape of hills, rock outcroppings, forests, and occasional homes.

"I'd like to live in that one. How about you, Mirjam?"

"Look out, that car's turning left!"

Since last night, Mirjam had been behaving strangely. She had traded her happy vacation mood in for a stubborn silence. If the kids asked her something, she didn't seem to hear. This morning, David had caught her staring out the kitchen window at the blank wall of the next-door apartment. It wasn't the right time of month for her period, but maybe her cycle had been thrown off by the changes in her routine, by the heat.

Approaching Nice, an apparently endless traffic jam brought them to a standstill.

"We should have taken the highway," said David. "I thought it'd be prettier on the coast road."

"Prettier," Mirjam muttered unhappily.

"Where are we going, Dad?" asked Bas.

"I just thought we'd take a little drive and—"

"Now it's a little *don't* drive," Mirjam interrupted him.

"—and see some more of the area. Otherwise, it's all just the same thing. Swimming pool, beach, swimming pool, beach—"

"I *like* the swimming pool and the beach," said Bas.

"Hey, we're moving!"

Past Nice, David stuck to the small roads and drove through Villefranche-sur-Mer and Beaulieu. "That means 'beautiful place,'" he told the kids. "And it *is* a beautiful place. Years ago, before you were even born, your mom and I stayed here." No reaction, not even from Mirjam, though back then they'd been madly in love.

They stopped for lunch in Monte Carlo, found a café, and ordered *croque monsieurs* all around.

"Why don't they just call it grilled ham and cheese?" Bas demanded, trying to lick away a strand of melted Gruyère that had dripped onto his chin, just out of reach of his tongue.

"They like to have their own names for things. The French are kind of stubborn that way."

Bas laughed. "Like you!"

"You watch out, young man. When we're back in the pool, I'm gonna *get* you. Is that okay with you, Mir?"

She shrugged. "Can you order me another glass of wine?"

"Are you—?" He cut himself off. She'd already had two, tossed them back like lemonade. Maybe this was a deliberate attempt to medicate herself out of her bad mood.

During lunch, David rattled on about Europe's tiny countries: Monaco, Andorra, Vatican City, the Republic of San Marino. Then, when they left the café, he led them past what he called "one of Monte Carlo's most famous buildings."

"You're not going in," said Mirjam. "You swore you wouldn't—"

"Daddy swore?" asked Bas.

"Of course we're not going in," said David. "Kids aren't even allowed. But look how elegant it is! You don't see anything like this in Holland."

Behind the ornate entryway, he knew, were the gaming rooms. To one side, a huge room filled with long rows of slot machines. Long ago—it seemed like a lifetime ago—when they'd been in Beaulieu, they'd spent an evening in the Casino de Monte-Carlo. Mirjam had looked on disapprovingly as David pumped a few hundred francs they couldn't really afford to lose into the one-armed bandits. "I know there's a jackpot in there," he said. She couldn't understand how he could let himself get so caught up in something so completely idiotic. "I'm not caught up in it," he protested, "I just think it's fun." Mirjam shook her head. "You ought to see yourself," she said, "all hot and bothered, like the only thing that matters in the world is that machine."

Even then, he'd known that the slots were kid stuff. "Gambling for Dummies," he called them. The *real* gamblers patronized the rooms on the other side of the entrance hall. Blackjack, poker, roulette. They weren't allowed in that part of the casino, dressed as they were in T-shirts, shorts, and sandals.

Now that he was so close, he could feel the old excitement stirring within, a symptom of the gambling addiction that had gotten him into so much trouble in the past. *I'll bet I can… I'll bet you can't.* He couldn't even trust himself to have simple conversations like that. The size of the wager never mattered—a Euro, half a Euro, it made no difference. It was the interplay between the possibility of winning and the possibility of losing that held him in thrall. And you could bet on anything, that was part of what made it so exhilarating, and so dangerous. If two of the kids were arguing which could stay under water the longest, you could bet on the result. Would their history teacher show up for school with or without a tie? Would class clown Frits Biemans dare to sneak up behind the popular Barbara Boonstra and unhook her bra, or would he chicken out?

Soccer pools and the lottery had never appealed to him. There was no immediacy to them. That wasn't real gambling…

On the way back to the resort, they had a flat tire. Mirjam and Romy parked themselves angrily on the curb. Bas, clearly impressed, stood watching David manipulate the jack. *You want to help? Yes, that's it, just like that! Not so fast, easy does it. See, you can lift up a car!* He chattered happily as David pulled off the flat and mounted the spare.

Mirjam's cell phone chimed as she got up from the curb. She turned away, brushing off the seat of her shorts with one hand and checking her screen with the other.

"What was that?" he asked.

"Oh, nothing, just Thera."

"Important?"

"No, she's going to a party this weekend."

"We're partying every day," said David.

"Lucky us," she said, her voice flat.

❧

She had no idea how she managed to go on playing the happy mother and wife with Steven's text somersaulting around in her head.

"I'm coming."

That was all, just two words.

She'd texted back two words of her own—"No, don't!"—but she knew it was pointless.

"I'm coming."

Two words, eight letters, an apostrophe, and a period—and that was enough to put a full stop to her peace of mind.

Several times during the course of the evening, David asked her where she'd gone to.

"Me? I'm right here."

"You know what I mean."

Now they lay in bed. At home, David was the one who always had trouble getting to sleep. Here, though, he dropped right off.

Not her, not tonight.

She lay beside him, wide awake, worrying about tomorrow.

Chapter 10

David paced the vacation apartment's living room, cursing. He almost tripped over one of the kids' toys and kicked it into the corner. If it broke, so what?

"Fuck, fuck, fuck!"

Maybe he shouldn't have taken the family to Monte Carlo yesterday. That had probably torched her off, reminded her of all the money he'd pissed away earlier in their relationship. The financial wounds he'd inflicted on their marriage were still far from healed.

Yeah, it must have been Monte Carlo that had triggered her. Last night, after they'd gotten back, she'd been silent and stubborn. She'd barely paid attention to Bas and Romy. She was off in a world of her own. She'd said a clipped good night, closing the door on a rerun of the previous night's lovemaking. This morning she'd seemed a little more like herself, but then the bomb had gone off.

While the resort's childcare staff kept the kids busy with a treasure hunt, she started in about his gambling. Within minutes, they descended into all-out war. She yelled at him, called him a shit who only cared about work and his own little pleasures. "Like right before we came down here, that night you stayed out till two. Imagine if *I* pulled a stunt like that!"

He tried to calm her down, but anything he said just added fuel to her flame. The couples in the apartments on either side of them were getting an earful, but Mirjam didn't seem to care. She was right up in his face, raving, and at last he grabbed her, wrapped his arms around her in an attempt to settle her down, but she punched fiercely at his back and shoulders and head like a madwoman. She seemed determined to make him hit her back, but he forced himself to stay in control of his emotions. He had never hit her, never, and he wasn't going to start now.

"Fuck you, you bastard!" she screamed. She grabbed a suitcase, tossed in some clothing and her purse, and fled out the door. Where did she think she was going? She didn't know anyone here.

Temporary insanity, that was the only possibility. *Give her half an hour,* he told himself, *and she'll be back, sobbing apologetically.* He would hold her close and comfort her. Mirjam, his Mirjam.

But she'd been gone for more than five hours. He'd called her cell, again and again, but she'd turned it off—something she *never* did. Maybe he should start calling all the hotels in Sainte-Maxime. *Has a Madame Driessen checked in?* Or maybe she'd use her maiden name, Madame Zighorst.

Eventually, the kids had thought to ask where Mommy was. He told them that he and Mommy had had a little argument, and that Mommy had gone away mad for a while.

"What about?" Bas demanded.

"It doesn't matter. We just had a fight. She'll be back in time for supper."

"Yes," Romy announced in her most grown-up voice, "'cause she'll get very hungry."

Now Bas was busy with his Xbox, and Romy was outside with a girlfriend.

He'd delayed opening a bottle of wine as long as he could stand it, but now he was on his second glass. He looked again at his watch: five fifteen. How long could she leave them here like this? How long would it take her to cool down? Once she did, he'd have to tread lightly, check out the lay of the land, see if they needed to talk about it, or if it might be best not to go there at all and let whatever it was slowly heal itself.

He jumped when his phone rang. Mirjam. The police—they'd found her, unconscious, by the side of the road. Then how did they get his number? Well, duh, from the contacts in *her* phone.

"Driessen," he said nervously, trying to make his name sound French. It came out "Dree-SAH," with a silent n.

"Is this D Squared?"

Hein. Although David didn't give his personal cell number out to clients, as a rule, he'd made an exception for Hein. Everyone made exceptions for Hein.

"This is David."

"'Allo, Monsieur Dree-SAAAAAH." Hein's pronunciation was even more exaggerated than David's. "Zees ees 'Ein speekeeng."

"What's up? Trouble?"

David heard a click, a burst of static, another click.

"Having fun down there by the sea, by the sea, by the beautiful sea? A little sun, a little swimming, good food and drink, playing with the kiddies, playing with the wife when the kiddies go to sleep?"

"Yeah, it's all good. Took a few days to decompress from work, from the shitty drive down, but now we're all relaxed. Great resort, lots of stuff for the kids to do. It's just… Mirjam and me… we—"

His voice caught in his throat.

He wanted to take Hein into his confidence about the fight with Mirjam, but he didn't want to come off the pitiful victim, deserted by his wife, albeit just temporarily.

Temporarily, he thought. *What does that even mean?*

What was that old saying again? Chinese, he thought. *The longest journey begins with a single step*, something like that.

If Mirjam ever left him for real, there'd have to be a first step, a single step out the door. Maybe this morning she'd taken that step.

"'Allo, 'allo, tu es encore là?" asked Hein.

"I'm here."

"And everything's okay?"

"Not really, no. But, you know, normally a man and his wife get a break from each other every workday. On vacation, though, you're in each other's face twenty-four seven, and sometimes that's a little too much, you know what I mean?"

"Absolutely. That's why I'm still single. But, hey, I'm not your therapist, I need to ask you something. They searched my house this morning. Warrant and everything. Good thing you've got those documents. Just tell me they're safe, okay?"

"Safe as money in the bank. No one but me can get to them."

"Excellent. Since you're my legal guy"—he paused for a moment—"I thought you should know. Don't worry about it, though. Have a good time with the wife and kids."

Did Hein add a little extra emphasis to the word "wife," or was that just David's imagination? "Will do, but what about the search? What's going on?"

"Ah, John van Bremen's been arrested. He's probably trying to bullshit his way out with a bunch of lies, about me, for one."

"That's not good." David wondered if Hein was telling him the whole story. A suspect is in detention, and somebody *else's* house gets searched? That seemed unlikely, but this wasn't the right time to ask if there was more going on than Hein had told him.

"Whatever. There was nothing there for them to find. They even took my hard drive, but there's nothing on it. They must think I'm the Artful Dodger. When are you back?"

"A week from Monday."

"Okay, I'll see you then. We've got a few things to talk over."

"Such as—?"

But Hein had already broken the connection.

∽

If only time would stand still. If it never got any later, they could stay together like this forever. It was horrible to think that each minute that ticked by meant one less minute left for them to enjoy together. And the clock ticked inexorably on.

This evening and tonight, though, she would be here with Steven, no one could take that away from them. He'd booked a room on the top floor of the Hotel La Belle Aurore, with a balcony looking out across the Gulf of Saint-Tropez. They'd ordered up a simple dinner from room service.

And now it was time for her to call. What lie had David dreamt up for the children? She had her own story prepared. But would it convince Bas and Romy? Was she strong enough to reappear before them as the mother who'd run away, not only from their father, but from her own son and daughter?

The melodramatic question was unavoidable: *Does this make me a terrible mother?*

"More wine?" Steven asked.

"No, thanks. I have to call before the children go to sleep." It would be easier to text, but that was the coward's way out.

"Of course."

She sat naked on the edge of the bed, her phone in her hand.

☙

He lay awake most of the night, snatching brief stretches of sleep between bad dreams. When he finally dragged himself out of bed, his body was stiff, as if he'd spent too many hours in the gym.

Mirjam had called at eight the night before. She needed a night alone, she'd said, to work through her emotions. "I have to get some fresh air in my head." She'd gotten a room in a little hotel in the heart of Sainte-Maxime. She didn't want to say which one, as if afraid he might come after her. "It doesn't really matter, does it?" She would return sometime the following day. He asked her what she meant by sometime. "You'll see me when I get there." He told her he was only asking in case he wanted to take the kids somewhere. "Don't try to pin me down, David. That's part of the problem." He hadn't known that. If you didn't pin people down to specific times, how could you ever get anything done? Imagine telling a client, *You'll see me when I get there.*

Bas and Romy didn't seem aware that there was anything wrong. Mommy was having a sleepover by herself… what could be more normal? He and Romy had picked up sandwiches for supper, and she'd rattled on just the same as always. "When Mommy comes back, can we go to the beach?"

He decided not to worry about the timing of Mirjam's return. It would be dumb to hang around the apartment all day waiting for her. He'd leave a Post-it on the door: "At the beach." That would be plenty.

In the morning, they went into Sainte-Maxime to see the *Musée du Phonographe*, with its collection of old bell-horned phonographs... but alas no statues of Nipper the His Master's Voice dog. He explained what gramophones and gramophone records were—*and then the needle goes down into the groove and vibrates*—and told the kids that his father, their grandfather, had had one—*except his didn't have such a beautiful horn*—but neither Bas nor Romy seemed all that interested.

On the beach, all was practically normal. The only difference was that David had to shoulder all of the responsibility for the children's entertainment and safety. He checked his watch often and kept verifying that his phone was on. She might appear at any moment. But Mirjam was unpredictable—perhaps the air in her head was not yet fresh enough. Might she call only to tell him she'd decided to stay another night at her hotel? And, if so, would *one* more night be enough for her?

Maybe she'd taken the bus to Saint-Tropez, enjoying her unanticipated day of freedom, and she'd return when she was good and ready with a new bikini from some chichi boutique.

He looked around the beach. Lots of bronzed bodies. Weird, he thought, how women's swimsuits got smaller while men's got bigger. Like many of the other men in sight, he wore a pair of water shorts that stopped halfway between his waist and knees. Some of the younger guys, teenagers and twentysomethings, wore colorful board shorts that extended *below* their knees. Meanwhile, the women's bikinis left little to the imagination. Mirjam had brought at least five of them with her. Five... he'd never understand the female mind. He'd packed two bathing suits and had wondered if he'd really need the second one. But this was one of the mysteries he'd learned not to question. What he intended as nothing more than curiosity, she interpreted as an attack on her behavior, and she reacted accordingly.

Maybe she was already back in the apartment or sitting at the poolside bar, nursing a glass of white wine or rosé. Was she feeling at all guilty? He certainly didn't plan to accuse her. It wasn't about guilt, anyway. The only thing that mattered was that the two of them find a way to get along. This vacation was supposed to mark the end of a rough patch in their relationship, but now they seemed worse off than before they'd come.

Down by the waterline, Romy was building a sandcastle with a knot of other girls. Bas was nowhere to be seen. Shit, he'd been sitting here fantasizing about Mirjam when he was supposed to be looking out for his kids. He struggled up out of his beach chair and began searching. No Bas. He checked with Romy, but she hadn't seen him.

His heart pounding wildly, his throat dry, he scurried up and down the beach. He wanted to call Bas' name, but knew that was useless. Bas was a fine little swimmer. Last summer, he'd taken lessons and done remarkably well. The sea was calm. There was no way anything could have happened, it was impossible that…

He didn't dare finish the thought. Instead, he resumed his reconnaissance, searching high and low for his son.

He finally left the beach altogether and went back into the resort grounds. And there amongst the apartments and cafés and shops he found Bas at last, perched on a half-broken beach chair beside a trash dumpster.

Relief won out over anger, and he scooped the boy up in his arms.

"I was looking for Mama," Bas said, "but I couldn't find her anywhere."

೮๑

David tasted his coffee. Although he normally didn't care for a strong drink, he'd also ordered a glass of Calvados. Today, he needed it.

It was nine fifteen, and the subtropical heat of the day had scarcely dissipated. Bas and Romy were back in the pool. The Calvados burned a pleasant path down his throat.

"You sure you don't want a sip?" He held the glass up towards Mirjam.

"No, thanks. That stuff knocks me right off my feet."

"I can carry you back to the apartment."

She smiled. "Bas and Romy would like that."

He took her hand, brought it to his lips, and kissed it.

"I'm such an idiot," she said, turning away to hide her shame. "I don't know what came over me. It was just all, I don't know, I just went a little crazy. I'm sorry, David."

"It's okay. Forgiven and forgotten."

They sat there and watched their kids playing in the water. When Mirjam had finally returned, late that afternoon, Bas and Romy seemed to find her reappearance the most natural thing in the world, as if their mother had simply stepped out to run a few errands, and now she was back. As casually as he could, David asked her which hotel she'd spent the night at. She said a name, but it meant nothing to him.

"Was it okay?"

She shrugged. "Alone's alone," she said.

He took a sip of his Calvados.

Romy came running up. She jumped onto Mirjam's lap, an earnest expression on her face. "Mama," she said, "promise you won't run away again?"

Chapter 11

In his search for precedents in cases comparable to that of Mrs. Rijkhof, David came across a decision in a 2009 case. A woman had killed her husband after years of both psychological and physical abuse. The curious circumstance was that the murder was also committed with a heavy frying pan. On Christmas Eve, the victim had a few too many and at last drove his wife to violent action by singing "Silent Night" over and over again, like a broken record. This pushed the woman over the edge. She fetched a pan from the kitchen and bashed her singing husband's brains in.

At which point his night went really *silent*, David thought.

He stretched, yawning as if testing his jaw muscles to see how far they could go, and gulped coffee in an attempt to drown his sleepiness.

He had lain awake for hours again last night, unable to quell the thoughts that whirled around in his mind.

Money… debts… Mirjam… bills… Hein… solutions…

There was always a solution to every problem, he knew, but the problem was *finding* it.

He forced his thoughts back to Mrs. Rijkhof. Her husband had never hurt her physically, but she'd suffered more psychological abuse than anyone could have expected her to tolerate. And where was it written that psychic violence was less damaging than the bodily variety?

Meanwhile, Mr. Rijkhof had at last shuffled off this mortal coil. "I go on vacation for three weeks and the shit hits the fan," David muttered when he got the news, his first morning back in the office. Now the charge against his client would probably be bumped up to murder.

In the 2009 case, the lawyer had moved to have all charges dismissed, contending that his client's use of force was covered by Article 41, Section 2 of the Dutch Penal Code: "Exceeding the limits of necessary self-defense is permissible in cases where it is the immediate consequence of overwhelming emotion occasioned by the original assault."

David made a note.

Outsiders assumed incorrectly that the word "assault" always and only referred to a sexual assault, but in fact the term included any attack committed with criminal intent. In this case, Mrs. Rijkhof's offense clearly wasn't an "immediate" response to violence, but that wasn't necessarily a problem, given a Supreme Court decision dating from 1988 that had recognized the legitimacy of the so-called "delayed violent reaction." Even if the "original assault" had occurred sometime previously, a compulsion to retaliatory action could still be introduced as exculpatory evidence, since emotions often take significant time to fade.

Still searching, David came across a case in which a defendant had been regularly mistreated by her husband over a period of years before finally doing him grievous bodily injury. He could probably use this one, too. He thought he might even have a chance of getting Mrs. Rijkhof off altogether, if he could make the case that emotional abuse was entitled to the same legal standing as physical abuse.

He felt a moment of uncertainty. In principle, he was defending a woman who wanted to be convicted of a crime she hadn't committed, although she *had* devised the murder plan with the actual perpetrator, making her at the very least an accessory both before and after the fact. Meanwhile, the woman who wielded the murder weapon hadn't even been charged.

How much latitude did he have here? It wasn't his job to serve something as abstract as "justice"—assuming such a thing even really existed—but to serve the best interests of his client. She had the right to his unconditional loyalty, and if she was willing to be convicted of a crime she hadn't actually committed, that was her choice. His only option was to respect it. The customer is always right—and when the customer *isn't* right, the lawyer's job is to act as if she is.

Joost peeked in around the edge of the door. "Meeting at eleven. Jeez, you run into a lawn mower?"

David put a hand to his short cropped hair. "Yeah, you know, it's more comfortable in the summer. Hey, I wanted to ask you…"

He let the sentence trail away. Joost was probably the only person he could take into his confidence about Hein Wesseling. But maybe it was better if no one knew, at least no one at the office.

"Yeah?"

"Never mind. I'll be right there."

David sat there, gathering his thoughts. Joost had been with the firm about a year longer than he, had in fact been responsible for bringing David aboard. He was his last remaining friend from the law school group that had hit the bars together, hit on girls together, gone skiing, played soccer, kept each other awake through the all-night cram sessions. Usually in that order. There'd been six of them, but one by one the others had dropped out of sight. They got jobs way out in the boondocks, married women who weren't interested in nights on the town with their husbands' old gang, aged out of soccer. These days, their only bond was their memories.

The only one he still saw was Joost—and even that friendship had become less intimate since Joost's divorce a year and a half ago. They too had grown apart, their lives moving in different directions. Joost's had become more turbulent; he talked about it, sometimes, and David was glad not to be in his shoes. He had a young girlfriend, and they were out clubbing on the weekends till late at night—or, more accurately, till early in the morning. The trendiest bars and dance clubs, where—as David himself had experienced, the one time he'd accepted an invitation to join them—the music was earsplittingly loud.

Joost knocked on the door. "Hey, come on! Your lawn mower head still in the south of France? Time to get back to work, buddy!"

Meeting, shit. Yeah, it was time to get back to the daily grind. He made a few last quick notes for his pleading, and then headed to the conference room, where the first fifteen minutes were devoted to the usual "What I Did on My Summer Vacation" stories.

Vacation…

The memory of Mirjam's temporary desertion distracted him from Joost's account of his exciting trip across Southeast Asia. Thinking back on it, it seemed to him that Mirjam had forced their fight. It was as if she'd been *looking* for an excuse to disappear. A few days after her penitent return, she'd ended a phone call with a hurried "Talk to you later" the second he came into the bedroom. As breezily as possible, he'd asked her who she'd been talking to. Her mother, she'd said. She didn't say why she'd broken the connection so abruptly.

He thought back to the lists of phone numbers Emiel's tech guy had fished out of her phone. He had a feeling there was something about that one number he'd dialed, the man who'd told him he had a wrong number and refused to give his name. Last night, he'd sat there with his phone in his hands, a Post-it with that number scrawled on it on the desk in front of him.

While vacation stories ping-ponged across the conference table, David's thoughts kept going back to his wife. The last days of their stay, her mind seemed to be elsewhere. They talked, she played with the kids, had a glass of wine with him in the evenings, but she wasn't really *there*.

Tonight, he'd get in touch with Emiel. *He* could find out whose phone number that was.

"How 'bout you, David?"

He looked up and felt his face flush. Hopefully no one would notice it beneath his Mediterranean tan.

Paul, Maarten Starrebeek's son and heir apparent was smiling at him ironically. "Where'd you go? You look like you're still there."

A polite laugh went around the table. It was an unwritten law that Starrebeek Junior's jokes were always officially funny. David thought he ought to have a laugh track, like a sitcom. Every time he came up with a new knee-slapper, all he'd have to do was push the button.

"Me? Same as last year, family resort on the Côte d'Azur. The kids like it and, if they're happy—"

"—then Mommy and Daddy are happy, too," Paul finished his sentence, underscoring the banality of the remark.

David wanted to pop Starrebeek Junior right in the nose, just like Hein had hit the jerk at the gas station. Hein would know how to handle an ass like Paul Starrebeek.

Hein…

Nobody here had the slightest idea of David's involvement with him, and that's the way he meant to keep it. Yes, they knew he'd represented him that one time, but that was it.

Paul launched into a long-drawn-out tale of his whitewater rafting adventure. That was about as independent as Little Paulie got. Otherwise, he just toddled through life, holding onto Papa's hand like a good little boy, doing absolutely nothing whatsoever to put his lovely future as senior partner at a respected law firm at risk. Paul was in his late twenties, married, and he'd already ensured the continuation of the Starrebeek name: a photo of his fat little baby graced the desks of both Junior and Senior. They probably had wet dreams of changing the sign on the door to read "Starrebeek & Starrebeek & Starrebeek."

"And then, right after a Grade Four drop, there was this _huge_ rock, you couldn't possibly avoid it. But we managed to survive." Paul gifted his colleagues with a boyish grin.

"Okay," said Starrebeek Senior, "let's move on."

An assortment of cases were brought up for discussion. Starrebeek believed in brainstorming. "A little romp amongst the legal challenges and opportunities," he called it. What it really boiled down to, though, was him pedantically steering the junior attorneys through the intricacies of their cases. He often introduced his comments with a trite phrase along the lines of: "In my extensive experience, I have found that…"

Then came the assignment of new cases. Starrebeek liked to think that the work was distributed democratically, but in practice he reserved to himself almost complete discretion over which attorneys would be assigned to which matters. Although David had his eye on an armored-car robbery, he wound up with a flasher.

"You seem to be cornering the market on sex crimes," said Starrebeek, apparently thinking he was doing David a favor, "so this indecent-exposure case should be right up your alley."

"Cornering the market?" David scowled. "I don't *think* so."

"You're on that rape case, aren't you? And last year there was that abuse thing."

"Doesn't mean I've cornered the market."

Starrebeek grinned. "I didn't say you've *cornered* it, David. I said you're *cornering* it. You've shown real potential in that area. You have a problem with sex?"

There was general laughter, and this time it wasn't merely polite.

⁊

From what Lucas could see, it seemed like Selma had now pretty much confined herself to bed. She was certainly there now, curled up in a fetal position, her back turned to him. He sat on the edge of the bed and laid a hand on her arm.

"Get away from me." She ran the words together, making the command almost incomprehensible. *Geddawayfromme.*

"I'm sorry." He moved over to her dingy tub chair, so old he could feel its springs threatening his butt. "Have you talked with your lawyer?"

No reaction.

He repeated the question.

"Yes."

"You went over what you're going to say in court?"

She mumbled something inaudible.

"What? I didn't hear you."

Unexpectedly, she rolled over to face him. At full volume, she said, "I'm not going."

"But," he began, then cut himself off. He went to her kitchenette and filled a glass at the sink. "Here, drink this."

She swatted the glass from his hand. It shattered against the bedframe, and water flew everywhere.

"Be careful," Lucas warned. "You'll cut yourself." The words were out of his mouth before he could help it, but she didn't react. "Just stay there."

He swept up the broken glass and mopped the water with a dishrag. There was a smell of decay in the room. Lucas wasn't sure if Selma had changed her clothes in weeks. Had she even washed them? He didn't want to set her off, so he didn't ask.

"Can I open a window? Let in some fresh air?"

"No."

"Why not? It's stuffy in here."

"I don't want them coming in."

Lucas swallowed.

"Them?" Who were "them"? And why would they want to come in? And how *could* they? The room was on the second floor. Anyone who wanted to come in through the window would need a ladder.

"Don't want who coming in?" he asked.

"Men. It's not safe if the window's open."

Lucas changed the subject. He asked Selma if she wanted to eat something, but she said she wasn't hungry.

"It's after six. I can order a pizza."

She shook her head.

"Maybe you should move in with Mom and Dad for a while," he suggested. Their parents would be spending four weeks in Holland during the winter. Their mother had come down for a week in June but had mostly hung out with her girlfriends. She'd met Lucas and Selma in town for dinner twice, but that was all they'd seen of her. Selma had made him swear not to say anything about the rape, and she'd acted perfectly normally both times the three of them had gotten together. She apparently didn't want Mom to worry about her. She'd chatted pleasantly about school, friends, her little apartment.

Now, Selma said she didn't want to go to Finland. "Mom'll just nag me about school. What am I taking, how do I like it, how are my grades."

This is progress, Lucas thought. *At least she's talking.*

He decided to risk returning to the subject of the court case. "It's really important you show up for the trial, Sel. Then you can tell the judges what happened, so they can hear it straight from your mouth. That always makes a better impression."

"I said no," she repeated stubbornly.

"Why not?"

"He'll be there."

"Who, Patrick?"

A pained expression twisted her face.

"You don't have to talk to him. You don't have to *look* at him."

"That's easy for you to say. You're not the one who got raped."

❧

With definite misgivings, David shook hands with his client, Geert Verstegen. He couldn't stop himself from wondering how recently the man had beat off with that hand, and whether or not he'd washed it since.

"Tell me what happened and why you're here," he said.

Verstegen offered a confused account of a woman who'd begun screaming when he walked past her in the park. Frightened, he'd run off, and two men had grabbed him, called 112, and held him there until the police arrived. "I didn't do anything!" he insisted.

"Then why did you run off when the woman screamed?"

"She scared me."

Another poor sucker who'd seen no evil, heard no evil, and done no evil—or at least that's what he claimed. Even losers like this had a right to legal representation, but why was *he* always the one who had to deal with them?

Verstegen's eyes filled with tears.

David tried to summon up at least a little empathy, but the repugnance he'd brought into the interview room with him got in the way. "According to the woman's statement, you jumped out from behind a tree with your dick in your hand and asked her"—he checked his notes—"'Ever seen one of these before?'"

"That's not true! I was… I was out walking in the park, and I had to take a leak…"

David knew where this was going. He'd heard almost the identical story two years ago from another exhibitionist.

"I went behind some trees," the man went on. "Maybe I didn't have my fly zipped all the way up when I came back out, and so she got a little glimpse of my, um, my private parts. And then all of a sudden she was shrieking."

"Uh huh." David knew this was how he'd have to present his defense, whether he believed the pervert's sad story or not. He asked Verstegen if he'd ever been arrested for a similar offense before. And—surprise!—he had been, but that had also been a misunderstanding.

It had happened about a year ago. He was in the bedroom of his ground-floor apartment, dressed in what he called his birthday suit because he'd just stepped out of the shower. He thought he'd closed the curtains, but apparently they'd somehow slid back open a bit, and a woman walking by outside had seen him through the gap in all his glory. A half hour later, the police were at his door.

"And you were convicted?"

"Yeah, falsely. I got six weeks. It was totally unfair. I was the one telling the truth, but they believed her."

"And you're going to tell the judge that what happened in the park was another 'misunderstanding.' After you urinated behind a tree, you accidentally failed to adjust your clothing appropriately, and didn't notice that there was a woman walking towards you."

The man nodded eagerly. "Yeah, exactly, that's what happened."

"You need to realize that the court will be irritated if the judge suspects that you're not telling him the truth, that you're just making obvious excuses, because men who get picked up on this sort of charge almost always come up with this sort of story."

❧

David got home around six. Mirjam was in the kitchen, cutting up vegetables.

"Hi, honey. Have a good day?" he said. He pulled her close and kissed her on the mouth.

"You better be careful," she said. "I've got a knife."

David went upstairs to go through his mail. A few bills, a postcard from Paul Starrebeek of all people, and an envelope with nothing but his name scrawled on it, the two Ds written extra large.

There were two sets of car keys in the envelope, title papers, a parking pass, and a sheet of expensive stationery on which was written: "Dear D Squared, Here's a little thank you for all your help. It's parked outside. That old rust bucket of yours really has to go. Hein."

He was hyperventilating, and it took him several minutes to bring his breathing under control. He looked at his hands and saw that they were shaking. He paced back and forth in his office, sweating.

He went to the bathroom, but despite the pressure in his stomach he couldn't do anything. He flushed the toilet anyway, conscious that the action was a metaphor. He was flushing away something invisible, something intangible, but something important and real.

If he accepted this gift from Hein, he was saying goodbye to a part of himself, something he couldn't exactly define but that represented an integral part of his character.

What if he declined to keep the car? How would that even work? Just return the keys to Hein? He'd laugh at him and refuse to take them.

And, anyway, hadn't he earned it? He'd done exactly what Hein had asked of him, and he'd done it specifically because he knew Hein trusted him. He didn't want to—couldn't!—betray that trust.

Maybe he should lay the whole situation in Maarten Starrebeek's lap? No, that would make things worse. He'd have to explain *why* a client had rewarded him so lavishly, and that would not make the senior partner happy. He'd heard those words many times during their weekly meetings, when anything unpleasant was reported. "That does not make me happy."

"Dinner!" Mirjam called up the stairs.

Dinner. He wasn't sure he'd be able to swallow.

In the dining room, at the table, she told him he looked pale.

"You're not coming down with something, are you?"

Chapter 12

"Right, that's the number. Can you get me a name?"

"You know, you can do this yourself. It won't cost you anything, and you—"

Emiel's sentence exploded into a coughing fit, and David jerked the phone away from his ear. He could practically smell the stench of heavy shag tobacco.

When Emiel recovered, David said, "I'd rather you do it. Maybe you can follow her for a couple of days, just during the day, until she picks up the kids." He felt like he was being smeared with a layer of sticky muck. But now that he'd come this far, there was no turning back.

"You're talkin' about real money here," Emiel cautioned him. "Four hundred a day."

David had an image of Humphrey Bogart in black and white, with a stack of unpaid invoices on a spike on his desk and a bottle of whiskey in the bottom drawer. All that was missing was "SPADE AND ARCHER" lettered backwards on the insides of the windows and a shadowy figure flitting past the pebble-glass panel on the office door, while a secretary with pale pink lips leaned provocatively over the desk so he could look down her inviting décolleté while she hand rolled him a smoke.

Emiel impatiently repeated his price.

"That's no problem," David said. The Alfa was worth at least fifteen hundred, and he could pay the tariff out of that.

"It's a pleasure doin' business with you."

"You'll keep it lowkey, right?"

"What do you think? I'm gonna walk up and introduce myself to your wife: 'Good morning, Mrs. Driessen. My name is Emiel Lensink, and your husband has asked me to shadow you unobtrusively for a period of time, to see if you might be boffing a person or persons unknown'?"

"No, of course not, but I—"

There was a loud knock at the door.

"I have to go. I've got a client waiting."

"Fine," said Emiel. "You'll hear from me."

David opened the door to Mrs. and Mrs. Van Middelheim thoe Harchem, for whom Hanna had made an appointment. He waved them to a pair of chairs.

The man remained standing, and glanced around the room with evident distaste, while his wife cowered behind him. Her tight gray curls were so perfectly arranged on her head that the slightest movement might dislodge them.

"Is Mr. Starrebeek not handling this matter himself?" said Mr. Van Middelheim thoe Harchem. It wasn't merely a request for information. It was a recrimination, made even more cutting by the affected tone in which it was spoken.

"He is not," said David formally. "Mr. Starrebeek has a very full calendar at the moment. He has instructed me to represent your wife in his stead. I have handled many similar cases in the past—with considerable success—

and I assure you that the full legal knowhow of Starrebeek & Starrebeek is at your disposal."

Van Middelheim thoe Harchem was unimpressed. "I should hope so. Otherwise, I'll be quite disappointed in Maarten."

David again indicated the waiting chairs. "Will you sit, please? Can I get you anything? Coffee, tea, water?"

"Let's get straight to the point," harrumphed Van Middelheim thoe Harchem. "The more quickly we can put this ridiculous matter behind us, the better." He nudged his wife toward a chair.

"I agree with you completely," said David. "Can you tell me exactly what happened, ma'am?"

In a brittle and often faltering voice, the woman described the events of the day in question. She had obviously been coached by her husband. She turned to him with frightened eyes after almost every sentence and went on only after he rewarded her with a nod of approval. She'd learned her lessons well and laid out the story in the hope of a passing grade.

As David expected, she claimed the whole thing had been a mistake, a foolish bit of carelessness on her part for which she was deeply ashamed. She had selected an assortment of, ahem, undergarments, and was browsing the shop for other possible purchases. She was distracted by another customer, who had asked her a question, and had simply forgotten to pay for the, ahem, lingerie she had chosen. Only when the store manager had followed her out to the street and demanded—quite rudely—to look in her handbag had she realized her error.

David nodded with all the compassion he could muster, and delicately raised the question of the previous incident, when Mrs. Van Middelheim thoe Harchem had been arrested for the theft of five, ahem, foundation garments. "Because this is a second offense," he said, "I'm concerned that the court may have reservations about your version of the events."

"Why would my wife steal a few trivial items?" demanded Van Middelheim thoe Harchem. "She could buy out the entire store, if she had a mind to."

"But she did remove the items from the premises without paying for them, sir. That, unfortunately, is a problem, and the fact that she's done it before makes it worse."

Van Middelheim thoe Harchem glared at David as if he'd been personally insulted. "We are relying on *you*, young man, to make it better. That's what I'm paying you for, and I'm prepared to pay whatever it costs."

℃

David slid behind the wheel of the shiny new metallic gray Peugeot 308. Not an overly ostentatious car, but several orders of magnitude better than the Alfa. It was four forty-five, an early day, but he had several files in his briefcase that would need his attention this evening—including the flasher.

"These smaller cases are part of your education," Maarten Starrebeek had pontificated on numerous occasions. "They give you a chance to learn the finer points of the profession. Don't forget. There are no small cases, only small attorneys."

The cliché made David want to scream. A few years back, Starrebeek Senior had hinted that an "eventual" partnership was a possibility, but David was beginning to realize that "eventual" probably translated to the Twelfth of Never. He'd since put out some feelers, looking for a place with a firm that might offer him more potential for growth. Some six months ago, he'd responded to an ad in the *Advocatenblad* and applied for an opening at Tonnaer & Bouman. In his interview, though, it became clear that he'd be starting just as low on the T&B ladder as he was at S&S.

But now bigger things were in the offing, worlds beyond the low-hanging-fruit sort of castoff cases that were beneath the dignity of the high-and-mighty Maarten Starrebeek. Cases that brought him not just a mingy paycheck but a new Peugeot 308.

Before he turned the key in the ignition, David just sat there for a few seconds, eyes closed, breathing in the heady aroma of automotive leather—what a difference from the stuffiness of the Alfa!—and running his hands appreciatively across the dash. Mirjam's first reaction had been surprise, but that had morphed quickly into rage. A brand-new luxury car? How did David think they were going to pay for it? And *now*, no less, when they still owed on their vacation rental and expenses.

He had a complicated story all prepared. Low down payment, some cash he'd been able to set aside, an overdue raise in the offing, the Alfa was on its last legs anyway… and, he grudgingly permitted himself to pretend to admit, he'd made one little wager which had paid off big-time.

Yes, honey, I know I promised I wouldn't, but it was just this one time, and look how it turned out!

She only seemed about half willing to believe him.

His cell phone rang.

"David Driessen."

"Hein here. Everything okay?"

"Um, sure, but, Hein, the car. You shouldn't have done that. I'm actually driving it right now, on my way to—"

"Something wrong with it?" Hein interrupted him. "You rather have something better? A BMW 5-Series, maybe, or something Mercedesish?"

"No, come on, the car's fantastic. I can't thank you enough. Hang on, I'm parking."

"I'll see you at the Stadium later." Hein said something that sounded like "Vakzuid."

"I didn't catch—"

But he was gone.

He called Mirjam and told her he'd be home an hour late. In ten minutes, he pulled into the Olympic Stadium. Hein might have meant the Amsterdam Arena, the biggest stadium in the country, but he'd specifically *said* "Stadium," not "Arena," and the Arena was way out by the Bijlmer, so he took a chance.

He left the Peugeot in the parking garage and, sure enough, there was a restaurant called Vakzuid set under the grandstands with a terrace overlooking the track. The place was almost empty at this hour. Two tables had been pushed together, and a group of young women and a few men seemed to be engaged in a business meeting, but Hein was nowhere to be seen.

David wasn't sure what to do. Wait here, or roam around the Stadium? He assumed that people like Hein scheduled meetings here all the time. He sat at the bar and ordered a white wine.

Half an hour later, Hein still hadn't put in an appearance. He lingered another half hour and, to calm his jitters, drank two more glasses of wine. Finally, he pulled out his phone and dialed the number from which Hein had called him. No answer. He left the restaurant and walked all the way around the inner perimeter of the Stadium. He wiped his forehead with his handkerchief.

His phone rang.

Mirjam.

He let it ring through to voicemail. He didn't have time for her now.

The last of the Stadium's office workers were heading out for the day.

David went back into the restaurant and looked around.

No Hein.

He walked around aimlessly for a while longer, then finally gave up and headed for his car. On his way out of the garage, he dinged a parked Audi's fender. He got out to examine the damage. There was a miniscule scratch on his own bumper, but the Audi hadn't gotten off that lucky. He'd left a sizeable dent in the right rear quarter panel. David looked around the garage, saw no one, and got back in his car.

∽

Two days went by without a word from Hein. Not a sign of life. David grew more and more concerned. He redialed that last number repeatedly, but there was never any answer.

Something was wrong, that much was obvious.

At five thirty in the afternoon of the second day, alone in the office, he took the envelope Hein had left in his care out of the safe. Maybe it held some clue of how to reach him. In the kitchenette, he steamed it open. A cliché, he knew, that you only ever saw in old movies and Agatha Christie novels—but it worked like a charm. Look at him: a sort of modern-day Miss Marple.

But it worked.

He went through the documents, primarily bills of sale, but also some IOUs and several contracts revolving around financial transactions he didn't bother trying to understand. The names John van Bremen and Ben Heuvelink both appeared on numerous pages. David's breath caught when he saw some of the amounts mentioned. There were several references to something called "Papaya," which seemed to be an unfinished resort on Curaçao.

On the spur of the moment, he decided to make copies of some of the documents. While he was busy with that, his cell phone rang.

"Got 'er," said Emiel.

"What do you mean?"

"Don't be naïve. The woman's cheatin' on you—at least, that's what it looks like to me. That phone number you wanted me to trace? Well, she's been to the guy's house twice in the last week, both times around noon. It's in the Nicolaas Maesstraat. She's got her own key—doesn't ring the bell, just lets herself in."

"Jesus." David almost lost his balance but grabbed onto the photocopier for support. "Are you sure?"

"Of course I'm sure. She stays for an hour or two. Couple minutes after she takes off, the guy follows. Speaks for itself, don't you think?"

No, he didn't think. It wasn't true, there had to be some other explanation. "Some kind of business thing," David said wildly. "An interview. Now that the kids are in school, she's looking to go back to work."

"Dream on," said Emiel. "You want to put that spin on it, you have my blessing. But since when does a lady interviewin' for a job have her own key to the building?"

David had to sit down.

Mirjam… another man… a lover.

He tried to drown out the image of Mirjam lying naked on an unfamiliar bed, a man with no face running a hand up and down the length of her body.

Emiel coughed. "Second time was a little different. Your wife let herself in, and then the guy got there five minutes later, all out of breath. Obviously runnin' a little late for the erotic rendezvous."

The erotic rendezvous. Why did Emiel have to put it so snidely? The facts were bad enough. His snarky word choice just made it worse.

"You want to know his name?"

David hesitated.

A name would make it realer—although the name of the street had already made it real enough. How many hundreds of times had David driven through or crossed the Nicolaas Maesstraat? He'd probably *seen* the man, whoever he was.

"Well?" Emiel persisted.

"Yes, fine, go ahead."

"Steven Veenstra. Works at an advertising agency, Veenstra & Watzlawick, so I guess he's probably a partner. Well respected. Divorced about three years ago. One kid, a boy. You want more?"

"What's the number of the house?"

Emiel gave it to him. "You're not gonna do anything stupid, are you?"

☙

His first instinct was to go straight to the casino in the Leidseplein and gamble away every cent he had. Or find a café and drink himself into a stupor.

With the greatest difficulty, he resisted both urges.

But on the way home he detoured through the Nicolaas Maesstraat, past Steven Veenstra's house, crawled along the road searching for a parking space but couldn't find one. So he went home, parked a hundred feet up the street from the house, and sat behind the wheel for long minutes.

Mirjam was in the kitchen, preparing supper, always a major undertaking since Bas and Romy had very different ideas about what they would and wouldn't eat.

"Hi, honey. Have a good day?" she said, filling a saucepan with water. He had no idea if she was serious, or mocking him with his own standard greeting.

He gave her a light kiss. He had to keep himself together. No scene, absolutely *don't* make a scene.

"It was all right," he said. "Some stupid woman got caught walking out of a store with ten pairs of panties she hadn't paid for in her purse."

As expressively as he could manage, he told her about the Van Middelheim thoe Harchems, but he only made it halfway through the story.

Mirjam looked the same as ever. You couldn't *see* a difference, but it was there. She was still his wife and the mother of his children, but at the same time she was someone he didn't know, a woman with a life he knew nothing about and didn't share. He wanted to hold her, press himself to her and never let her go. He wanted to feel like they belonged to each other again.

"So what did he say then?" She gentled pasta into the boiling water.

"Who?" He almost asked her if she meant Steven Veenstra.

"Mr. Van Middleschool from Haarlem."

"Van Middelheim thoe Harchem," said David. And then, imitating the man's arrogant voice: "I hope I can count on your providing a competent defense, young man, so that my wife and I may quickly put this unsavory situation behind us without any unfortunate consequences."

Chapter 13

While Geert Verstegen, the flasher, repeated his confused story of the inopportune call of nature, the zipper zipped too late, and his shock when the lady in the park began to scream, David was watching the court clerk, an extraordinarily lovely woman, possibly half Indonesian, who he was seeing today for the first time. She offered him a friendly smile, and he returned a nervous grin. It was her smile that brought him back to this morning's surprising phone call. Hein hadn't said one word about their missed connection at the Stadium, and David wasn't about to bring it up himself. At three, they agreed, they would meet at a café in the Amstelveenseweg.

David gave his client's statement a veneer of truth by pointing out that there was in fact no public bathroom in the park or its immediate environs. Then he emphasized the absence of any corroborating witnesses—it was his client's word against the complainant's. Because of the previous conviction, though, the prosecutor demanded a heavy sentence: five months, of which two would be suspended.

Verstegen glared at David, reproaching him for not getting the case summarily dismissed.

&

"I need your help," said Hein, after ordering them each a cappuccino. "I like the short hair, by the way. Now you need to lose the glasses. You thought about Lasik? Or contacts?"

"Help with what?" asked David.

"At four o'clock, I need you to sign some papers at the notary. I take it you'll pass as a man of unimpeachable character?" He put air quotes around those last two words. They were fine words, words that meant something.

"Of course." David had trouble holding his curiosity at bay. What papers? Why did *he* need to sign them? What lay behind this request? Because there was guaranteed to be *something* significant behind it.

"Should we set this up through my office? So they can bill you for my time?"

"Won't be necessary," said Hein. "You trust me, right? Because I—"

The cappuccinos were brought by a buxom waitress. "Gentlemen," she smiled pleasantly, setting down the cups and saucers.

When she was out of earshot, Hein picked up where he'd left off. "Because I trust you, David. One hundred percent. You're a guy I can count on—and you can count on me, too. I know it, and I think you do, too."

"Absolutely. But these papers. What do they—?"

Hein interrupted him. "All will be explained. Later, at the notary. And this time no invoice, by the way. I'll pay cash, it's easier."

"It doesn't work that way," said David. "Hein, this is way out of my wheelhouse."

"Welcome to *my* wheel-and-dealhouse," Hein laughed. "Look, D Squared, you want to make a little extra money this afternoon, or not?"

"I can always use a little extra money, but—"

Hein laid a hand on his arm and eyed him narrowly. He seemed to see right into David's innermost thoughts. It was the same intense gaze he'd noticed that first time he'd seen Hein, in the gallery at Barry's hearing. "I think you could *definitely* use a little extra money right about now. And I want to help you, you understand that?"

"I do."

"We'll both come out ahead on this one… together."

Hein squeezed David's arm, not painfully but with force. It was as if he was transferring energy from his own body to David's. David wanted to throw an arm around Hein's shoulder, but he felt like that would be a sort of capitulation, and he didn't want to give in so easily.

"I have to be sure everything's on the up and up. Just because we're, ah, friends—"

"That's exactly what we are: friends."

"—that doesn't mean we're in business together," David continued, "especially not if it could get me in trouble with Starrebeek."

"There won't be any trouble," said Hein. "I'll take care of that. Starrebeek won't know anything about it. That's best for you, isn't it? I mean, you don't think Starrebeek really cares about you, do you?"

"Well, no, but—"

"That's settled, then." Hein gave David's arm another squeeze. Then, changing the subject, he asked about their trip to the Côte d'Azur, and listened with apparently genuine interest to a couple of David's stories.

Halfway through the flat-tire anecdote, Hein cut him off. "Something's wrong," he said flatly.

David shook his head. Talking about Sainte-Maxime had called up memories of Mirjam, their fight, her flight—and the devastating information he'd gotten from Emiel. But that was personal, private, not something he wanted to talk about with Hein.

"No, *something's* bothering you, I can see it."

"Not really." David didn't know what to expect from Hein if he unburdened himself about Mirjam, but he wasn't sure he could keep his emotions in check. There was already a lump in his throat that wouldn't let itself be swallowed away, and there were tears gathering at the backs of his eyes. He'd seen suspects burst out crying in the middle of their testimony. If only he had Hein's strength and self-confidence.

"Not really, or really not?"

Again, David shook his head. He was this close to losing it, but thankfully Hein seemed to know just how far he could go and didn't push the subject any further.

&

As they were leaving the notary's office, Hein said, "Let's grab a drink."

It wasn't a question, a request, a suggestion—it was a statement of what was going to happen next. "We've earned it with all these nice transactions."

Transactions, yes, that was the word. A nice word. In an hour and ten minutes, David had become the nominal owner of three buildings, then resold them for a profit of a hundred and twenty thousand Euros, which was deposited into a special bank account opened there on the spot, from which the money was then transferred to a numbered Swiss account.

The notary, with his stately façade and sober gray suit and vest, and the gold watch and chain he clicked open to keep track of the time, seemed born to occupy his prestigious office, the dark wainscoting lined with classical paintings. A secretary had served coffee and tea, with sugar and cream in ornate silver vessels.

Why, David thought, had *he* not studied notarial law?

There in the notary's office, he asked himself yet again if he shouldn't pull back, if his friendship with Hein was really worth the risks he was taking.

But *were* there any risks? Given the confidence-inspiring and thoroughly respectable appearance of the notary, it seemed impossible. Business was being done, yes. Ingenious business, lucrative business. But was it monkey business? The comfortable ease with which Hein arranged everything set his mind at rest.

Nothing could possibly go wrong.

Hein held him back as he was about to cross the street to his car. "You're coming, aren't you?"

David checked his watch. Quarter past five. He probably ought to be home by six.

"Let me call the house first."

"Sure."

Mirjam picked up so immediately he thought she must be sitting by the phone.

"I'll be a little late," he said.

"Okay. Any idea *how* late?"

"Can't say for sure… it's a complicated case." *That was certainly true*, he thought.

"No problem. I can always heat up your dinner for you."

"See you later."

She seemed unusually agreeable. Maybe she was feeling guilty.

"All set," he said.

At Hein's favorite café, they drank whiskey. David didn't often care for hard liquor, but this was a special occasion. The pretty waitress from their previous visit was there, behind the bar. Hein managed to get her phone number, which she scribbled on a beer coaster with obviously feigned reluctance. "You never know," he winked at David. After a second drink, Hein suggested they go elsewhere for a bite to eat.

David suspected it would turn out to be another late night. Hein seemed to be making up their agenda as they went along, but his apparent spontaneity was usually an act. There was always careful planning beneath the surface.

It was clever, the way Hein played it. He could learn a lot from Hein. This way, you could just surprise people, and then simply overwhelm any opposition. Without even knowing he was lecturing, Hein was teaching him life lessons more valuable than anything he'd taken away from his years at the university.

He called Mirjam again. He was going to be later than he thought. He had to see a client, and, after that, he'd probably have to go back to the office. He'd grab something to eat along the way.

When he hung up, Hein was studying him critically.

"Something wrong?" David said.

"Don't ever say more than you have to," said Hein. "Every unnecessary detail can come back to haunt you. What if she calls your office? You should turn off your cell. Better to be *un*reachable than reachable at the wrong time or place. A lot of people get tripped up that way."

David did as he was told.

"We'll leave your car and walk a little. Get some fresh air."

In the restaurant Hein steered them to, they shared a dozen oysters.

Maybe Mirjam would call a sitter, David found himself thinking, and go see her—her lover. Or she'd invite him over, and they'd do it in his own bed. His own bed, why hadn't he thought of that before? Probably *trying* to delude himself into ignoring the prospect. He forced himself to stay in his seat, but what he wanted to do was jump up and rush home. He could see himself bursting into their bedroom and finding Mirjam entwined with that fucking Steven Veenstra. That "fucking" Steven Veenstra. He remembered a case in which a man in a situation like his had stabbed his wife and her lover to death with a butcher's knife. The scene unspooled in his mind, and he imagined bright red flowers blooming on the white bed sheets.

Hein was waving his hand before David's face. "You here? Or dreaming of all that lovely money you just made?"

"Sorry, I was thinking about a case I've got coming up. Rape, at least according to the so-called victim."

"I know the story." In a singsong voice, Hein chanted, "First she said she would, and then she said she wouldn't." He took a sip of his wine. "You tell your client he needs to stay away from the cockteasers."

"I'll get him off." David said it as if he was sure.

"I'm sure you will. The kid got suckered. He shouldn't have to pay for a fuck gone wrong."

"That's my take."

After the oysters, they had wagyu steaks, then coffee with a twenty-year-old cognac.

"For dessert," Hein said, "we'll head out to Vinkeveen."

David hesitated. "I don't know if I—"

"Hey, you're not gonna flake out on me, are you? Are we pals or not?"

❧

"Feel like doing a line?" Hein asked as they were about to walk into the club.

"A line?"

Hein tilted his head.

"Oh," said David. "No, thanks, not my thing."

He didn't want to admit that he'd never even tried coke. In his student days, he'd taken a hit off the occasional joint, but as a nonsmoker he hadn't really enjoyed it.

"Yeah, I hear you. It's a hell of a kick, though, every once in a while. You ought to give it a try."

They walked around the side of the club. There was a rickety bicycle rack holding one rusty old bike without a rear wheel; the club's employees obviously didn't bike to work. Hein took two small paper packets, a square mirror, and a thin metal straw about four inches long from his pockets.

"How about it?" said Hein.

"No, you go ahead."

The situation reminded David of sharing a contraband beer behind the school with his buddies when he was fourteen.

Hein unfolded one of the packets, tapped out a line of white powder on the mirror, and snorted it up through the straw. He threw his head back and held his breath for a long moment. Then, "Good stuff," he exhaled. "Best you can get."

He tapped another line onto the mirror and handed David the straw. "You want to suck it as deep into your nostril as you can."

David did what he was told. He felt like Hein was proctoring a final exam he had to pass. His eyes welled with tears.

"Attaboy," said Hein. "Enjoy it. This shit's worth every cent it costs." He tapped his jacket at heart height, and David knew he was tapping his wallet. "But we had a good day today."

Inside, the place wasn't crowded. Soul music purred sensually from invisible speakers, a perfect soundtrack for David's mood. That was odd, because every song seemed to be about unattainable love and lost love, but David was feeling great. He sank into an overstuffed armchair and gazed around the room at the other customers and the hostesses. Hein was already chatting up a stunning blonde at least four inches taller than him. She laughed so infectiously at some story he was telling her that David, even though he couldn't make out a word, joined in.

Everything was clear and beautiful. What was the name of that girl he'd talked to, last time? Nikki? Something like that. He thought of Mirjam. She sat beside him and told him everything was going to be okay. "That's how strong my love is," sang Otis Redding.

But Otis was dead. No, don't think about that. What was the point? He was feeling better than he'd felt in months.

He looked over at Hein, who winked at him, his hand on the blonde's hip. They stood so close together you could hardly see any light between them. Hein toasted him with his glass. David laughed—it was good to laugh again, here with all these fine folks around him—and held up his own glass.

"Is the glass half full or half empty?" he whispered. That was the sort of thing that asshole Starrebeek always said. He really ought to give old Senior a good swift kick in the nuts. *What do you say now, huh, with your big fat mouth? You always know better… treat me like your little slave… well, those days are* gone, *Starry, gonegonegone. I'm taking over. Hein'll put up the cash, and I'm scraping Starrebeek right off the windows.*

The armchair's carmine upholstery was so soft. He caressed it with his fingertips and brushed the hand of a woman who was sitting on a plush ottoman beside him.

"Who's Starrebeek?" she asked. "I never heard that name before."

Oops, he'd apparently been talking what he thought he'd only been thinking. The woman was on the short side, but well endowed for her height. Were they real?

"Nobody," he said. "Doesn't matter." Didn't matter about the breasts, either, certainly not to the guys who went upstairs with her. The shape, the shape was what mattered, the softness of the skin, the ripeness, the sensitivity of the nipples. He wondered if silicone made a difference. He'd have to look into that.

Something she'd just said caught his attention. "First? First what?"

"I said is this your first time here?"

He laughed.

"What's so funny?" She was smiling. Sweet little thing, he thought, with those sweet big tits. Big tits, nice knockers, great rack. He giggled.

"What *is* it?" She stroked his cheek.

Suddenly the name came to him. "Nicole," he said. "Is Nicole here?"

"She's not working tonight. But I am…"

∽

Mirjam called him at seven, and Steven promised to keep the evening open and await further developments. When the kids were asleep, she called again.

"I don't know where he is or when he's coming home. I'm guessing late."

"How late?"

"I don't know. He didn't say."

Mirjam thought she could hear him breathing on the other side of the city.

Steven broke the silence: "Let's take a chance."

That was typical Steven.

At nine, he entered her home for the first time. She tried to see the place through his eyes. The couch and chairs were due to be replaced. One of the table lamps dated all the way back to David's dorm room. He hadn't been willing to part with it and still used it for reading. Steven wouldn't like the Herman Brood print. He'd think it cliché. And what about the wall of family photos? The kids, her and David, the four of them on vacations, day trips, parties, birthdays, with both sets of grandparents. The wall presented them as everything a loving family should be.

Steven pulled her to him, kissed her, pressed her so close it hurt a little.

She asked him if he wanted something to drink.

"You know what I want."

∽

By the time he and Hein were in the cab, the effects of the coke had faded, although his heart was still pounding. His body felt heavy, and he was exhausted.

"Good time?" asked Hein.

David nodded.

"You were flying."

David knew he should be grateful—Hein had paid for everything—but he couldn't find the right words.

Now that the euphoria had passed, his conscience began to poke at him. But, shit, look at what Mirjam was doing. She wasn't just holding hands with advertising boy. So now he'd paid her back.

But didn't that give her permission to go on?

No, what he'd done was different, a one-shot deal with a woman he'd never see again. He stretched out his fingers. Those breasts had been bigger than his hands. The nipples had seemed incredibly sensitive, but maybe she was faking it. Her orgasm, too? He sighed.

"Any regrets?"

"No, not really."

"'Cause you've got nothing to be sorry about," Hein told him.

He wasn't sorry, but David couldn't decide what exactly he *was*.

They took the Rijnstraat into town. Hein told the cabbie to stop at Victorieplein, and he got out there.

"Next Saturday, we're going fishing."

"I," David began, but Hein had already slammed the door. David watched him strike off briskly towards the Churchilllaan.

He gave the driver his address. When the cab stopped in front of his house, the meter read seventy-three Euros. He handed over a pair of fifties.

"Keep the change," he said.

Hein would have said the same thing, in the same carefree tone.

Chapter 14

David couldn't shake loose the memory of the girl sitting there so despondently during the pre-trial hearing. Who could say what impact the incident—to give it a neutral name—would have on the rest of her life?

No, he couldn't think of it like that. It wasn't his problem, not a cross he had to bear. The moment he put on his black robe and tied his white neck band, he stopped being David Driessen and became someone else, a someone to whom the only thing that mattered was winning.

Patrick was playing his part to perfection. The image of a normal young man in neatly pressed trousers, dress shirt, and simple sport coat. He had a pat answer ready for each of the judge's questions. "If I'd known what would happen, Your Honor, I would never have gone upstairs with her," he said, just the right note of contrition in his voice.

The public prosecutor produced the usual song and dance, droning on about "the victim of this brutal rape," and how she'd been "shattered by her traumatic experience." She was so emotionally damaged that it was impossible for her to be present in the courtroom—a further confrontation with the perpetrator would be far too stressful.

David objected to the use of the words "victim" and "perpetrator."

"It's for the court to determine whether a crime has been committed here, or if we're dealing with consensual sex which Ms. Groothuis ultimately regretted, leading her to invent her story of a rape."

"Sustained," the presiding judge said.

❧

Lucas listened from the public gallery, growing angrier by the minute. It was infuriating how Patrick's lawyer twisted everything, manipulated the facts, made Selma look like a liar, lasered in on that period after it had ended with Eric-Jan and she'd dulled the pain of a broken relationship with a couple of harmless flings. He was painting her as a whore and Patrick as practically a saint. Wouldn't hurt a fly, university graduate, lots of friends, the occasional girlfriend.

The court would announce its ruling in two weeks. Lucas waiting outside the courthouse for a quarter of an hour, and then Patrick and his lawyer came through the revolving door and headed for the parking garage.

Lucas followed them, stayed about thirty feet behind. They were talking animatedly. Patrick laughed at something the attorney said. Probably joking at his sister's expense. The bastards. Half concealed behind a pillar in the garage, he watched Patrick slide into the lawyer's car.

❧

David blinked. Clear vision without glasses—when was the last time he'd had *that*?

They wanted him to keep the trial contacts in for two hours, then return to Specs & Lens—it sounded like a comedy team!—for further consultation with the optometrist. The eye exam hadn't taken as long as he'd expected. The main concerns were the strength—or weakness—of his eyes, and their general condition. Then a pleasant optician had showed him how to insert and remove the lenses. He'd practiced clumsily under her patient supervision—it would have been easier if she hadn't been watching him like a hawk.

His first thought had been to opt for Lasik surgery, but he'd Googled the procedure and learned that in rare cases it could go wrong, resulting in *worsened* vision or even blindness. He could just picture himself shuffling along behind a seeing-eye dog or flailing about with one of those long white canes, and ultimately decided that, no matter how slight the risk, it was a risk he didn't want to run.

Two hours. He'd taken the afternoon off for what he thought of as Step Two of the David Driessen Makeover. So what should he do to pass the time?

Like most of his colleagues, David bitched and moaned that his workdays were overbooked. Give him some unanticipated free time, though, and he didn't know what to do with it.

He'd had Emiel on the phone yesterday and gotten the confirmation he'd needed but feared. He'd observed Mirjam more closely than usual all evening, but she didn't seem any different.

He was the one who had changed, and he knew it was the changes he was feeling on the inside which had motivated him to start making some changes on the outside. He didn't tell Mirjam of his decision to trade his glasses in for contacts.

Without consciously choosing the destination, he found himself walking in the direction of the Nicolaas Maesstraat. He pulled up across the street from Steven Veenstra's building. It was ten to three. What were the odds of Mirjam being there now? Probably small. She had to pick Bas and Romy up from school at three thirty.

He crossed the street.

There was a row of buzzers next to the door, and "S. Veenstra" was listed on the second floor. He pressed the bell, with absolutely no idea what he would say if there was a response. *This is Mirjam's husband.* Sure, and then what? *I want you to keep your goddamn mitts off her?*

S. Veenstra would laugh in his face, kick him down the stairs, call Mirjam to report her husband's ridiculous behavior. No, he wouldn't let the bastard make a fool of him like that. He'd taken enough shit already.

There was no response to his ring.

He tried again—and again nothing.

He pulled out his phone and Googled Veenstra & Watzlawick. Their office was only two blocks away. He still had an hour and a quarter before the friendly folks at Specs & Lens expected him back. He had to fill the time somehow.

He found the office building and stood across the street watching the front entrance for fifteen minutes. He had no idea what he expected to see. The name VEENSTRA & WATZLAWICK was painted on the windows in large block letters. Veenstra's partner probably wasn't even called Watzlawick. The unusual name had probably been selected only as a contrast with the ordinary "Veenstra." If there even *was* a partner, he might be Visser, or Smit—or, for that matter, Spade, or Archer. "Veenstra & Spade"—no, that was too bland for the world of advertising.

David didn't even know what Veenstra looked like. If the door swung open and the man himself emerged, he wouldn't stand a chance of recognizing him. This morning, he'd actually consulted Google Images, but there were dozens of Steven Veenstras, everything from newborn babies to retirees.

On the spur of the moment, he crossed the street and rang the bell. A buzzer buzzed, and the door clicked open. He found himself in a large open office, where he would have expected some sort of reception room or counter. The walls were hung with poster-sized reproductions of ads for laundry detergents, coffee, a nature club. Two young women and a man sat behind desks. One of the women, with a head of auburn curls and a pair of horn-rimmed glasses, asked if she could help him.

"Is Mr. Veenstra in?"

She pushed her glasses a fraction of an inch higher on her nose. "Do you have an appointment?"

"No, but I was in the area, and I thought, well, I thought I'd drop in and take a chance."

"May I ask what this is in reference to?"

David noted the absurdity of her asking him if it was okay to ask him. A social nicety, silly as it might be. "It's a personal matter."

The other woman and the man looked up from their computers.

"So you're not a client?"

"No, I'm not."

"Then I'm not sure if—"

The woman glanced at her colleagues. The man nodded.

"Well, let me see." She typed something into her computer. "I can put you in for next Tuesday morning at ten fifteen. Will that work?"

David pretended to consider it, fished out his iPhone and tapped the screen randomly as if he were checking his calendar. "Yes, that's fine. Tuesday at ten fifteen."

"And you are, sir?"

"Harry Krook." It was the first name that popped into his head. He'd gone to grade school with a Harry Krook; the poor kid had been hit and killed by a drunk driver.

"May I have a contact number, in case Mr. Veenstra has to cancel?" Her glasses had slipped down her nose again. Too heavy, perhaps.

David made up a number.

୧୬

"I'm getting contacts."

"What?" Mirjam had no idea what he meant.

"Contact lenses. No more glasses."

"Oh. Well, if you think you'll like them." It was an indifferent reaction, and she backed up and tried again. "I mean, I'm used to you in glasses, but I'm sure you'll look good without them."

David poured them each a glass of wine. "Cheers."

She continued snapping string beans and didn't respond, and, when he stayed where he was, leaning against the doorway that connected the kitchen to the dining room, she asked him if he was checking to make sure she was doing it right.

"Me? How would I know?"

"I have no idea."

He went into the living room, where Bas and Romy were in front of the TV. It was Romy's turn to control the remote. They'd gotten the idea from a parenting magazine. The kids traded "remote duty" on alternate days, and whoever turn it was got to select that day's viewing. It was a simple system, and it put an immediate end to their television turf wars… though not to their daily disappointments, since each child had favorite programs the other couldn't stomach.

David grabbed the paper and went up to his study, as far from the screeching racket of the American cartoon show as he could get. But he still couldn't concentrate.

What would happen if he suddenly said Steven Veenstra's name aloud, completely out of the blue? *So, did you see Steven today? How's it going with you and Steven?*

He'd love to see her reaction, but he didn't have a clue where to go from there. He would have laid his cards on the table—and then what? What would she do? Confess? Probably not. Burst out weeping? Get mad? Go on the offensive? Maybe she'd storm out again, leave him alone with the children. *I've had it, David. I'm going to Steven's.* And then?

He considered a series of scenarios. None of them had happy endings.

There were three possibilities.

First, they could get divorced, the kids would stay with Mirjam, and he'd move into some pathetic bachelor pad, the sort of nothing little place he'd often visited to question suspects and potential witnesses.

Second, they'd get divorced, Mirjam would move in with Steven, and he and the kids would remain in the house.

Neither one of those options satisfied him. Mirjam was his wife, dammit, the mother of his children. She was the only woman he'd ever really loved, the only woman he *would* ever love, he knew that without hesitation or doubt. It was sentimental and foolish, he knew *that*, too, but it was what was in his heart.

The third possibility—and, without even realizing he was doing it, he held up three fingers to an invisible judge—was that Mirjam would break off her affair, but she'd resent him for forcing her to end it with Steven, and their marriage would never be the same.

He took a long swallow of his wine. There was a burst of whining from the living room, but it ended before he could hoist himself out of his chair.

There was, he realized, a fourth possibility. Things could simply go on as they were. He would have to figure out a way to tolerate Mirjam's extramarital relationship.

"Extramarital."

He said the word aloud, softly, tasting it on his tongue.

No, he couldn't possibly live that way.

He'd read about the Swinging Sixties, when "Free sex!" was the battle cry of the liberated generation prior to his, and open marriages were common. It was supposedly healthy for couples to grant each other permission to do whatever they wanted, whenever they wanted, with whoever they wanted to do it. Horrible. Just the thought of it was unbearable. He refused to share his wife with another man. His love for her was too intense, too all-encompassing. *Hey, sweetie, you have a good fuck last night with X—or was it Y—or was last night Z?*

No, never.

☙

David sat in his study, going over the Rijkhof documents for the umpteenth time, though he already knew the details of the case backwards and forwards. A few more days, and then the trial. He'd made an impassioned plea to release her on her own recognizance pending the court date. There was zero danger of her re-offending, no abuse of the legal system would be occasioned, and the chances were that, even if she were convicted, her sentence would be shorter than the time she'd already served if not suspended entirely. But the court had not been moved by his arguments, and Mrs. Rijkhof remained in detention.

He had visited her again in jail. She seemed to be handling her incarceration without the least bit of stress.

He got up and went into the hall. Television sounds filtered up from downstairs. He crept halfway down and saw Mirjam sitting with the kids as if everything was perfectly normal. He crept back up to his study. What should he do? He went back over the possibilities yet again.

Mirjam did what she felt like doing, as if he didn't matter, as if his happiness meant nothing to her, as if he didn't even exist for her any longer. And he had to suck it all up, act like there was nothing wrong, let no one know that he was suffering.

Why?

Nothing seemed to matter anymore.

He pushed the case file to the side of his desk, switched on his computer, surfed over to *888casino.com* and typed in his username and password.

Chapter 15

The charge was murder, with a secondary charge of manslaughter. The prosecution was apparently so sure of its case that it had filed no charges less than manslaughter. Mrs. Rijkhof seemed not to understand.

The presiding judge—chief of the three justices who would hear the case—summarized the facts that had been presented during the pre-trial hearing, including the testimony of the witnesses who had described the lengthy and systematic psychological abuse to which Mr. Rijkhof had subjected his wife, and read out extensive passages from the psychological report on the defendant.

One of the statements, perhaps the most telling, came from the neighbor, Maaike Vlietstra. David had spotted her in the public gallery, though he knew she belonged at the defense table.

He'd lain awake last night, unsure what to do about Mrs. Vlietstra, and, before leaving the office for court this morning, he'd discussed his concerns with Joost.

"I know she's the one who swung the frying pan, not the defendant," he'd said.

"What you *know* doesn't matter," Joost had reminded him. "Your job is to represent your client, I don't have to tell you that. If this is how she wants to play it, that's her business. You just stand by her and do your best. That's what you're there for."

In this case, David felt, what he was there for was flat-out wrong. He felt that way about a lot of what he did—especially what he was doing for Hein.

But *that* he didn't discuss with Joost.

The oldest of the three judges asked Mrs. Rijkhof why she hadn't simply left her husband if—as she had testified—he'd made her life a living hell.

"I couldn't. I knew he'd never let me go. I tried to leave him, two years ago, but it didn't take him three days before he found me."

"And *when* he found you, what did you do?"

"I went home with him. What else could I do?"

At the end of his closing argument, David emphasized that his client had lived for years in fear. "Her husband controlled her life, her spirit, everything. She was completely subjugated, and that is a well-known psychological syndrome. They lived together in a pathologically symbiotic relationship, what the psychiatric literature describes as 'parasitism,' with Mr. Rijkhof as the parasite and his wife the host. This condition is attested to in the psychologists' reports."

A symbiotic relationship.

He thought of Mirjam. Was he himself unhealthily dependent on her— or she on her lover?

One good shot with a heavy frying pan… that was enough to kill a man. Though Steven Veenstra was decades younger than the late Mr. Rijkhof, and maybe his skull was harder…

The presiding judge broke into his thoughts: "Are you done, Mr. Driessen?"

"Ah, no, Your Honor, my apologies."

He picked up the thread of his argument. The charges against his client were unwarranted. At worst, this was a case of assault. Since *that* charge was not mentioned in the indictment, however, the court had no choice but to acquit Mrs. Rijkhof of the charges that *had* been filed against her.

If the court *should* decide that the defendant's actions rose to the level of manslaughter—and this, David said, would greatly surprise him—then the "delayed reaction" precedent should be taken into account. He reminded the court of the witness testimony to the victim's lengthy mistreatment of the defendant.

"Therefore," he concluded, "I ask Your Honors to dismiss all charges and order my client's immediate release from custody."

જી

"What *do* you want?" There was a plea in Steven's eyes, an expression she found hard to resist.

"I don't want to lose you. I'd rather—"

Mirjam had a dramatic finale for that sentence in mind—*I'd rather die!*— but she didn't say it. Too pathetic, and who would even believe it?

She snuggled deeper into his shoulder, her hand on his belly, her fingertips stroking a patch of dried sperm. She could stay for another half an hour, no more. And then? What about the hours, days, weeks, months to come?

She wanted to say something, something sweet, something tender, but despair blocked off the words.

"You could ask him for a divorce," Steven said, his tone subdued, as if he was afraid to pronounce the D word.

"Divorce?" It was the first time either of them had acknowledged the possibility aloud, although they had edged around it, like animals circling a prey they were afraid to confront.

"We can't go on like *this*," he said.

Her muscles cramped, her fingers clenched. Was this their last afternoon together?

"Well?" Steven demanded.

"I don't know. David… the kids… what would it do to them?"

Every time she thought about it—and she'd thought about it often in recent days—she panicked. She was afraid of drowning in a flood of chaos.

Steven worked himself into a half sitting position, propped up on one elbow, and her head fell away from his shoulder. "Honestly, Mir, I don't know how much more of this I can take. I hate to pressure you, I know how hard it is for you, how much I'm asking." They gazed at each other longingly. "It'll be worth it, you know that."

She sighed.

"All the lies," he said, "the stolen hours, the hiding. I just can't do it anymore, baby."

She held a finger to his mouth. "Me, neither."

He kissed the finger and pulled her hand from his lips. "When you're divorced, we can be together all the time, do whatever we want. I won't have to sneak away from the office like a thief in the night. I think they're starting to suspect something's going on." He frowned. "And you won't have to go on lying to David, making a fool of him. You don't *like* cheating on him, do you?"

"No."

"So it's David or me. You're going to have to decide—I can't do it for you. All I can do is wait for you to choose." He sounded completely powerless.

"I'm *scared* to go through a divorce, Steve. David's a lawyer, he knows how to twist the system so everything works out best for him. If he's even ten percent in the right, he futzes around until the other ninety percent goes his way, too. He'll wind up with full custody of the kids, I know it!" Her eyes filled with tears.

"We'll get you the best divorce attorney in town."

She held him close with all the strength at her command. "I don't want to lose you," she cried. "I don't ever want to lose you."

∽

It was a quiet Saturday morning. The city hadn't yet awakened. A few early birds were biking down the street. People on their way to first-shift jobs, a teenager with a paper route. It was a crisp September day, the sky filled with the standard Dutch clouds that occasionally permitted a glimpse of the sun.

David asked where they were headed.

"The Amsterdam-Rijn Canal," said Hein. "If it's quiet, there'll be fish. I'm not one of those nuts who needs to drive an hour out into the country and hang out with a dozen other fanatics who'd rather stand there bullshitting about rods and reels and lures than actually *fish*. Half of them are kitted out with all sorts of electronic gear that does everything for them but bait their hooks. Not my style."

Hein had picked him up in the Van Baerlestraat, near the City Concert Hall, in a brand-new Mercedes. David had figured it would be better to meet there than have Hein come to the house. To explain his early absence to Mirjam, he'd invented a client all the way up in Groningen. "Big case," he'd said. "Something to do with insider trading. I don't know all the details yet."

As he said it, he knew he was violating Hein's Golden Rule: keep it simple, don't tell people more than they need to know.

But he couldn't stop the flow of words. He'd take the train, he said, so he could work while someone else did the driving. Impossible to say how late he'd be home.

These last few days, Mirjam had been even more distant than had become usual for her, as if she was rehearsing for life after divorce. Again and again, David had made up his mind to tell her he knew about Steven Veenstra, but each time he'd pulled back.

Today, he'd arranged for Bas to go to fencing practice with a friend. He felt like he was now responsible for everything: the house, the kids, money, safety, security, you name it.

And yet...

"We'll just cut through Diemen," said Hein, "and we're there."

They parked on a residential street and walked the last hundred yards to the canal. Hein carried their rods, and David struggled with a tackle box in one hand and a pair of camp stools in the other. There was no one in sight in either direction except one guy off to the east on a folding beach chair, gazing out at his bobber. Or at least that's what it looked like he was doing. He might just as well have been sleeping.

"Here you go," said Hein, handing over one of the rods. "Simple stuff, nothing fancy. That's the reel, and that's the line. You catch something, you reel it in. Got it?"

David nodded.

"Okay, bait. Fish are like people, you have to lure 'em in or they won't bite." Hein tossed him an exaggerated wink. He unscrewed the lid from a jar of writhing grubs. "Need me to show you how to bait a hook?"

"Please."

"Just hold the little guy still and shove it up his ass."

David swallowed while Hein skewered the wormlike larva. "You don't want to kill it. If it's still squirming when it goes in the water, the fish are more likely to fall for it. Live bait, that's the ticket." Another wink. "You want to do your own? Not yet? Okay, you set up the chairs—you can handle *that*, right?"

When they were settled in, their hooks in the water, a sense of peace descended on David. He understood that this was the point for Hein. The fishing was secondary, just an excuse he used to justify getting far from the madding crowd for a while, leave the daily bullshit behind and just chill out by the canal. Sure, he might actually catch a fish every once in a while, but he didn't worry whether he did or didn't, and it didn't matter. "If I *do* hook anything," Hein had told him, "I throw it back. I want to *eat* fish, I go to a restaurant. You don't get swordfish or tuna out here, anyway. Not many shrimp, either."

"Lobsters?"

Hein smiled. "Yeah, no." He produced a thermos. "Coffee?"

David nodded.

"You'll have to imagine the donuts."

After about an hour, Hein got a bite, a silvery thing about four inches long.

"Bitterling," he announced. He worked the hook from the little guy's mouth and tossed him back in the water.

"Doesn't that hurt it?" David asked, trying to keep his voice light.

"Not really. Human lips are full of nerves. That's what makes 'em so sensitive—which is why we get off on kissing." Hein pursed his own lips and made kissy noises. "But fish have practically no nerves in their lips, so they can't really feel anything."

He and Mirjam almost never kissed each other anymore, and never as passionately as they had at the beginning of their relationship. But with Steven Veenstra…?

He wanted to call her, right then and there, but he shook off the compulsion. He stared for long minutes at his plastic float, bobbing up and down on the canal's gentle wavelets. There was nothing to see on the far side of the water, nothing to distract him from the question that preoccupied him: What was he going to *do?*

He felt like he was standing in front of a locked door and couldn't find the key. He could break it down, but then what?

He jerked back to the present, dimly aware that Hein had asked him a question.

"What?"

"I said what's wrong? You look so serious, so… well, morose. Is that your normal Saturday morning face?"

"I…" He hesitated.

"Can't talk about it?"

David was silent.

"Don't have to if you can't. I don't want to butt in on anything that's none of my business. It's not our, ah, transactions, is it?"

David shook his head. And without warning, the tears came. Dammit, he was bawling like a baby. What would Hein think? Hein was the last person he wanted to see him like this. He wiped his face with the sleeve of his jacket and sniffled.

Hein slid off his camp stool and knelt beside him. "Hey, come on, man, what is it?"

David shook his head. "Just give me a minute."

"You in trouble? What's going on?"

"It's Mirjam." He spat out the name as if he'd held it in his mouth for too long and it had gone sour.

Hein took a flask from his tackle box. "Take a slug of this. It's good cognac. Really ought to drink it out of a warm glass, but it's good like this, too. Sometimes better." He returned to his stool. "Mirjam," he said softly. "That's your wife, right?"

David took a long pull of the brandy. It burned its way down. He drank some more. It was like a thread of fire connecting his mouth to his stomach. There was still nothing to see on the far side of the canal. The grassy dike just sat there, unchanging. He found a handkerchief and blew his nose.

Then he told Hein about Mirjam and Steven Veenstra, everything he'd gotten from Emiel, everything he knew.

Hein threw an arm around his shoulder. "Jesus, D Squared, what a fucking mess. What are you going to do?"

"I don't know. What *can* I do?"

"Tell her she's gotta end it."

"I'm scared she'll pick him over me. And *then* what do I do?"

❧

They sat at the bar at Café Schemer, where Hein was a regular. People kept coming over to chat with him about business, buildings, acquisitions, payments, and the associated problems. John van Bremen's name came up repeatedly, and the references weren't always positive. "That thing with John? I got that all worked out. He won't cause you any more trouble," Hein told a bulldog of a man with a bushy mustache. Maybe the mustache compensated for his short stature, gave him an alternate way to make an impression.

Around two that afternoon, Hein had said he'd had enough fishing for one day. David wanted to go home, but Hein cautioned against it. "You're supposed to be in Groningen, remember? It's way too early to go home."

The names Mirjam and Steven had not been mentioned again, and David was grateful. Hein knew when to put up and when to shut up.

The world beyond Café Schemer might as well have ceased to exist. Here, it was just the two of them, a pair of like minded guys. Friends.

Soft, pleasant music swam from the café's sound system. They ate tuna sandwiches.

"Fish," said Hein.

A man handed him a pile of glossy brochures. "Hot off the presses," he said, grinning, and Hein clapped him jovially on the shoulder and introduced them. "Peter Vollings, entrepreneur—you don't mind if I put it that way, do you, Pete?—and this is my good friend and legal adviser, David Driessen."

They shook hands and said "Pleasure" simultaneously.

"This calls for a drink." Hein signaled the bartender, a young man who looked more like a recent seminary graduate than a mixologist, though David had seldom seen anyone as handy with a cocktail shaker.

The young man set three glasses of Johnny Walker Black on the bar and added bowls of cashews and roasted almonds.

"Success," Hein toasted. He showed David one of the brochures. "Check this out, man. This is gonna be our golden goose."

The four-color flyer advertised the Papaya Resort, "where fantasies become real," owned and operated by Curaçao Property Development, Ltd. David thought he recognized the name from the documents Hein had entrusted to his care. Beautiful photos of luxury houses, "the vacation paradise you've always dreamed of." Swimming pools, views of the stunningly blue Caribbean, a smiling black waiter serving drinks to two bronzed beauties in perfect bikinis on a terrace surrounded by palm trees and lush purple bougainvillea, a row of pastel houses lining the harbor of Willemstad. "Available for rental or outright purchase," an inside headline announced, over a paragraph detailing a series of reasons to buy: "Curaçao not only boasts an extraordinarily welcoming meteorological climate but also an advantageous financial climate. Curaçao Property Development, Ltd. has arranged a variety of options for both absentee investors and those looking for a year-round residence on this lovely island, where New World charm blends with colonial heritage to provide a treasure chest of Dutch amenities."

"What do you think?" Hein asked.

"Looks like a great place for a vacation with—"

David cut himself off and swallowed something that wasn't there.

"—with Mirjam and the kids?" Hein finished for him, after a pause.

David's face was anguished.

Hein laid a hand on his shoulder. "Chin up, D Squared. I promise you, it's all going to work out just fine."

David nodded dully and downed the last of his whiskey.

Hein caught the bartender's eye and pointed at their glasses.

"You can stay any time you want," said Hein. "Normal rental price is twelve hundred a week, but for you, let's call it five hundred. If you're smart, though, you'll buy in. Right now, we're returning twenty percent a year on investments. I'll show you the figures."

"I haven't got anything to invest," David smiled weakly. He was ashamed to have to admit this. "I can't even pay my bills. And what would I tell Mirjam?"

"She doesn't have to know anything about it."

David looked at him quizzically.

"The way it works," Hein went on, "you don't put up your own money, anyway. You take out a low-interest loan, say five percent, so you wind up ahead by fifteen percent a year."

"No bank's going to lend me money, I know that for a fact."

"Maybe not a bank," said Hein.

"Who, then?"

"What about me?"

David had to let that sink in. "What?"

"*Me*. It doesn't have to be complicated: you tell me how much you want to invest, and I take care of it for you."

The little man with the mustache tapped Hein's shoulder.

"What's up, 'Stache?"

"We're ready to start. You coming?"

"You in?" Hein asked David.

"In what?"

Hein nodded towards the back of the café. "Back there."

There was an unobtrusive door set into the far wall. It opened into a narrow corridor that led to a spacious, nicely decorated room that held a roulette table and a couple of blackjack tables ringed with barstools.

A black woman with an enormous Afro stood behind the roulette wheel.

"Good evening, gentlemen," she said.

Chapter 16

"What do you think?" The optometrist smiled encouragingly.

David blinked. "They feel good." In the mirror, he saw both himself and a stranger, a single reflection that showed two versions of David Driessen, the old and the new. He wondered what Hein would say.

When he got back to the office, the receptionist cocked her head. "You look different. Did you get a haircut?"

David did a little pirouette.

"New suit?"

"Nope."

"I know you didn't have a beard. Mustache?"

He remembered the little man at Café Schemer, 'Stache, who did odd jobs for Hein. What sort of jobs, it was probably better not to know. "See no evil," as Starrebeek Senior never tired of saying.

"I give up, then. What is it?"

"Glasses," David said.

"But you're not—oh! You got contacts?"

"Just now."

"Well, duh." She was embarrassed. "They look good. I mean—"

"Thanks."

There was a note on his desk: could he go to the police station at eleven to talk with a robbery suspect? The guy was one of Joost's clients, but Joost was out sick.

"Weekend flu," David muttered. Recently, Joost and his new girlfriend had flown south for four days in Barcelona. This weekend they probably had another little outing planned—and, since Joost had used up all his vacation days on a five-week tour of Southeast Asia this summer, he'd probably called in sick to squeeze out an extra day. So David got stuck with yet another stupid case.

He skimmed through his e-mail. Nothing important.

Barcelona…

Before Bas was born, he and Mirjam had been there, a day trip from the apartment they'd rented in Cadaqués. Mirjam's purse had been snatched while they stood watching a fire-eater on Las Ramblas. Fortunately, there wasn't much in it, except a wallet and a few hundred pesetas. It had been a shock, though, the idea that you could be robbed like that, in broad daylight. Mirjam had thrown herself into his arms, wailing, right there in the middle of the busy pedestrian street. They'd had a future then, long before Steven Veenstra made his first appearance in their lives.

This weekend, they'd mostly avoided each other after he got back from Café Schemer, as if denying each other's existence.

It had done him good, an hour at the roulette table. He'd needed the distraction. And Mirjam would never know a thing about it. Hein would never betray him.

Hein had loaned him five hundred Euros to play, and, after paying him back, he'd still wound up more than a hundred and fifty to the good. Out on the street, Hein had pressed a wristwatch into his hands. "Take it," he'd insisted. "It's a Rolex, not a fake, I swear. I can't let my business associates see my lawyer wearing that piece of shit." He glanced down at his trusty old Swatch. He couldn't swank around the office with a Rolex on his wrist, but he'd be sure to wear it from now on around Hein.

He sent a couple of quick e-mails and reported the hours he'd spent on the Rijkhof case to Hanna for his time sheets. Then he got in his car and drove to police headquarters.

ভ৹

Just as he pulled into a space in the Marnixstraat parking garage, his phone rang. He didn't recognize the number.

"David Driessen."

"It's Hein. You free tonight?"

"Sure," David said, wondering what excuse he could use to explain another absence from the home front. Another client meeting? Well, given that Hein *was* a client, that was actually even true. A new thought struck him: What if Mirjam thought he was having an affair?

"Couple things I want to talk over with you."

"Such as?"

"I'll tell you tonight. My car's in the garage under the Museumplein. Meet me there around four."

"I can—"

But he was talking to a dead line. David sat there for a minute with the phone in his hand before climbing out of his car.

ভ৹

Idriss el Machoufi had a big bandage on his forehead.

David consulted his copy of the arresting officer's statement. "According to the shopkeeper, a Mr. Weiner, you came—"

"Weiner? You mean Whiner." Idriss laughed hoarsely. "How come they don't let you smoke in here?"

"You came into his store," David continued. "You closed the door behind you, stuck a pistol in his face, and ordered him to give you the money from the register. 'All the *doekoe*,' it says here."

"'*Doekoe*'? I'm no Surinamer." Idriss stared at the table and never once looked David in the eye.

"When he started screaming, you ran—"

"You think I am afraid of that jerk?" Idriss snorted and made a spitting sound.

"—but he was faster than you and... let me see." David skipped ahead, made a few notes, and then summarized: "He grabbed you, threw you to the ground and held you down. Your bad luck, turns out he used to take judo. Another customer came in the shop and called 112. Your pistol—"

"That peashooter was not mine."

"The pistol—which turns out to have been a starter's pistol, and which the police believe was yours—was found in a corner of the shop. Did you drop it when Mr. Weiner jumped on you?"

Idriss bent forward, as if he were talking to the table. "This whole thing is bullshit. You know that, right?"

"What happened, then?" asked David.

"Wallah, I come in the shop, I swear, I just want to buy a pack of Marlboros, and that bastard go crazy on me. Maybe he think I'm somebody else—you know, all Moroccans look same-same. So then he start to scream and I want to run away, and then he grab me and push me down. Look, he do this to me, the bastard." He touched the bandage on his forehead. "You file charges on *him* for me. He have to pay."

David scribbled "unprovoked attack" on the statement.

"Shit, man, all I want is a pack of smokes."

"I see."

"You no believe me, right? You Dutch, you never believe us. We Moroccans, we always guilty."

David knew that Idriss had a prior conviction for purse snatching. He'd been the passenger on the back of a scooter, his nephew was driving, and he'd yanked the pocketbook right out of a woman's hand. He was still on probation for that offense so, for this new violation, he'd certainly do at least six months. And it would be prison time, not a juvenile detention facility, since Idriss was now nineteen. A semester at Prison U would teach him how to be a *real* criminal.

"What about the pistol?" asked David. "How did that wind up on the shop floor? Did the gnomes put it there?"

"What means 'gnomes'?"

"Never mind. How did the pistol get there?"

"How do I know? Somebody put him there. Not me. They find my fingerprints on him?" Idriss looked up triumphantly. He was playing his strongest—and perhaps his only—trump.

David's spirits sagged. How was he supposed to present this punk to the court? Arguing cases like this one, he sometimes felt like he was standing there naked.

That would be a good name for a book: *The Naked Defender*.

David paged through the case file. "It says here you were wearing gloves. Why?"

"Because it's fucking *cold* in your fucking country."

ↂ

"This is Lucas."

"Lucas, it's Heleen. Heleen ter Bruggen."

He'd known it would be her. The trial was two weeks ago, so today was The Day, when the judges would render their verdict. "Well? How much did he get?"

It was quiet on the other end of the line. "I'm sorry. They acquitted him."

"Acquitted?" He'd always known this was a possibility, but now that he heard the words spoken aloud, they floored him. He closed his eyes, breathed deeply. "They can't do that. He did it, the bastard raped my sister. They can't just let him get away with it!"

"That's how they ruled, though. They say there was too much doubt. On the road, you're not supposed to pass unless you're *sure* it's safe, and that's pretty much the way the court system works. No conviction if there's a reasonable doubt of guilt."

"That's such a crock of shit. This was *rape*, not reckless driving."

"I can't reach Selma. I left her a voicemail and asked her to call me back, but I thought maybe you could go see her? I honestly don't have the time right now. I'm sorry."

She wasn't sorry, the stupid bitch. She'd fucked up the case, and now she was too chickenshit to deliver the bad news herself. "What about an appeal?" he asked. "Is that an option?"

"The Public Prosecution Service says no. And we don't think a civil suit for damages would be fruitful. It would just mean more stress for your sister. At this point, we recommend she take the court's verdict as closure and try to move on with her life."

Closure. Move on with her life. Yadda yadda yadda. All that was missing was *look on the bright side*.

"I have to go, Lucas. Again, I'm very sorry. I thought we had a good case, but Patrick's lawyer managed to convince the court otherwise."

Lucas sat there with the phone in his hand for long minutes.

Patrick's lawyer. That goddamn piece of shit.

Although he suspected it was pointless, he called Selma.

And, sure enough, got her voicemail.

❧

"So, where are we off to?" asked David.

"It's a nice day. Let's just drive."

David guessed that Hein had something particular to discuss, but he knew they'd get to it when the time came. They headed towards The Hague, then took the A44 through Sassenheim and the N444 to Katwijk aan Zee.

"Nicer than the beaches at Zandvoort and Scheveningen," said Hein. "Here you can walk on the promenade without slipping on some kid's spilled ice cream every ten seconds."

Hein was wearing Ray Bans, but David had to squint against the sun, which hung low in the sky out over the sea. A brisk wind stirred the sand. Most of the people still on the beach were walking dogs. One man was apparently a professional. A pack of seven or eight dogs frolicked around him. Sure enough, a little further on they saw a van with "Donald Dog Walkers" lettered on the side. Another D Squared.

Hein threw an arm around David's shoulder. "Thought any more about Curaçao?"

"I don't know," he said. "I'm pretty strapped for cash right now. I don't know if I can—"

"No, I get it. I totally understand. That's the way I used to think. Don't spend more than you've got in the bank. You bite off more than you can chew, you might wind up choking."

David nodded. "And it's even harder right now."

"The economy, you mean?"

"Well, that, too, but mostly what's going on with Mirjam. It's not exactly the Cold War, but it's a pretty cold peace. I think something's going to happen. I keep feeling like she's about to say something."

Hein scooped up an empty Coke can. "What do you think that'll be?"

"She's leaving me. She's chosen Steven Veenstra. I think that's the way things are headed."

Things are headed that way, he thought, *and they're ticking.* A bomb was getting ready to explode, and it would blow everything to hell, everything he'd based his life on, his entire future.

Hein dropped the can in a trash barrel lettered "Together We Can Make The Netherlands a Neater Land."

He squeezed David's shoulder. "Chin up, D Squared. Don't let this drag you down, man. You walk around all passive and scared, for sure she won't want you."

"I know, but—"

"Let's rustle up a couple of drinks and a bite to eat, huh? Huis ter Duin, I think the national soccer team stays there when they've got a home game. Those bastards make way too much money. And for what? Kicking a ball? You're more talented than any of them, and what do *you* make? Hey, how come you're still wearing that shitty watch?" Hein unstrapped it from his wrist. "Let's dump it." There was another trash barrel ahead, and Hein held the end of the watchband between his thumb and forefinger as if it were a dead rat and dropped it in the bin as they passed.

❧

Selma didn't respond to his ring. Lucas tried the other bells. Finally, the door clicked open. At the head of the stairs was a girl he'd never seen before.

"I'm looking for Selma, my sister. I think her buzzer's broken."

The girl seemed skeptical.

"Look, here's my ID. Same last name, Groothuis."

"Okay."

He knocked on Selma's door, but nothing happened. He knocked again, harder.

"Go away!"

Her voice was muffled, as if she was yelling into a pillow.

Lucas pushed the door, and, to his surprise, it swung open.

The curtains were closed, and the room was almost dark. Selma was lying on her bed. Lucas wanted to sit on the edge, but decided to keep his distance, at least at first. He moved a pile of clothes and books off a chair and sat down.

"I'm not gonna beat around the bush, sis." He cleared his throat. Get it said, and then they could begin figuring out how to process it. "They let him off."

"I knew they would."

"They should have made him pay for what he did, at least a couple of months in the slam. I ought to—"

He didn't dare finish the sentence. Ought to what? What *could* he do that would be of any help to Selma? His Selma, his closest companion from the moment of their birth.

The least he could do was make sure that justice prevailed. That was the phrase, wasn't it? None of that "eye for an eye, tooth for a tooth" crap, but you couldn't just let a shit like Patrick Hamilton get away with it.

Selma said nothing. She was wearing a long-sleeved T-shirt, so he couldn't see her wrists. She wouldn't…

He didn't dare even *think* it.

"Maybe we could go out and get something to eat?" he suggested. "Or have you got anything here?"

Selma shook her head.

"I bet you haven't eaten anything in days."

"What difference does it make?"

☙

David was home by eight thirty. Hein dropped him at the door. In the restaurant, they'd talked about Curaçao and the Papaya Resort and the many financial advantages of an investment with a guaranteed return of twenty percent a year and probably more. Hein had shown him the accountant's report. "It's all right here. Look at these numbers."

On the way home, Hein had made a proposal that would put an end to what he called David's "clerkship" at Starrebeek & Starrebeek.

"You could make a lot more money if you had your own practice. You ever give that any thought?"

David acknowledged that, years earlier, he'd discussed the possibility with Joost.

"Why didn't you do it?"

He danced around the question, not wanting to admit that he'd been scared of the responsibility.

Hein seemed to read his mind, though—of course, he saw through everything—but he let it lie and said only that he wanted to help. "I've got my eye on a nice building. Cheap. I can provide the clients. A couple guys you met at the café need a lawyer from time to time. Why not you?"

David could already see it: a modest little office with a big brass plaque beside the door. "David Driessen, Attorney at Law." Just that, nothing more. Start on his own, bring in another lawyer when he got big enough to need one, then a third. Build steadily, make more money, stop wasting time on bullshit cases.

Hein's phone rang as they were passing the airport.

"What? Tonight?" He listened intently. "Fine, Theo, you go ahead. I'm out of it, and I'm *staying* out of it." He ended the call.

☙

"I'll have to get used to it," said Mirjam.

"You think I look okay without glasses?"

"I think you look fine."

She didn't sound very enthusiastic, but at least she'd *noticed*. She offered to warm up some leftover pasta in the mike.

"Thanks, I already ate."

They sat in the living room. David read the paper. He couldn't see the cover of her book, but it wasn't *Eyeshadow*. Had she finally finished it? Or maybe she'd just given up on it, like she'd given up on him?

He watched her out of the corner of his eye, spied on her, really, analyzing her appearance. Small movements, facial expressions, as if they would reveal her plans.

Could he simply sit by and let her pull the plug on their marriage? Hein would never have let things get to this point. He would have done something about it long ago.

At ten, he turned on the news. The second story was introduced as "a murder in the Amsterdam underworld." A mobster identified only as "John van B." had been gunned down as he was leaving a restaurant in Amsterdam-East with his wife, who had also been wounded in the ambush. The shooter had fled the scene on a motorbike. The police had no solid leads at present, but there were rumors of internecine warfare amongst the city's criminal element.

"John van B." That was obviously John van Bremen. The name had come up a number of times in David's conversations with Hein. But he wasn't sure exactly how they were connected.

❧

He opened his eyes. The clock radio read one twenty-eight. He had awakened, sweating, from a bizarre dream. He'd been feeding coins into a slot machine, the old-fashioned kind with the handle on the side, the kind that used to eat up not only his allowance but whatever he could bum off his friends. And he remembered being chased by some sort of gang. At the end of the chase, his path had been blocked by an immovable steel door. He banged his fists against it, and that was when he'd woken up.

Mirjam lay sleeping beside him.

He crept quietly into the bathroom and drank a glass of water. He examined his face in the mirror above the sink. He had the impression that the birthmark below his chin had gotten a little bigger. Maybe a melanoma. Skin cancer. That meant surgery, or chemo.

"Goddammit," he whispered.

He took an Ambien but couldn't get back to sleep.

John van Bremen, Steven Veenstra, Hein, Papaya Resorts, his own practice, a new future, kissing Starrebeek goodbye, should he have his doctor take a look at his birthmark?

His thoughts flew in all directions, came together, split apart, merged and separated, blended and divorced. Everything was connected, it was all one boiling stew.

Three fifteen, dammit, and it all kept whirling around in his brain.

Half an hour later, he couldn't stand it anymore.

He sat up in bed and yelled Steven Veenstra's name.

Chapter 17

That morning, getting the kids to school was almost more than she could handle. For starters, yesterday's sunshine had given way to a chilly drizzle. Someone must have told the weather gods about last night.

Preparing their lunches, getting them into their jackets, putting down a minor squabble that threatened to turn into something more serious (how Bas hated her standard reminder: "You're the oldest, so you should know better"), unlocking their bicycles (since their return from France, Romy absolutely refused to ride in the child seat on Mirjam's carrier bike, now permanently chained to a streetlamp), pedaling to school, dropping them at the door (a wave and a quick goodbye for Bas, a kiss for Romy, all according to their instructions)…

And then? The overture to her day had gone more or less according to form, but now what? It was hard to pick between the various necessary evils. "The paradox of choice," wasn't that the *nom du jour* for it?

She could go home and hope that David had already left for the office, but he probably hadn't. When she and the kids had taken off, he was still in bed. She could head over to Steven's—even if he was gone, she could let herself in—but that seemed cowardly.

She called his cell and got his voicemail. Then, still standing in front of the school, she tried his office. *No, Mr. Veenstra's not in yet. His first appointment's not until eleven. No, I'm sorry, I don't know how to reach him. Have you tried his cell?*

Latecomers slipped past her as she stood there, wondering which way to turn. A mother rushed up the walkway carrying a forgotten lunchbox.

ひ

Thera tugged at Mirjam's sleeve. "Hey, where'd you go?"

"Theer," said Mirjam, her voice strangled.

"What is it, honey?"

She threw her arms around her friend, splashing Thera's jacket with her tears.

Ten minutes later, they were in Thera's newly refurnished living room, each with a cup of espresso.

"Okay," said Thera. "Tell me everything."

And Mirjam snuffled her way through an account of the events of the previous night. How she jolted awake when David suddenly shouted Steven's name. How he seemed to know all about the secret she'd thought she was protecting. How he begged her to break off the affair. How she told him that doing so would be like cutting out a part of her heart.

No, she hadn't used those specific words. He was already so angry, she was terrified he might do something violent.

"He was out of his mind. I wanted to go downstairs and sleep on the couch, but he wouldn't let me. He locked the bedroom door and spent the rest of the night threatening me. Said he was going to take away my kids because I was cheating on him. It was horrible."

She burst out again in tears. Thera tried to comfort her. "It's all going to work out, honey, really." But Mirjam's confusion and grief were too overwhelming to be blotted away with a few trite phrases.

When she finally calmed down, Thera asked her what she was going to do.

"What *can* I do?"

"You're going to have to choose," Thera said, confirming what Mirjam already knew. "Either break up with Steven or divorce David. By the way, I saw David yesterday. Did he get Lasik?"

"Contacts."

"He was on the other side of the street with some guy who looked amazingly like him. Was his brother in town?"

"David's an only child."

∽

Before reporting to his work-study job at ten, Lucas went over to the student apartments where Patrick lived. He wasn't sure what exactly he'd say or do if Patrick was there, but he trusted himself to rise to the occasion. Oddly, Patrick's name no longer appeared on the list of residents posted beside the front door.

Lucas pushed a buzzer at random. Nothing happened. He flipped up the mail slot and put an ear to it. There were noises, as if the house itself were waking from a sound sleep, and somewhere inside a window went up.

He stood, backed away from the door and looked up. A sleepy head emerged from a room on the second floor.

"Who're you looking for?"

"Patrick Hamilton. Is he home?"

"He doesn't live here anymore, the creep." The boy started back inside.

"Wait a second. Can you let me in? I'd like to ask you a couple questions."

Several minutes passed. The boy with the sleepy head opened the front door. "Jesus, that was some party last night. My mouth tastes like an Apache loincloth."

"Do you know where Patrick's living now?"

The boy peered at him through half-closed eyes. "Why do you want to know?"

"I—he owes me some money."

"Join the club. He left here a month behind on his rent. You can kiss whatever he owes you goodbye."

"You don't know where he went?"

The boy pulled a pack of shag tobacco from the back pocket of his ratty jeans and began to roll a cigarette. "New Zealand, I think."

"New Zealand? Why? What's he got there?" Shit. The bastard had flown the coop the second he got acquitted. Gone literally to the far end of the world, as far from here as you can get. The fucking chickenshit.

"Dunno. I guess his dad's there. Hamilton. He came from there originally, I think. Came here, married a Dutch woman. You got a match?"

"I don't smoke. When's he coming back?"

"Never, I hope. His folks are divorced. He went to live with his dad. I think that's what Jasper said."

☙

Ten forty-five.

When Mirjam got out of bed at seven thirty this morning—he had no idea whether or not she'd finally gotten any sleep—he'd rolled over and dropped back into a deep and dreamless slumber. His cell phone was downstairs. The office had probably called, but he hadn't heard it ring.

He went cautiously down the stairs. Not a sound. Mirjam probably wasn't home. That was just as well. He didn't think he could handle a repetition of last night's scene. She'd been absolutely furious, as if *he* was the one to blame. Maybe she thought he'd played a dirty trick on her by discovering her unfaithfulness. She'd asked him how he knew. "I know. What difference does it make how? Are you going to deny it? All the phone calls, the secret *rendezvous?*"

She'd had the balls to say he didn't know—couldn't know—anything about *rendezvous*. Again he'd asked her if she was denying it. "That time you were supposed to be at your parents and I called them? You're telling me you weren't with him then?"

She looked primed to spring at him, her hands curled halfway to fists with sharp red claws. He grabbed her by the arms and threw her onto the bed, maybe a little too roughly, but at that moment he lost all control.

"It's true, isn't it?" he shouted. "It's all true. You've been cheating on me for months."

She lay there, eyes squeezed shut, panting wordlessly, but her silence spoke volumes. And then another piece of the puzzle fell suddenly into place.

"In France, in Sainte-Maxime, you spent that night and the next day with *him*!"

Her lips were pressed tightly together.

"You picked that fight so you could get away from us, so you could run off and fuck him."

Her nod was so tiny he would have missed it if he hadn't been looking for it. He turned away from her to keep himself from beating her. "Jesus fucking Christ, I can't believe it."

Now, alone in the house, he made some coffee, but it didn't take away the filthy taste in his mouth. Sour, bitter.

There were two messages from the office in his voicemail. After a second cup of coffee and a cheese sandwich, he felt able to call back. "Sorry, Hanna, I'm sick." It wasn't hard to make his voice sound hoarse. "Couldn't get out of bed this morning, that's why I didn't call in."

"Should I cancel your appointments?"

"Yeah. For tomorrow, too." He wanted to tell her he was taking the rest of the week off, and next week as well, but that seemed premature.

"What's wrong? Something serious?"

"I think it's the flu."

"Take care of yourself!"

He wondered where Mirjam was. Maybe after dropping the kids at school she'd gone straight to Steven Veenstra and was there now, blubbering in his arms. And then having sex with him, of course. Breakup sex? Would she dump him, now? He doubted it. She hadn't said it in so many words, but it was clear. Their marriage was dead. If anyone was getting dumped around here, it was him.

❦

David puttered aimlessly around the house for hours, moving furniture, setting it back where it belonged. He tried to read the paper but couldn't even concentrate on the article about John van Bremen's murder. He had a little more to eat and drank too much coffee. He opened his laptop and surfed over to the online casino, but his head was on a different wavelength. When he got to three hundred Euros in the red, he saw that his heart wasn't in it and quit. He remembered the croupier in the gaming room at the back of Café Schemer. She'd nodded pleasantly and pushed stacks of chips across the table.

Place your bets, please, gentlemen.

There was an almost-empty glass of cognac beside his coffee cup. He couldn't remember having poured it, and certainly not having drunk most of it.

He pulled on a jacket and went out. There was a dead pigeon in the street, crushed and bloody. A crow was pecking at the mess. The bad taste in his mouth made him feel like he'd also been eating run-over pigeon.

He roamed the streets of Amsterdam-South for more than an hour, going nowhere. This was his world, but it was a world that had turned against him, a world in which he was perhaps no longer welcome. A little flat in the Indische Buurt or Bos en Lommer, was that his future? He wouldn't be able to afford much better than that. How much alimony would she soak him for?

It began to rain. So what else is new? The Vondelpark was practically deserted, except for joggers and people walking their dogs. Maybe he'd get himself a dog, so he'd have some company for the quiet evenings that lay ahead. Weekends he didn't have the kids, he could take old Rover out to the Amsterdamse Bos, get some fresh air. He'd meet some attractive woman out walking with her golden retriever. Single, like him.

Single.

What an awful word.

Their dogs would romp together, chasing each other, rolling in the grass, play-biting each other's fur while he and the woman managed to get past the uneasy early stages of a new romance. The shining sun, the green grass, the trees all around them in every direction. Anything was possible. At least, that's what you supposed at such a moment. Or hoped. Or maybe you already knew better.

He ate a veggie sandwich and drank a glass of white wine at *'t Blauwe Theehuis* in the park. As if by some master plan designed to rub his nose in his misery, the other tables were filled with happy couples. Three o'clock. Didn't these people have anything better to do? Work, school, clean up their damn houses? Bas and Romy had to be picked up at three thirty. He assumed Mirjam would see to that. A young woman at a table by the window broke into peals of laughter. He had to force himself not to walk over there and ask her what the hell was so funny.

He got up and paid at the bar.

His jacket felt damp, but the rain had stopped. Anything was possible. He wouldn't make a conscious decision—he'd simply let his feet take him somewhere.

They took him to the Café Schemer.

If you didn't know the place was a café, the exterior wouldn't give you much of a clue. The word "Schemer" was engraved on a small metal plate above the doorbell, as if a Mr. or Mrs. or Mr. and Mrs. Schemer lived there. No neon sign advertising beer above the door. No "Café Schemer"—or anything else, for that matter—painted on the plate-glass windows. Heavy curtains behind the windows, closed, concealing the interior from sight.

The last time, with Hein, he hadn't noticed the anonymity of the establishment. He knew that, as an employee of the distinguished law practice of Starrebeek & Starrebeek, he had no business here. But that very knowledge drew him in.

A doorman responded to his ring. "Are you a member, sir?"

David shook his head.

"A guest, then?"

"Yes, of Hein Wesseling's."

The doorman stepped back and waved him inside. "That's good enough for me, sir. Come right in."

There weren't many people there. Two men were talking at the end of the bar. A man and a woman sat at a table, heads together, enrapt in a whispered conversation. He couldn't hear a word they said, but it was apparent they were at odds with each other. From time to time, the man shook a warning finger in the woman's face. She played with a pack of cigarettes, sliding one out, turning it around and around between her fingers, returning it to the pack.

The man who looked like a clergyman was back behind the bar. David asked for a whiskey, and the barman chanted the names of the available brands like a litany.

"Johnny Walker," he said. "Rocks and a splash of water."

He was savoring his first sip when Hein came in, followed by the little man with the big mustache. Perfect. David had had a feeling Hein would turn up, that he wouldn't abandon him in this time of trouble. He would have done the same if their roles had been reversed.

Hein seemed delighted to see him. "But shouldn't you be at work? Nothing shaking at the courthouse? No vital contribution you need to make to keeping the wheels of justice oiled? Or did old Starrebeek kick you loose? If he did, he lost the best goddamn attorney he'll ever have."

"I'm sick."

"I see that." To the bartender, he said, "I'll take a dose of whatever medicine you prescribed for him. Beer for you, 'Stache?"

They toasted. "Shall we sit?" Hein led David to a small alcove in a corner of the room. "Trouble at work?" he asked.

David shook his head.

"At home?"

"Yeah. All hell broke loose last night."

"So now she knows you know."

A knot of men came into the café. Hein waved at them. When one of them headed over, though, Hein shook a finger to hold him at bay. David thought he recognized him from somewhere, but he wasn't sure.

Hein noticed David noticing. "That's Theo, Theo Wildschut." He sipped his whiskey. "Okay, so the cards are on the table. What's the next move?"

David didn't know. A divorce would be a disaster, he said, but they couldn't go on as they were.

"She's not gonna give Veenstra up?"

"I don't think so. She's totally—"

"—in looove," Hein finished the sentence, drawing the word out so it sounded both silly and beneath contempt.

"That about sums it up."

"So the only answer is for Veenstra to put an end to it himself," said Hein. "Yeah, put an end to it." With a satisfied grin, he tossed off his drink and pushed the empty glass to David's side of the table. "Doctor says internal application of medicinal alcohol is strongly indicated."

David went to the bar for another round. As he turned back with a glass in each hand, he almost bumped into the black croupier, who was standing there sipping a Coke. Her Afro seemed even fuller than last time.

"You playing later, Hein?"

"Sorry, I'm not Hein. He's over there."

"Oh, my bad. Are *you* playing?"

Jesus, those eyes, that body, that voice. Sultry and strong. He remembered a long-ago night in some popular hangout, when a fellow law student made a comment under his breath about a girl with a similar voice: "Christ, she talks with her pussy."

"Well?" she smiled. "See you later on?"

"I think so."

He liked the feel of Café Schemer. The soft music, the people, their voices, the chatter, the occasional laughter—it disarmed David, comforted him, set him at ease. He didn't know what exactly Hein had meant just then, but he was confident that if Hein said so, all would be well.

When he got back to their table, Theo Wildschut was there. 'Stache was a few steps away, watching Hein and Theo protectively, a glass of beer in his thick paw. A thin line of foam hung from his mustache.

Hein introduced David and Theo, and they shook hands. The conversation between the two of them seemed just about over.

"So," Hein concluded, "you weren't there."

"Nowhere near. I was at my in-laws in—"

"Better you than me."

"—in Alkmaar. Nowhere near John. That guy was contagious."

"Yeah, he had every sickness in the book. Some of them deadly."

Theo laughed.

Although the conversation sounded like code, David thought he could follow the general thrust. It seemed wise to keep his own mouth shut.

"Come on," said Hein. "Let's go in the back for a while."

He elbowed David in the ribs, but it was a love tap, not a blow. Maybe a little heavy handed for a love tap, but what could you expect from Hein? At least you knew he meant it.

ↄ৲

David had eaten—Hein had had Thai food delivered—and drunk, gambled and gamboled. The only thing missing was Lady Luck, who had failed to put in an appearance. Every time he lost, the compulsion to bet again—in bigger and bigger amounts—grew stronger. His numbers were due, he told himself, again and again.

He borrowed money from Hein, and, when the black croupier stepped in, his luck finally did change. Within half an hour, he'd won back everything he'd lost and was five thousand Euros ahead. He'd never won so much in a single session before. "Unlucky in love, but lucky at cards," they said—or, in this case, at roulette.

He was sure his winning streak would continue. But when the Afro was in turn relieved by a tall, pale man with a pinched face, he lost everything he'd won in a few brief spins of the wheel.

He borrowed again from Hein, positive the pendulum had to swing back in his direction, and shoved his wagers onto the black and red numbers convulsively, trying to get his mojo back.

It was all the stupid croupier's fault.

One more spin, he thought desperately, and he could still come out ahead.

Mirjam had betrayed him, but the game wouldn't do the same. Somebody had to put an end to… to Steven Veenstra? No, that's not what Hein had said.

He put a thousand Euros on Bas' birthday and another thousand on Romy's.

And then, hesitantly, another thousand on Mirjam's.

This was it, his last chance.

The little white ball raced around the wheel, skittered over the eighteen, over the three, over the twenty-seven, and kept rolling, hopping, bouncing in and out of the red and black pockets.

And then it dropped and stayed put as the wheel slowed interminably to a halt.

David turned away from the table as the crowd gathered around the felt made noises of excitement and disappointment.

His body began to tremble, first his arms, then the rest of him, his head, his knees.

Three thousand Euros in one go. He'd never lost anything close to that amount before. Spots danced before his eyes, little black spots and colored balls that burst into festive fireworks. He staggered, and felt a strong hand take his elbow.

"Hold on," Hein whispered in his ear. "It's not as bad as you think. Just don't lose it, not here, you don't want to look like a schmuck. Try to laugh a little. Not too loud, don't overdo it, just a friendly little laugh."

With a tormented grimace on his face, David let Hein lead him outside. He sucked fresh air deep into his lungs.

A couple of cars drove by, a motor scooter without a muffler. Across the street, a young couple strolled arm in arm. Sooner or later they'd learn that love doesn't last forever.

When he thought he could speak without screaming, David asked, "How much?"

"Sixty-five hundred." Hein's voice was neutral. *Move along, ladies and gentlemen*, his tone said. *Nothing to see here.*

"Jesus, there's no way I—"

"It's not so bad," Hein interrupted him. "Don't worry about it. Couple of little jobs, and we're even."

David wanted to ask what he meant, but instead said, "I think I need to walk a little."

"Good idea, stretch the legs, good for the circulation. Let's head over to the Vondelpark."

They walked off together. It was fifteen minutes before either of them spoke.

"You okay?" asked Hein.

"I'm not sure."

"Got some time tomorrow?"

"I guess. I already called in sick."

Hein came to a stop. "Feel like driving to Belgium?"

"Belgium?"

"Yeah, that exotic land south of Breda."

"Why Belgium?"

"Business. Maybe a little fun."

"Why do you need me?"

"I don't *need* you. It'll be nice, get away for a day. You ask me, you could use the distraction. And you'll learn a little more about the business. That'll come in handy."

"What kind of business?" asked David. "Come in handy how?"

Hein moved in close and looked him straight in the eye. It was a steely gaze, and David couldn't look away.

"Don't ask so many questions, D Squared. Just go with the flow, and all will be revealed. Hey, I'm glad you're wearing the Rolex. Makes a good first impression. You know what they say: you never get a second chance…"

David remembered the first impression he'd had of Hein, back during his half-brother's hearing.

"How's Barry?" he asked. "He keeping out of trouble?"

Hein laughed. "More or less. He's in Ibiza, working at a club. I set it up for him. Probably good for him to stay out of Holland for a while."

Chapter 18

After they passed Breda, David asked, "What's in Zeebrugge?"

"Lot of ships," said Hein, keeping his eyes on the road.

David knew it was pointless to ask any further questions.

But after a while, Hein volunteered more information. "The controls are tighter in Rotterdam than in Antwerp, and tighter in Antwerp than in Zeebrugge. Capeesh?"

Behind them, 'Stache chuckled. He'd offered to drive, but Hein had said, "Right, and run us into another ditch. Thanks, but you can sit in the back." That meant David got to ride shotgun, and he was happy to be up front with Hein.

"I need a smoke," 'Stache said for the third time in ten minutes. "Can we fuckin' stop?"

"The only thing you need," Hein said, "is to shut your mouth, otherwise *I'm* going to shove something in there, and it won't be one of your fucking cancer sticks."

"I just want to—"

With a squeal of tires, Hein braked the Mercedes to a stop on the shoulder of the highway. "You want to get out here? You can smoke all you want 'til the cops pick you up."

'Stache fell silent, abashed and, when they pulled off the highway for coffee at a rest stop outside Antwerp, he went in with them instead of hanging out in the parking lot with a cigarette.

They got to Zeebrugge around twelve thirty and drove straight to the harbor, where all three of them remained in the car. From their vantage point, they had a good view of the customs shed and the hustle and bustle around the ships and containers. Nobody spoke. David felt like a tourist.

After half an hour, Hein said, "Go take a look over there."

"For what?"

Hein sighed deeply. "Just go."

There was a stiff wind, this close to the sea. David and 'Stache strolled over to the customs office. Inside, several uniformed officers were working. 'Stache lit a cigarette and inhaled greedily. "Jeez, I needed this."

David shivered. He'd left his scarf in the car.

"Everything okay?" Hein asked when they returned to the Mercedes.

"Fine."

Hein tapped the horn four times in quick succession.

Five minutes later, the office door opened, and a man came toward them.

"Let's go, 'Stache," said Hein.

They got out of the car. David knew his presence was not required, probably not even desired. The idea that Hein trusted him enough to let him come along—even though not all the way along—gave him a good feeling, a warm feeling. At the same time, he knew he didn't really belong there. This was forbidden territory, but he quickly pushed that thought to the back of his mind. Everything was different with Hein around. If Barry was Hein's half-brother, what was *he*?

The three men came together about thirty feet from the car. The third man gesticulated angrily; it looked like they were arguing. But Hein laid a firm hand on his shoulder, and he calmed down.

"So, that's taken care of," said Hein when he was back behind the wheel. "They kick up a fuss, now and then, suddenly want more money or whatever, but you can't let it get to you. I mean, shit, they're getting paid to do nothing, how much they think that's worth? Anyway, I tack on an extra ten percent, and that keeps 'em happy for a while."

The man Hein had placated went back into the customs shed. Zeebrugge, a harbor town, had containers coming in from all corners of the globe, and minimal control. David figured he knew what was going on, but he kept his thoughts to himself.

'Stache was still outside the car, smoking another cigarette.

"Why'd you bring *him*?" asked David.

"Looks better," Hein explained, "have a little muscle at your side. They don't know what he might have tucked in his back pocket. I do the talking, and they're all worried what *he* might do. Me, they don't worry about. It all works out fine."

When 'Stache got back in the car, Hein drove into town. They pulled up at the Mermaid Café.

"I'm thirsty," Hein said. "Time for a nice Belgian beer."

They found a table. A waitress with ruddy cheeks, looking like she'd just come in from a brisk walk on the beach, took their order.

"*Awel, madammeke*," said 'Stache, putting on a broad Flemish accent for the occasion, "we'd be much obliged if you'd bring us three pints, for we've got a hankerin' for Belgian beer."

David saw Hein's expression tighten.

When the girl walked off, Hein got up, circled behind 'Stache, grabbed his wrist, and yanked it up hard behind his back, hauling the little man groaning to his feet. Hein applied more pressure, and 'Stache squeezed his eyes shut against the pain.

"You think that's funny?" he snapped. "Mocking the way she talks?"

'Stache shook his head.

"I can't hear you, you little prick."

"No!" 'Stache yelped.

"When she comes back, you're going to apologize, very politely. We Dutch have a shitty enough reputation here as it is, without you making things worse."

'Stache bobbed his head up and down.

"I can't hear you."

"*Okay*, I'll say I'm sorry."

Hein released him, and 'Stache collapsed into his chair. "Almost pulled my fuckin' arm out of the fuckin' socket," he moaned, jaws tight.

"Next time, I *will*."

☙

David and Hein sat in the restaurant in the Grand Casino in Knokke. Hein had pressed a stack of fifty-Euro notes into 'Stache's hands and told him to find his own way home. Then he and David drove the five miles up the coast to Knokke.

"We'll spend the night," Hein said. "Okay with you?"

He booked them in at the Hotel La Reserve, near the casino. David called home from his room. "I'll be back tomorrow," he said, playing it Hein's way: no reasons or explanations, just a simple statement of fact.

The Knokke casino. For some reason, David expected the formality of Monte Carlo, though he knew that the Dutch casinos had gone fully casual in recent years, with patrons dressing more down than up. In the entry hall, stern doormen waved newcomers to a welcome counter where IDs were checked and admission cards issued. David noticed that the identity card Hein laid on the counter bore a name he'd never seen before. He couldn't quite make it out, but it began with the letters LIGT. Ligthart, maybe?

The elevator was operated by a hunched-over little old man, well past retirement age, in a uniform that hung loosely on him. David didn't know if it was customary to tip him; playing it safe, he pressed a five-Euro note into the old man's hand.

The main gaming room had seen better days, and the jeans and untucked shirts of the players didn't seem out of place. Still, there were reminders of former glory, like the ornate chandeliers that illuminated the tables, vestiges of better times.

The restaurant at least made an effort to maintain some sense of grandeur, with silver cutlery and the wait staff in long-sleeved white dress shirts and black vests who appeared at your side the moment you wanted them. They both ordered shrimp croquettes as an appetizer—"You don't eat shrimp croquettes on the Belgian coast," Hein announced, "and you haven't actually been here"—followed by thick steaks in béarnaise sauce.

Hein returned to the idea of David opening his own practice. He sketched out the possibilities with sweeping gestures, painting a picture of an exciting and lucrative future. It was certainly tempting. Why should David go on slaving for that bloodsucker Starrebeek? Why be satisfied to go on as low man on the totem pole, with nothing more than vague promises of a someday partnership? Why not grab this chance?

Hein had found an even better possibility for office space. Still not on one of the central canals, but in the Rivierenbuurt, a respectable neighborhood. Until recently, a small manufacturing company had kept its headquarters there.

There was always plenty of work for a good attorney, and Hein's connections would get him going. A bank loan would be no problem, with Hein as co-signatory. David sputtered a protest, but Hein waved away his every concern. "I know what you're capable of, I know your character, I trust you—I've told you all this before. That's why I want to help you. It makes me sad to watch you hang on with Starrebeek… you're wasting your time and talent."

David nodded. He belonged in Hein's world, a world that, until now, he had rarely experienced. Maybe embarking on this new adventure was a risk, but it was exactly the kind of risk he'd been dreaming of. And anything would be better than staying at Starrebeek.

Last month, he'd checked in with a couple of old classmates who'd gone into criminal law, just to see if they knew of any openings, but the economic crisis seemed to have trickled down as far as the local law firms. If he wanted to make a fresh start, he'd have to suck up a pay cut. Yes, there might be something available at a well-known office in Friesland, but who wanted to be buried way the hell up there in the sticks?

"How are things with the wife?" asked Hein.

"Hopeless. She's getting ready to file for divorce. This other guy, Veenstra, he's all she can think about. I can see it—the way she looks, the things she says. I'm just an obstacle in her way."

An obstacle that has to be cleared out *of her way,* he thought.

"Have you talked about divorce?"

"Not yet. It feels like we're almost there, but neither one of us has the guts to say the word first. It's too big… too much. So we just avoid each other. It's like we're rehearsing for a split."

"You can't keep dancing around it. That's no way to live. You know that."

David understood that Hein was trying to cheer him up, but he wasn't ready to be cheered. Not yet.

"Want to hit the tables?" asked Hein, after they finished their coffee and cognac.

David hesitated, but convinced himself that this time he'd be more careful.

"Okay." He knew that, at the roulette wheel, he wouldn't be plagued by images of Mirjam with her other man, by thoughts of a lonely life in a dreary bachelor flat, by a thousand schemes to save his shattered marriage… and on and on and on.

"Let's get in the mood first," Hein suggested. "Make the world a little brighter."

Just before they pushed through the door to the men's room, with no one else in sight, he handed David a small paper packet.

∽

First the familiar confusion. David didn't know where he was. He felt around. No one there. Slowly it came back to him: he was in a hotel in Knokke. He opened his eyes, but she was gone. He was normally a light sleeper, but he hadn't been aware of her leaving the room. He must have been really out of it.

What was her name again? Jeanine? A typical Belgian name. She looked like Nicole from Vinkeveen, maybe that had been the attraction.

He couldn't remember much about the sex, and with a growing sense of shame he thought he might have fallen asleep—although the white powder was supposed to pep you up, especially in bed.

David wanted to leave Knokke as far behind as possible. He didn't want to have to think about last night, and he definitely didn't want to have to think about the evening that had preceded it—so of course he couldn't think of anything else.

How much had he lost? More than ten thousand Euros... *more* than ten thousand.

Fuck, fuck, fuck!

It had been a rerun of the last time. First he'd played carefully, winning small amounts, and then he'd gotten into a groove where everything seemed possible and success was inevitable. He'd started betting bigger, taking chances, losing, trying to make it all back by bumping up his bets, higher and higher, and finally the reality of it when the bottom fell out and he was in freefall. Long before that point, he wasn't playing with his own money anymore. Hein had generously loaned him several thousand.

Was it several? David wasn't sure, and he didn't want to know. Hein had reassured him: "Not a problem... we'll work it out. Don't get all bent out of shape. I know something that'll cheer you up." He'd made a few calls, and they went back to the hotel, where two lovely women were waiting for them. One was Jeanine, the other Juliette. Jeanine had long blond hair; Juliette short dark curls. They laughed in the same happy, open way. David drank more whiskey than he could hold.

It was crazy, absurd, idiotic—but he couldn't shake the idea that he had betrayed his marriage, that he had cheated on Mirjam.

He sat on the edge of the bed for ten minutes, elbows on his knees and fingertips holding his brains inside his head, and then he got to his feet, groaning. He looked down at his limp penis and wondered if he'd used a condom. His stomach was rumbling. He felt bile rising in his throat and made it to the bathroom just in time to fall on his knees before the toilet.

೧

Hein dropped him home around three. "I want to go over a few things with you on Thursday."

"What things?"

Hein shook his head. "I thought you liked surprises."

"Fine, okay, where?"

"Vakzuid. Four o'clock."

No one was home. David expected to find Mirjam preparing to move out: suitcases packed, the things they'd bought together divided into His and Hers piles, legal documents awaiting his signature. But none of that was in evidence.

He went upstairs to lie down. He was dead tired, but his mind wouldn't stop racing.

Man, though made of body and soul, is a unity.

Bullshit.

There was no unity of body and soul for him, and the *dis*unity made sleep impossible.

He suddenly remembered the piece of paper Hein had told him to sign. It would prevent future difficulties, or something like that. Had he signed it, or not? And what *was* it again?

At three fifty, he heard the front door open and Mirjam and the kids come in. He heard their voices—Romy's the loudest and most excited—but couldn't make out what they were saying. What should he do, stay in bed as if he were exhausted or go down and play the sympathetic husband, trying one more time to regain his wife's lost affections?

The decision was made for him. He heard Mirjam on the stairs.

She opened the bedroom door. "Oh, you're home."

"Yeah, pretty beat." He kept his voice low and trembly, as if he could barely speak. That ought to awaken at least a smidgeon of interest, get her to ask why he was so tired.

"We need to talk," she said flatly.

"Mmmm."

"We can't go on like this."

"I know."

"All right, I'll let you sleep. We'll talk later."

He wobbled downstairs at six thirty. Mirjam was in the kitchen, stirring something in a saucepan He told her he didn't feel well and wouldn't eat with them.

She had no reaction.

He stood there in the doorway. He wanted to fix this image in his memory: his wife—could he still even call her that?—making dinner for the family. How many times had he seen her this way? Hundreds, maybe thousands? They'd been married for twelve years, so that was…

He tried to do the math, but his brain was sluggish. Twelve years was around four thousand days. Had he watched Mirjam at work in the kitchen an average of once every other day? Well, say once every *four* days. That was still a thousand times.

"What are you staring at?" Mirjam took the spoon out of the pan and rinsed it in the sink. "You're creeping me out."

"I'm going back upstairs. Headache."

※

She repeated the words she'd used before: "We can't go on like this."

"Mirjam, be reasonable. *Think* about it. We've been married twelve years, we have two kids, a house, everything—"

David's last word hung in the air. He wanted to say more, but "everything" summed up exactly what he was feeling.

"It's all I *can* think about," she said. "My brain's about to explode from all the thinking." She cupped her hands over her ears, as if that would hold her head together.

"We can't just give up." He wanted to propose a new beginning, forgive and forget, they could remodel the house, put in a kitchen island, a new furnace, heated flooring; a winter getaway, just the two of them, Morocco, maybe, or Egypt. He'd have to borrow the money from Hein, but that wouldn't be a problem, Hein had money to burn.

No, he decided. None of that would get Mirjam to change her mind.

"People grow apart," she said firmly. "It happens all the time. Why shouldn't it happen to us?"

David took a sip of water. His stomach was empty—*he* was empty, he felt like he didn't fit properly into his own body. If he was hanging in a museum, he'd be titled "Man in Trouble."

Hein would know what to do. Hein always knew what to do. He should call him, ask for his advice, but you couldn't call Hein. It was safer that way.

"Hey," Mirjam broke into his thoughts. "Are you there?"

He nodded.

"Thousands of marriages break up every year, David. It's not—"

"No."

"Excuse me?"

"I don't want a divorce."

He thought of his parents. He'd visited them last week. His mother kept track of all the family birthdays, anniversaries, deaths. "In four months," she'd pointed out, "you'll be married twelve and a half years." That wasn't a big deal in other countries, David knew, but in Holland it was. An eighth of a century! "Are you throwing a party? Or just celebrating with Mirjam and the kids?" David had told her they hadn't yet decided, it was still a ways off. "It'll be here before you know it," his mother had said.

What would he tell his parents, dammit, their friends, his colleagues? He sighed.

"You'll get over it," Mirjam said.

"This is just a bump in the road, Mir. You think you're in love with this guy, you're like a teenager, not thinking straight. But—"

She cut him off. "I'm thinking absolutely straight, David. Our marriage is over. We've gone as far together as we can go, and now it's time to go our own ways. We have no future."

"That's not true! You can't just walk away. We can't let... *us* just go to hell."

"There is no 'us' anymore. There's just *you* and *me*."

David got up, as if it was his turn to address the court. "And Bas and Romy," he said. "What about them? They're just *kids*, they need a real *family*."

"We're not a real family, David. We're a fake family. We've been a fake family for a long time."

"But we can get it back, if you give it a fair chance. There's too much at stake here just to give up."

She turned away.

"Look, if we have to, we can"—it was hard for him to say this, hard to admit they couldn't handle it on their own—"we can get some therapy… marriage counseling or whatever. Sometimes you need to bring someone else into the picture, a psychologist, somebody who won't take sides, who knows how to help repair the damage."

He sat on the arm of Mirjam's chair and took her hand.

Her whole body stiffened.

Chapter 19

Lucas Groothuis, Lucas Groothuis.

David thought he recognized the name, but he couldn't place it. It had something to do with an old case, but he didn't remember a defendant, victim, or witness by that name.

His secretary Hanna had made the appointment for ten thirty, hoping that he'd be well enough to return to work today. And here he was, though his mind was in turmoil.

David consulted with Joost about a case that required his presence in Alkmaar this afternoon. Intent to inflict grievous bodily harm and attempt to commit arson in a psychiatric clinic in Castricum. A patient had attacked two of his nurses and then tried to set his room on fire. During Joost's tedious explanation of his experience with a similar case, David's thoughts drifted back to last night.

Mirjam's resolve had seemed to waver when he'd started in on the kids. This, he thought, was her Achilles heel. They *had* to stay together for the sake of the children, who would be the real victims in the event of a divorce. "Not if we set it up right and make a fair agreement we're both willing to honor," she finally countered.

Divorce. Mirjam seemed completely set on it. As far as she was concerned, the marriage was already over. When that got through to him at last, he laid his main demand straight on the table. He wanted full custody. Mirjam promised to do everything in her power to see that he didn't get it. She would hire an attorney who specialized in divorce cases, and David would have to see how well he could do against that caliber of adversary.

"How do you think you're going to pay him?" he'd demanded.

"I don't have to pay him. Steven's taking care of it. And it's not a him, it's a her, an old friend of Steven's. She handled *his* divorce." It was the triumphant way in which she said it that hurt the most.

Back in his own office, brimful of Joost's wise counsel, he tried to erase his aggressive thoughts about Steven Veenstra by fantasizing about opening his own practice. They would rent the office space, decorate it, hire a secretary, maybe a part-timer at first. If only Mirjam would… no, forget Mirjam.

His telephone rang.

"Mr. Groothuis is here. Shall I send him back?"

"Sure."

Lucas Groothuis, it turned out, was just a boy, in his early twenties at most. David introduced himself.

"I know who you are. I saw you in court. You had glasses then."

"Have a seat." David waved the boy into a client chair. "What can I do for you?"

"Patrick Hamilton."

"Patrick Hamilton?"

"You represented him."

He remembered. Patrick Hamilton had been accused of raping that girl, Groothuis, Selma Groothuis. This must be the brother, or maybe a cousin. But what did he want? The case was closed. Absolute acquittal, no appeal, case file off to the Starrebeek archives with a notation indicating a win for the home team.

"You defended him," said Lucas Groothuis. "You got him off."

"I didn't 'get him off.' The court declared him not guilty of the charge against him. What I did was present arguments pointing out that the evidence against him failed to demonstrate guilt beyond a reasonable doubt."

"My sister doesn't lie. She never has. You made her look like some kind of whore who—"

"Hold on, there."

"—who jumps into bed with every guy she sees."

David shook his head. He should have checked with Hanna to see what exactly his ten thirty wanted from him. If he'd known what was coming, he would never have agreed to see the kid. This sort of meeting never accomplished anything—at least, nothing positive.

"Do you deny it?" Lucas insisted.

"I did exactly what I'm required to do for every client, no more or less, and that's to provide the best representation I can. If there's any question about the evidence presented by the prosecution, then I *have* to bring it to the court's attention. I don't have a choice."

Lucas Groothuis glared at him. "Patrick Hamilton raped my sister, and that's why he left the country, the coward. He knew I'd—"

"Knew you'd what?"

The youth seemed to realize he might have said too much. "Nothing," he muttered.

"You'd avenge your sister's honor? You'd *get* him?"

Lucas turned away.

But David wouldn't let it go. "You'd punish him yourself, since the judge wouldn't do it? Take the law into your own hands?"

Lucas Groothuis jumped to his feet. "I don't have to listen to your shit, all your legal bullshit. That motherfucker destroyed my sister's life. She wasn't strong in the first place, and now that acquittal, that just ripped her apart. I don't know if she'll ever get over it."

"I understand and I'm sorry," said David. "It must be awful for her, but there's really nothing I can do about it. The case is closed."

Lucas took a step toward him. The boy seemed ready to fly at him.

If looks could kill, David thought, *I'd be dead.*

"It's not even *close* to closed. That's just more bullshit."

"I think we're done here," said David. "Let me show you the way out."

☙

His hands were shaking. His cup chattered against his teeth as he tried to bring his breathing under control.

Lucas had read stories in which "a red haze" descended before a character's eyes, but he hadn't believed such a thing could happen anywhere outside of fiction until it happened to *him* there in the lawyer's office.

How had he gotten *here*, to the university cafeteria? By bicycle? On foot? He couldn't remember having locked up his bike. It was probably stolen by now.

He began to feel a little better, took a sip of his cappuccino. A girl sitting at one of the nearby tables looked up from her laptop. He smiled.

Nothing wrong here, folks, I'm just drinking coffee while my sweet sister's life falls to shit.

The arrogance of that fucking attorney, like he's the only person in the world with a brain! He didn't give a rat's ass about the truth. All he cared about was notching another win on his belt. He didn't bother thinking about the poor losers he ran over.

Lucas figured the bastard probably drove a sporty little red convertible, lived in a lovely home in Zuid or Het Gooi with the wife and one point seven kiddies, while Selma…

He dropped his head and pounded a fist on the table. His cup rattled in its saucer, and his eyes welled with tears.

When he looked up again, the girl with the laptop was watching him.

☙

At five minutes past four, stuck in traffic approaching the Coen Tunnel, David called Vakzuid and asked them to tell Mr. Wesseling that Mr. Driessen was running late.

"Tell Mr. Driessen that Mr. Wesseling is late?"

"Other way around," said David. "This is Mr. Driessen. I'm meeting Mr. Wesseling."

"Ah, sorry, I got it."

"Jerk," said David when the connection was broken. Who knew if the message would be delivered correctly? The psychiatric patient he'd met with didn't seem to have understood a word he'd said. A transcript of their conversation would work perfectly in the Theater of the Absurd.

He finally made it to Vakzuid at four thirty. A cold wind swirled around the Stadium, and David buttoned his jacket. Where had he left his scarf? He'd searched for it at home this morning but couldn't find it. He knew he'd had it with him on the drive to Zeebrugge. Mirjam had given it to him last year for Sinterklaas… probably the last Sinterklaas present he'd ever get from her.

Hein was waiting for him. David was prepared for a half-serious reprimand for his late arrival, but Hein didn't even mention it. "Glad you made it, D Squared! Jesus, you look like you've been rode hard and put up wet. Wine, whiskey, or beer?"

"Whiskey." David hoped a drink would take the edge off. "But cut me off after one. I feel like I'm still paying for Knokke."

Hein ordered for them and settled back in his chair, looking at David as if he was expecting something. David had no idea what he was supposed to say or do.

"Your wife, Mirjam," Hein said at last. "How's that going?"

"Straight to hell."

"You deserve a break, my friend. Something fun. Feel like going to see Ajax next week?"

"Ajax?"

"Don't *tell* me you don't follow soccer, buddy. The Champions League? It's a big game."

"Oh, gosh, I don't know…"

"Come on, man, I've got Skybox seats. Glass of champagne, yummy snacks, nice people. People you'll want to know when you open your own practice. Next Wednesday. You can make that, right?"

"Sure, thanks."

Their drinks arrived.

"To the new office," Hein toasted.

"Well…"

"Hey, you were all over this when we were sitting with those two babes in the bar in Knokke."

David sipped his whiskey. He had only fuzzy memories of what all they'd agreed to, what documents Hein had showed him, before he'd staggered up to his hotel room with Jeanine—or was it Juliette? "I have to give it some more thought, Hein. I've got so much going on, my head's spinning. You know what I mean?"

"I know exactly what you mean." Hein patted his knee. "You're having a rough time. I'm taking that into account. But this is your chance to get a fresh start, to really get your life in gear. You know, sometimes a crisis turns out to be the best thing that can possibly happen to you. You shake up the bottle, and that's what gets you the fizz."

"Like champagne," David smiled.

"Bingo. You remember that building I told you about, in the Maasstraat? That place'll be perfect for you. And there's room to expand, if it all works out. And it's all gonna work out fine, guaranteed. You can trust me."

David was silent.

"You *do* trust me, D Squared, don't you?"

"Absolutely," David said quickly. "Of course I do."

"Hey, you know what, let's go take a look. We can be there in fifteen minutes. It doesn't hurt to look, right?"

❧

Selma had gotten out of bed and was sitting in a chair. Lucas tried to catch her eye, but she turned away. He wanted to tell her what the attorney had said, but she wasn't interested. "It doesn't matter anymore," she whispered. "Stop looking… stop looking at my arms." She pushed her sleeves up and showed him that she hadn't cut herself.

"Let's go out," her brother proposed. "It's a nice day. We could go into town. I need to buy a shirt. Want to go with me?"

"I'm not in the mood, Lucas."

"Tell you what. There's some band from Curaçao playing at the Bimhuis tonight. Grupo Fresca, something like that, a salsa band."

He hoped to remind her of their childhood, when their father had been stationed on Curaçao and they'd lived in a big house in Julianadorp. They were around ten years old, and their lives had been blessed by the sun, the sea, the beach, and the freedom to do whatever they liked. Nowadays, if he ever mentioned Julianadorp to his friends, they thought he meant the dinky little village here in Holland, south of Den Helder. But *their* Julianadorp had been a paradise.

Selma seemed not to have heard him.

"What do you think? Want to go? I'll check online and see if there's tickets."

☙

"So, what do you think? Looks fantastic to me."

"It's very nice." David was trying not to sound negative.

"But you're not sure," said Hein.

"Not a hundred percent." David took a few steps back and looked the building up and down. "Fruits and vegetables on one side, fish on the other. I don't know if this is really the right location for a law office."

Hein shook his head. "You're just looking for excuses. I don't think you're ready to go out on your own."

"You may be right. With everything I've got on my plate right now, I don't know if I can handle this." He wondered why Hein was so insistent about it. Because *he* would profit, too? Or was he just trying to be a friend?

"You're wound up too tight," said Hein. "You should see the way you look. You need to relax. Go to a movie or something. Take a colleague to a café."

David shrugged. A colleague? Like who? The only eligible candidate was Joost, but with his new girlfriend he wouldn't be interested in a guy's night out.

"You know what? I don't have anything on for tonight. Let's you and me go into town."

"But—"

"You rather stay home? No? Yeah, I thought so."

☙

David's schedule had become unpredictable lately. He came home late, had to leave without notice, sometimes was gone overnight. Mirjam had no clue what he was up to—and didn't much care. Maybe he had another woman. Maybe he was trying to pay her back for *her* affair. No, impossible. He was fighting tooth and nail against a divorce, probably hoping that her relationship with Steven would play itself out. How could he be so naïve? She knew how sharp he was in his profession, but he was still a child emotionally. She used to find that endearing, but now it was just annoying.

Tonight he'd come in at six thirty, too late to sit with Bas and Romy in front of the TV before dinner. At the table, he'd put on the jolly attitude of a father enjoying the company of his wife and their children, but it was all so forced, like he was a bad actor in a cheap Dutch TV show. He had an appointment at eight thirty, he'd announced. "With who?" she'd asked, with feigned interest. "It's a business thing… sort of a half-client, half-friend." He hadn't mentioned a name, but what difference did it make?

Now the kids were in bed. Peace, a chance to think, but she couldn't stop herself from calling Steven. She needed to hear his voice.

He didn't pick up, neither his landline nor his cell. She waited five minutes and tried again. Nothing. It didn't seem likely he'd be there, but she tried him at Veenstra & Watzlawick and got the office's answering machine.

She began to feel uneasy. It started in her stomach and grew from there, until it filled her whole body. Could Steven and David have bumped into each other somewhere? Or, worse: could they have arranged to meet, to talk things out? She had to know what was going on, had to do something, take *some* kind of action.

She was sitting on the sofa, an unread newspaper in her hand. It took her ten minutes to make up her mind. She could leave the kids alone for a quarter of an hour.

She shrugged into her jacket, got on her bike, and went to Steven's house. She pressed the bell, but there was no response. From the street, she could see a light burning in the living room of his second-floor apartment. Maybe he'd gone out in a rush and forgotten to turn it off?

She took out her key but hesitated. Maybe Steven wasn't answering his phone or doorbell because he didn't want to be disturbed. If she let herself in…

A phrase of David's popped up in her mind: "illegal entry." They hadn't made plans to see each other tonight, and maybe he had other company. If she walked in on him unannounced…

She decided to go home.

The kids were fine, both sound asleep.

It was going to be a long and restless night, that was for sure.

She poured herself a glass of wine, but it tasted sour. She looked at the label. A good Bordeaux, from a good year.

There was a talk show on TV, an obese woman trying to lose half her body weight. She flipped through the channels. An episode of an American crime series, another American crime series, Dr. Phil pontificating about difficult in-laws, a cooking show, an American sitcom, a Dutch sitcom. She knew "sitcom" was short for "situation comedy," but there was nothing funny about the situations these characters found themselves in, at least nothing that seemed funny to Mirjam. Two actresses pretending to be ordinary housewives, but they were gym rats with sophisticated Amsterdam accents who thought they could pass themselves off as working class by talking loudly and chewing gum.

She shut off the TV and tried the wine again. It didn't taste any better.

She reached for her phone. Straight to voicemail on both his home line and his cell.

It was ten twenty. Not too late to go over there again. She went upstairs and checked on the kids. They were both still sleeping peacefully.

&

The music was wonderful. People were out of their chairs, standing in the aisles and clustered around the bar, swaying to the beat, pumping their fists in the air, dancing. Even Selma seemed to be loosening up a little. Lucas spotted the hint of a smile on her lips.

"What do you want to drink?" he shouted. "Something tropical?"

"Just a Coke," she said in his ear.

He could barely hear her over the music.

When the band took a break, she went to the ladies' room. She was gone for a long time, still not back when the second set started. She wouldn't have gone home on her own, would she? Lucas had the coat-check thingie, so that didn't seem likely.

Embarrassed, he opened the ladies' room door a crack and looked in. The round indicators on all six of the stalls read "Vacant."

"Selma?" He tried to say it loudly but at the same time not loud enough to frighten anyone.

From behind, someone tapped his shoulder. He spun around and found a girl squinting at him suspiciously.

"I'm looking for my sister," he explained. "She's been gone a long time. I'm starting to worry about her."

The girl shrugged and pushed past him to the mirror to freshen her lipstick.

Lucas roamed around the huge Music Hall on the IJ, of which the Bimhuis was only one section. At the coat check, he asked if anyone had seen his sister. He tried to describe her, but there wasn't really much to distinguish her from the hundreds of other young women there that night. Medium-length hair, blue-gray sweatshirt, jeans, sneakers.

He checked the café-restaurant, which offered a grand view of the lake. A passenger ship strung with hundreds of twinkling white lights was heading west toward IJmuiden. Lucas saw a small figure at the terrace railing, watching the ship sail by.

His heart pounding wildly, he searched for a door leading out to the terrace.

"That way, sir," a girl carrying a tray of drinks pointed. "But it's cold out there."

Lucas never let Selma out of his sight for a second, and at last he was standing beside her.

He put his arm around her. "Jesus, Sel, what are you doing out here?"

She didn't seem to hear him. She said nothing, just followed the passing ship with her lifeless eyes.

❧

They went to see the new Robert De Niro film. De Niro played an aging cab driver trying to write the Great American Novel.

"He was better in *Raging Bull*," said David.

"And *Goodfellas*. Remember that scene where these Mafia bosses are sitting around this big round table—I think it was Las Vegas—and he's got this baseball bat?" Hein put his fists together as if he was holding a bat himself. "And he beats this one guy's skull in, because he was selling him out to the cops?" He put some gravel into his voice and quoted a line from the film. "'I get nowhere unless the team wins.' Then wham, wham, wham!"

"Yeah, that was classic. *The Untouchables*, though, not *Goodfellas*."

"Don't tell me about De Niro, my friend, I'm an expert."

"Even the experts make a mistake, once in a while, and—"

"You telling me I'm wrong, David?" He was smiling when he said it, but all the emotion had suddenly disappeared from his voice. And Hein never called him David. It was always "D Squared," or "man," or "my friend."

David knew that Hein *was* wrong. He'd watched *The Untouchables* on DVD just the other night, after Mirjam and the kids were asleep, and he'd especially relished the baseball-bat scene, had for a reason he'd been unable to put his finger on been reminded of Hein. In fact, that was what had led him to suggest *Being Flynn* for tonight.

But something in Hein's flat tone warned him to be careful.

"No," David said lightly, "I always get those old gangster films mixed up in my head."

They stopped for a drink at a café in the Willemsparkweg.

"Let's take that corner table there," said Hein.

They settled in.

David started to say something about the movie, but Hein interrupted him.

"That envelope I gave you that time, you still have it?"

"Of course. It's in the safe at Starrebeek."

"You haven't opened it, just to see what all the fuss was about?"

Despite Hein's exaggerated wink, David hastened to assure him that he absolutely hadn't. "We *never* look at stuff clients ask us to hold for them. Strictly forbidden, the boss would rip me a new one."

When they left the café, Hein suggested another fishing trip for Saturday. David looked uncomfortable.

"Or Sunday," said Hein, "so you can take your boy to fencing on Saturday."

David snapped to attention. How did Hein know about Bas' fencing lessons? He couldn't remember ever having mentioned the subject.

❧

Standing at his front door, Mirjam dialed both of Steven's numbers yet again. Nothing. The living-room light was still on. She used her key and started up the steps. The building was completely quiet.

She hesitated on the landing between floors, couldn't shake the sense that she was making a mistake.

Looking up, she saw that Steven's apartment door was open a crack. He would never have gone out without locking the door, he was much too careful. Something was wrong.

She told herself to turn around and go home, but when she took her next step it was up, not down.

She touched the doorknob and stood there, holding it. Should she push it open or pull it shut? She didn't know.

It was hard to breathe, hard to swallow. There was something in her throat, maybe her own uncertainty. She heard the wail of a siren in the distance.

The noise somehow decided for her. She pushed the door.

The first thing she saw was red, so much red. There was red everywhere she looked.

Chapter 20

It was one fifteen, and the lights were still on. Once again, Mirjam had forgotten to turn them off when she went to bed, as if their electric bill wasn't high enough already.

He hesitated in the foyer. Maybe she hadn't gone to bed yet, was waiting up to start another confrontation. Waiting up, anger building inside her, and for what? Because *he'd* discovered that *she* was stepping out on him.

Sally butted his leg with her head, meowing for attention. He dropped to his knees and stroked her. The kids' backpacks were on the floor. Home all day, no job, and she couldn't find the time to clean up after Bas and Romy or the energy to make them do it themselves. Too busy mooning around the house, dreaming of her fucking lover. Or was this some kind of coded message? He picked up the backpacks and hung them on the coatrack where they belonged.

He found Mirjam in the chair by the living room window. She didn't look up when he came into the room. He still had his jacket on, ready to bolt for the door if he had to. She sat there, completely motionless, her eyes dead and empty, her pale hands folded in her lap.

David jumped to the worst conclusion he could imagine. "Did something happen to the kids?"

She didn't respond. It was like she wasn't even there.

David repeated his question, louder this time.

She made no sign of having heard him.

He put a hand on her shoulder and felt her recoil. "Mirjam! What's wrong? Where are Romy and Bas? Say something!"

He rushed out of the room and up the stairs. Both children lay peacefully sleeping in their beds. He sighed out the breath he hadn't realized he was holding. Bas rolled onto his side and made a strange mewling sound. He was having one of his odd little dreams, David knew, and he wished he could climb into his son's head and join him there. Bas often told David about his dreams, and some of them seemed too perfectly constructed to be real. Sometimes he wondered if the boy made them up. At school, he wrote stories that always earned the highest possible grades. A budding writer, his son? David hoped not. He knew from his conversations with a former client that most authors were barely able to scratch out a decent living.

He wanted just to sit there at the end of Bas' bed and watch the boy sleep, but he tiptoed out of the room and down the stairs.

Mirjam hadn't stirred.

"Okay," he said, "the kids are fine. What is it, then? Your parents? Uncle Bas or Aunt Josje? One of your girlfriends? Thera or Evelien?"

It took him completely by surprise when she leapt up and pummeled him with her hard little fists. "What did you do?" she hissed. "What did you do to Steven?"

He pulled back before she could rake his face with her nails.

❧

"You've made—how should I say this?—negative or perhaps even aggressive statements about Mr. Veenstra?"

The detective, who'd introduced himself as Inspector Tom Biesterbos, seemed perfectly friendly, but his demeanor didn't correspond with his words.

Mirjam had talked with the policeman earlier, while David took the children to school. She'd probably filled him full of suspicions—maybe even accusations—concerning David's role in the murder of Steven Veenstra.

Certainly she'd accused him last night. "You killed him! You killed him!" she'd shrieked, over and over. He tried to bring her to her senses, but it took a long time before she wore herself out and collapsed onto the sofa. It was a miracle that the children had been able to sleep through it all.

Of course he'd protested his innocence, but his words didn't seem to get through to her. At last he was able to get enough of the story out of her to begin to get a sense of what had happened. She'd gone to Veenstra's house, let herself in with her key, went upstairs to find his apartment door open, and gone in to find him on the floor, dead, bathed in blood.

The newspapers didn't have the story yet. There was a brief report on NU.nl, but no word of a suspect. Whether or not anything had been stolen from the apartment was left unstated. Steven Veenstra was described as "a successful advertising executive," the winner of two gold Effies, founding partner of the well-respected Veenstra & Watzlawick agency.

David had slept on the couch in his study, although there hadn't been much actual sleeping involved.

"Did you consider Mr. Veenstra an enemy?"

No, he wanted to say, *he was my best friend, I'm devastated by his death*, but he knew better than to make sick jokes in the middle of a murder investigation.

"I hated him," he acknowledged. "How would you feel if *your* wife was—?"

Biesterbos interrupted him. "I have a husband," he said, "not a wife. But go on."

"I hated him, I don't deny that. But if I started knocking off everybody I hate, I'd be the Dutch Ted Bundy."

Biesterbos smiled patiently.

"He destroyed my marriage," David went on. "Mirjam and I have been talking about getting a divorce."

"A contested divorce, your wife told me?"

David nodded.

"It would have been better for you if Mr. Veenstra simply wasn't in the picture anymore?"

"Jesus, come on, Inspector, that's a cheap shot. What do you expect me to say?" He felt insulted, like Biesterbos was underestimating his legal ability. "I've sat in on too many interrogations to fall for that sort of trick."

"This isn't an interrogation, sir," said the detective.

"No, of course not, it's just an ordinary friendly chat with a kind of creepy subject matter, right? Fine, then. You want a cup of coffee?"

"Mr. Driessen, you understand we're in the first phase of an investigation here. I don't want to jerk you around and haul you down to the station, that seems unnecessary at this point."

"At this point," said David drily. "Well, *I'm* gonna have some coffee."

In the kitchen, he fixed a cup of Nespresso. Leaning against the counter, he considered how the situation must look to Biesterbos. Here's David Driessen, faced with the biggest crisis of his married life, confronted with a divorce he doesn't want, and all of a sudden, completely by coincidence, his rival drops off the face of the Earth. Well, not exactly. Sometime soon, his rival would be buried *under* the face of the Earth, so that wasn't exactly the same thing. Anyway, if he were Biesterbos, *he'd* consider Counselor Driessen a prime suspect in the Veenstra murder, no doubt about it.

In the living room, the detective stood gazing out the window.

David coughed.

Biesterbos turned. "Mind if I ask you a few more questions?" he said.

David looked at his watch, though he knew he had nothing but time. He'd called the office and told Hanna to cancel his appointments for the day so he could deal with "a family emergency." She hadn't asked him what sort of emergency. "Fine," he said. "Go ahead."

"Given your profession, sir, you already know I have to ask—"

"—where I was last night?"

"Yes, sir."

David had given this some thought. Could he use Hein as his alibi? He knew, with a level of confidence approaching certainty, that Hein would prefer to avoid conversations with the police—and he wasn't thrilled about the prospect, either. The sort of friendly relationship he'd developed with Hein wasn't really appropriate between lawyer and client—and he *was* still formally serving as Hein's attorney. If word of their personal relationship got out, one or both of them might suffer. Better to leave Hein out of it.

David said he'd gone to see Robert De Niro in the second evening screening of *Being Flynn* at the City Theater.

"Alone?"

"Yes. With everything that's been going on with Mirjam, all the talk about divorce and what to do about the kids and all, I just needed to get away by myself. Take a break from all the stress."

"I understand. And I'm sorry to have to ask, but—"

David knew that Biesterbos wasn't the least bit sorry. He was just doing his job, asking the standard questions.

"—is there anyone who can confirm that?"

David shook his head.

"You didn't see anyone you knew?"

"No, no one."

"Do you have your ticket stub? It wouldn't really *prove* anything, but still…"

Hein had bought their tickets. David had never even touched them.

"No, sorry, I threw it away."

☙

Mirjam lay in bed. She felt completely empty. Nothing could affect her anymore, nothing mattered. She would go on for the sake of the children, but there was nothing left for *her*. The bullets hadn't just ended Steven's life. They'd also ended hers. The damage couldn't be seen from the outside, but that only made it worse on the inside.

She would take care of the kids, do the household chores, all of that. She didn't have the energy right now to go forward with the divorce. She wasn't sure she had the strength to attend Steven's funeral. How would she even know when it was? Or where? They'd know at Veenstra & Watzlawick, but she wasn't in any condition to call them.

She'd left a comforter and a pillow in David's study. She couldn't stand the thought of having him next to her in bed. There had to be some link between Steven's violent death and David. He'd gone out around eight, claiming he had an appointment at eight thirty. "A business thing," he'd said. "Half-client, half-friend." That was conveniently nebulous.

Last night, her emotions in disarray, she'd been positive that David must have done it. But now that the horror had begun to subside, she wasn't quite so sure. Where would he have gotten a pistol? Maybe that wouldn't have been hard for him, with all the criminals he met in his line of work. But could he have actually pulled the trigger? That just seemed so completely out of character. David was always afraid of violence, like that time at a party some years back, when some bodybuilder who'd had two or three too many had grabbed her ass. David had seen it happen, and he didn't do a thing about it! She'd insisted they leave, and on the way home she let him have it.

"You saw the guy," her husband had protested. "He could have beaten the crap out of me. And for what? Because he groped you for one second at a party?"

"What if he raped me?" she'd raged. "Would you stand up to him then?"

But she couldn't let go of the thought that, one way or another, David had *something* to do with the murder. Otherwise, it was all too big a coincidence.

Almost three hours until time to get the kids from school. Maybe that was something to hold on to, the simple routines of day-to-day existence.

Hopefully David was already gone.

☙

David sat at his desk. The office was a whirlwind of activity, but there was nothing for him to do. He checked his Rolex, and it was only three minutes since the last time he'd looked.

Tomorrow he had court. A kid, age around twenty, arrested for possession of and trafficking in cocaine and heroin. David leafed slowly through the case file. The amounts involved were nominal, but, since this was the boy's third arrest on similar charges, he was facing significant prison time. Not much here for David to grab on to. His client had been caught red-handed. It was a familiar story. Guy's on welfare, he does a little dealing to pick up some extra money—and maybe to get his hands on some product for his own delectation. He knows the risks and, sure enough, it all goes south. Some of them get away with it for longer, others are so dumb they don't bother taking even the most basic precautions.

He wondered how Hein got hold of *his* stuff. Certainly from someone he could trust, not some nobody like this morning's client.

His phone rang. Hanna said that a Mr. Wesseling was holding for him. Funny, think of the devil, and there he was.

"This is David."

"I'm in the Prinsengracht, parked right outside number 743. Can you be here in five minutes?"

"Okay, I—"

He was talking to a broken connection.

⁓

Smiling, Hein took a flask from his inside jacket pocket. "Bourbon. Something a little different, for a change. You look like you could use it. Cheers!" He put the flask to his mouth, then handed it over.

He reached around and plucked a copy of the evening newspaper, *Het Parool*, from the back seat. It was folded to an article headlined "Adman dead man in A'dam." The piece was illustrated with a photograph of Steven Veenstra and a small reproduction of a poster advertising laundry detergent. "For the cleanest wash, wash with Klean," the poster read. Clever. It would stick in people's minds, and of course that was the point.

"For the safest life," said Hein, "don't mess with D Squared's wife."

David had no idea how he was supposed to react to that. He took another hit of the bourbon.

"Hey, save some for me."

For the cleanest wash, wash with Klean. That was probably a pretty decent slogan. What laundry soap did Mirjam buy? Surely not Klean.

"You're looking down, man. Why? Seems to me this is a win for you. You ought to buy the guy who capped Mr. Veenstra a drink." Hein gave David a meaningful look, but David wasn't sure exactly what meaning it was full of. He had a suspicion, but he didn't dare say it aloud.

He unfolded the paper and read the article. It was hinted that the victim had come home and surprised a burglar. And then all the usual clichés: the police were withholding further details pending investigation, the homicide squad was pursuing several leads, but no suspect had been identified as yet, and the detectives were not ready to make an arrest. Then came a brief précis of Steven Veenstra's life and successful rise from assistant copywriter to founding partner of one of the most important ad agencies in The Netherlands. Divorced, one child, a boy. The fact that he was having an affair with a married woman at the time of his death was not mentioned.

David refolded the paper. "They were at the house this morning. Biesterbos, young guy."

"To be expected. What did you tell him?"

"I was at the movies… alone."

Hein nodded approvingly. "I figured you'd say something like that. You know how to play the game, D Squared. I've been right about you all along. Together, we're invincible, right?"

"Absolutely."

David watched the city traffic crawl past. Mostly bikers, maneuvering alongside and between the bumper-to-bumper cars. In the same manner, *he* was wending his way around and through the various obstacles that lay in his path.

"Pretty soon now," Hein said, "we're going to have to make a decision about your new practice. You haven't forgotten, have you? I found a new space, way better than that dump in the Maasstraat. We're not going to rush into it, but you have to strike while the iron is hot, you know?"

Strike, thought David. *Why 'strike'?*

"And that investment in Curaçao, too. Remember?"

"Of course I do."

"We'll talk about it. Right now, I gotta go."

David understood that he was being dismissed.

Before he could shut the door, Hein said, "Oh, yeah, fishing on Sunday, right? I'll pick you up at seven."

Chapter 21

Mirjam walked through the house like a robot. Like a badly programmed robot. She dropped things, put the laundry in the wrong drawers and closets, burned their dinner, forgot to get bread at the supermarket, left Bas and Romy's lunches behind when she took them to school. She ignored David as much as possible and let the kids do whatever they wanted. The house was turning into a dump, and David was afraid to say anything about it.

It was only at mealtimes—which were completely disorganized; to Bas' delight, she served pasta for dinner three nights running—that she seemed to notice David's presence in the house. If he came into the living room late in the evening and found her parked in front of the TV, she got to her feet without a word and went upstairs. Since the death of Steven Veenstra—and David always thought of it as *the death*, rather than *the murder*—what had once been their bedroom had become her private domain, off limits to him. It was bad enough they had to share the bathroom.

They put certain agreements in place. Mirjam informed him via e-mail that it would be his job to take the kids to school on Monday, Wednesday, and Friday mornings. She made other pronouncements, and it was clear that they were to be received as Holy Writ: you will do this job on this schedule, and that job on that schedule, and there will be no discussion, let alone negotiation.

He tried to talk reason with her. "What if I have to be in Utrecht, say, at nine on a Wednesday morning? Then how am I supposed to—?"

"Figure it out," she said tonelessly, and she turned around and walked away.

One advantage was that, as long as he played by her rules, he could do whatever else he wanted. He was never challenged, and never had to explain himself.

On Sunday, he and Hein went fishing, this time on the north side of the North Sea Canal. The hours by the water were relaxing. David had never much believed in old saws like "Don't underestimate the value of Doing Nothing," but that afternoon, just him and Hein and their hooks, he for once began to appreciate what Winnie-the-Pooh must have meant. Even the boats motoring by failed to disturb the mood—in fact, they added a pleasant accent to it. Like last time, Hein had brought food, coffee, and booze.

The only problem came when David actually caught a fish. He couldn't believe it at first. His bobber disappeared beneath the surface of the water, and he felt a jerk on his line. "Reel it in!" yelled Hein, laughing. He did, and the problem was getting the hook out of the squirming creature's mouth. "You took it, you unhook it," said Hein. "That's an unwritten law, D Squared, and you know the drill: the unwritten laws are more important than the written ones."

While David struggled to release it, the stupid fish flopped around like it was having an epileptic seizure. All that talk about fish not having nerves in their lips sounded great, but he was sure the wildly flailing critter must be in agony.

He finally managed. The fish looked dead by now. He lobbed it into the canal and couldn't tell if it swam away or sank like a stone.

On the way back to the car, Hein spotted a leather shoulder bag lying half hidden beneath a bush. There was a wallet inside, and in that an assortment of ID cards and bank cards in the name of P. Smit—and two hundred Euros in cash. Not one of the cards showed an address or phone number.

"P. Smit," said Hein. "Maybe Peter? That's probably the most common man's name in Holland."

They stopped at the police station in Zaanstad and turned the bag in. Then Hein dropped David at home.

"I'll pick you up at Starrebeek on Tuesday, four o'clock. I want to show you that office space I told you about. It's perfect, you're gonna love it. We have to grab it before someone else gets it, trust me."

Before David could react, Hein had driven off.

He watched the Mercedes go, and suddenly a memory from before the kids were born washed over him.

He was on a high bridge over a deep valley, and a raging river rushed by far below. His throat was dry, and his heart beat wildly against his ribcage. Mirjam was down there, watching him, camera at the ready. She wouldn't think any less of him if he chickened out. So why jump? For himself, to prove he had the guts? Was that a good enough reason to bungee off this enormous height? It was all perfectly safe, the guide assured him, adjusting his harness, slapping him encouragingly on the shoulder. "Come on, man, you can do it!" Adrenaline coursed through his veins. He stepped carefully onto the little platform and knew that he was going to jump.

✧

"Think carefully," said Biesterbos. "Did Mr. Veenstra ever mention having an enemy, anyone he was having a problem with?"

"Yes," said Mirjam. "David."

"I don't mean your husband."

"I do."

"I'm talking about other people, Mrs. Driessen. Your husband doesn't have much of an alibi, but there's absolutely nothing at the crime scene to link him to the murder, not a fingerprint, nothing. Nobody saw him in the area around 10 PM. We haven't written him off, but, if we focus in only on your husband, we might miss out on other possibilities. That's what we call tunnel vision."

Mirjam sighed. Like she didn't know what tunnel vision was. She was *in* that tunnel, and she knew that it led—maybe not directly, but still—to David. It *had* to.

"I'm sorry we haven't made much progress," Biesterbos said.

"I *know* he had something to do with it," Mirjam insisted. "I'm absolutely positive."

"I'm sorry, ma'am, but you can't—"

She cut him off. "I'm not saying he *did* it. I don't think he's the kind of man who could actually shoot somebody, he's too much of a coward, but he's *involved*, somehow, that's what I'm trying to tell you."

"Involved how?"

Mirjam decided to lay her hypothesis on the table. Generally, David defended only petty criminals, but maybe some of them were capable of stepping up to more serious offenses, or had connections who were.

"Maybe he hired someone to do it," she said. "You read about that, murder for hire. David knows a lot of underworld figures through his work, and—"

"Yes, but—"

"—and maybe it wouldn't have been hard for him to find someone, a drug dealer, maybe." She could see it, David tracking down some gun for hire, meeting clandestinely in a dark alley or a low class bar.

☙

It was all happening so quickly, and maybe that was for the best. Any slower, and he might find himself trapped in the molasses of doubt. And it would be pointless now to object to Hein's suggestions. If he didn't want to start his own practice, he should have put his foot down and said so in the first place. But Hein had convinced him, and was himself proof of the wisdom of his personal philosophy: Sometimes you just had to put the hammer down and take it full speed ahead.

Last Tuesday, they'd checked out the building, and Hein was right—it was perfect. It was on the ground floor of a five-story building, formerly home to an import/export business that had gone bust. Above it, the rest of the building had been divided into apartments. Not in the *Grachtengordel*, the area inside the city's four main canals, but in Amsterdam-South, between the Van Baerlestraat and the Hobbemakade, right off the Roelof Hartplein.

They'd had dinner nearby, in the restaurant at the Okura Hotel, and discussed the situation. Financing would be no problem. Hein was prepared to cosign the mortgage. He was sure the seller would come down fifty thousand Euros, so he'd offer a hundred thousand below the asking price and negotiate from there, see what happened.

Afterwards, they went to Café Schemer, where David played for high stakes. He won a little and lost a lot. Hein generously staked him to more, which quickly shrank to less and then nothing at all. But Hein didn't seem concerned.

They got gloriously drunk. Arms slung across each other's shoulders, they staggered out to the street, abandoning the two sweethearts who'd played up to them at the bar.

"Too wasted to screw," Hein said, pronouncing the words with exaggerated care. "Right, bro?"

David wasn't sure he'd heard him right, but he slurred "Mush too wasted" and kissed Hein on the cheek.

"Shit, fags," one of the women said. "You go have fun, then, boys."

David woke up with a splintering hangover. The alcohol had dried up the blood in his veins, and he couldn't sleep past six. He'd collapsed on the couch in his study, still dressed, hadn't even kicked off his shoes.

A long shower, alternating between scalding and frigid, did him little good. He felt like he'd been pressed between two panes of glass and had no control over his body. Bas and Romy had to take *him* to school, instead of the other way around.

Back home, he returned to his couch. In this condition, he wasn't just a danger to himself but to the world at large. And this afternoon was Mrs. Van Middelheim thoe Harchem's pretrial hearing. He couldn't possibly ditch it. When he closed his eyes, he saw her flouncing around the courtroom in flimsy lingerie. She sat on the edge of his bed. "Oh, honey, you having a rough morning?" She stroked his hair. She looked just like Nicole from Vinkeveen. Maybe he'd go back there with Hein sometime soon. Not tonight, tonight was the Champions League game, 7:30 at the Willemsparkweg, don't forget. "You want me to come lie with you? Should I change into something else? I have lots of these. No? Not enough room on the couch? Can't you sleep in your own bed anymore? Sleep tight, then. Sweet dreams. Everything will be fine when you wake up, I promise."

ↇↄ

Mrs. Van Middelheim thoe Harchem sat there like a chick fallen out of its nest, with fluttering little wings and a chirping beak. She wanted nothing more than to fly away to safety, but that was no longer an option.

David had spoken with her—or, really, with her husband—in the corridor outside the courtroom. "You have to get the charges dropped," the man had said. "She'll never survive a prison term."

David figured that, if she'd managed to survive being married to him, a few weeks in stir wouldn't kill her.

At the request of the investigating magistrate, who pronounced her name as if it tasted bad, Mrs. Van Middelheim thoe Harchem told her version of what had transpired at the lingerie shop. She repeated the story she'd previously told David almost verbatim. He assumed she'd spent most of yesterday and this morning rehearsing for this afternoon's performance.

David glanced behind him. Her husband sat in the first row of the gallery, nodding encouragingly. Jesus, one row back, off to the side, sat Hein. He smiled when he caught David's eye. What was he doing here?

As she completed her recitation, the defendant managed to squeeze out a couple of tears. "So unfair," she murmured, "so unfair."

The prosecutor stuck strictly to the facts as presented in the indictment, and David offered the obvious defense: the accused had absolutely no intention of stealing the goods in question, she clearly had the means to pay for them, everyone makes mistakes now and then, an understandable slip, to err is human, no reason to punish her, blah blah blah.

The magistrate gave her forty hours of community service.

David tried to make his escape as quickly as possible, but Mr. Van Middelheim thoe Harchem intercepted him. His wife was at his side, looking as stricken as if she'd been sentenced to the guillotine.

"Community service!" Van Middelheim thoe Harchem bristled. "Forty hours! Do they really expect my wife to pick up trash in the park with a bunch of junkies?"

"Maybe there's—"

"Or wipe the buttocks of demented old people in a nursing home? He can't be serious. *Look* at her! She's incapable of handling the humiliation."

From the corner of his eye, David saw Hein go out the building's revolving door.

"It's a scandal," Van Middelheim thoe Harchem rumbled. "They haven't heard the last of this. I'm calling Maarten. Obviously *you* are out of your depth here."

තා

David had never been in a skybox before. It was like a chic little café, with one whole wall a huge-screen TV showing a soccer match. The only difference was that the TV was a plate-glass window, and the players were right down there on the field. David was introduced to the other guests, including Theo Wildschut. "My legal advisor," Hein said. "He helped me acquire those buildings in the Rivierenbuurt."

"Maybe you can help me with a few things," Wildschut said. And, to Hein, "It's a shame John's gone."

Hein grinned. "Yeah, a dead shame."

The other team scored the first goal, but then Ajax tied it up. There was polite cheering in the skybox, unlike the insanity that broke out in the stadium, barely audible through the thick glass window. Someone popped open a bottle of champagne, then another. Wildschut was treating the company to two bottles for each Ajax goal. David bought into a friendly pool, betting a thousand Euros on a 2-2 tie. Everyone else had the cash on hand. Hein fronted David's share.

They clinked glasses. "You weren't really all there this afternoon, were you?" Hein asked. "I don't think you really bought her story, the panty lady."

"Did *you* believe her?"

"Of course not, but it was interesting. She could wipe her ass with fifty-Euro notes, and she's stealing underwear? What's up with that?"

David checked the action on the field and sipped his champagne. "Too slippery," he said.

"What is?"

"Fifty-Euro notes. You couldn't wipe your ass with them."

Hein punched his shoulder. "At least you can still crack a joke, D Squared. How're things going at home?"

"Hopeless. She won't even look at me. It's like I don't exist."

"Yes, yes!" Hein was watching the field, where Ajax had the ball and was moving it steadily forward. "No!" He winced in pain and turned back to David. "What did you say?"

"It's like I'm invisible. She doesn't see me."

"But Veenstra's out of the picture. That worked out perfectly."

"What do you mean, 'worked out'?"

"You know what I mean." Hein winked.

And the thought David had been avoiding was suddenly impossible to ignore. He had to ask Hein if he was right about it, but he simply couldn't muster the courage. It would sound like an accusation. And he'd learned by now that, in these circles, you never discussed such matters explicitly. It didn't matter if you were dealing in suspicions or certainties, everything was insinuation, allusion, like Wildschut's comment about the murdered John van Bremen.

An anorectic girl came up to them with a tray of sushi.

"You ought to have some yourself," Hein told her. "You look like you could use it."

She shook her head.

As she tottered off on her spike heels, Hein muttered, "Skank."

David asked where the bathroom was.

"You leave," Hein said, "you'll miss a goal, guaranteed."

He was all alone in the men's room. After he peed, he examined his face in the mirror over the sink. Did he look any different, now that he knew? More like Hein?

He decided to leave the stadium, go home, start over. This time, things would be different. Mirjam would believe in him, in their relationship, in their life together.

He heard a roar in the distance.

He went back to the skybox and sat next to Hein. "Two to one, Ajax. I told you. You piss in a hole, you're missin' a goal."

⁊

Lucas read the text: "Please contact the Lijnbaansgracht Police Station. Sanne Vos."

Police. Had he done something wrong? Some sort of traffic violation? Unlikely. Maybe that bastard lawyer had accused him of threatening him.

It took him twenty minutes to get to the station on his bike. Sanne Vos was gone for the day, her shift over. Phone calls were made. Lucas had the impression he was being jerked around. After a while, they seemed to have forgotten about him. In a corner of the room, an officer was watching a soccer match on a laptop. He'd never been all that interested in soccer. Now baseball, that was another story. If it had been a World Series game, he'd be looking over the cop's shoulder. Or the Baseball World Cup, which the Dutch team had stunned the world by winning in 2011, beating out twenty-five-time international champion Cuba. He didn't understand all the hoopla about soccer. It was a violent game, constantly interrupted by fights. Baseball was so much more peaceful. And there was so much more *to* it, they understood that in the States. In the Antilles, too. There was a guy from Curaçao on his team, Humphrey, a fantastic catcher and a jackrabbit on the base paths.

Two officers were steering an aggressive dirty bum with a crusty beard and an overfull plastic grocery bag in each hand out of the station.

"I'll get you fuckers," he screamed drunkenly. "Me'n my brother, we'll mess you up."

"You're scaring us," said a young inspector. He turned to Lucas. "Help you?"

"I'm supposed to see Sanne Vos. She texted me, told me to come in. I don't know why."

"Sit tight. I'll see what I can find out."

It took a long time. That could mean anything. Maybe they just weren't very competent. Or it was nothing, a mistake. But it could be *something*, something big. As if a sheet had been whipped off a statue in a public park, it was suddenly revealed to him. Something had happened to Selma.

He stood up and began to pace.

It was almost fifteen minutes before the young inspector returned, this time accompanied by an older officer. "You're Lucas Groothuis?" the older cop asked. He had a dried-out, drawn face, its hard lines carved of stone.

"Yes. What—?"

"Come with me, please?"

They went into a little sort of conference room.

"What is it?" asked Lucas. "Is it Selma?"

The officer looked away, as if there was something important hanging on the wall. He sighed deeply and turned back to Lucas.

"I'm sorry, son. There's no easy way to say this. Your sister is dead."

Lucas blinked, uncomprehending. "What?"

The older man said it again, more slowly, stretching out the words, as if he'd cut them apart and was now pasting them back together into a sentence. "Your sister, Selma Groothuis, is dead."

"But—"

"Tonight, shortly after 7, she jumped from the top floor of the student apartments in the Korte Leidsedwaarsstaat." It sounded like he was reading a news report from a teleprompter. "She went out a back window, so she wasn't found right away. She probably died on impact. We don't think she suffered any pain."

Lucas sat there, his mouth open. He stared at the man across from him. He had to take it back. If he took it back, then it wouldn't have happened. Like running a movie in reverse: you saw some guy at a café, drooling coffee into a cup, filling it to the brim, setting it down on a saucer so a server could pick it up and take it away, walking backwards…

"I'm truly sorry," the officer said.

Why should he be sorry if nothing bad had happened?

"Your sister left a note. She said we should tell you first, then your parents. We understand they're out of the country?"

Chapter 22

The service was well attended. Dozens of people were there, divided into groups of three and four. Some of the mourners chattered animatedly, as if they were at a party, waiting for servers to come around with a tray of cocktails and canapés, but most of the conversations were whispered, as if secrets were being shared. Occasionally, a shrill half sentence or burst of quickly repressed laughter rose above the background noise.

Mirjam stood by herself; she knew no one there, and no one knew her. She'd never met any of Steven's employees, and had no idea which was his partner, Igor Watzlawick—who'd adopted that intriguing name when they'd gone into business together, Steven had told her, but had been born and raised as Henk Bakker. Maybe it was the chain smoker with the long gray hair tied back in a ponytail. She didn't recognize him from the one time she'd been to the office, to apply for that job. She hadn't gotten the position, but she'd gotten the boon. They'd never actually discussed the job; it hadn't seemed important anymore, once they'd connected.

The older couple were probably Steven's parents. The woman seemed on the verge of collapse, and the man was having trouble keeping her on her feet. And that exotic woman—there was something Indonesian about her— must be the ex-wife. All Mirjam knew about her was that she was a clerk at one of the courts. Maybe David had met her.

That made the frisky six-year-old the ex held tightly by the hand Steven's son Sjoerd. Sjoerd Veenstra, named for Steven's father. She recognized him from a photo on the desk at Steven's house. Steven had rarely talked about the boy; all she knew was that he'd been diagnosed with ADHD. Steven's custodial weekends were more work than play, and often left him completely exhausted. He looked like Steven, a young Steven. She wondered if he and Bas would get along. Mirjam wanted to approach the boy, to say something to him, but she couldn't imagine what that might possibly be.

What would happen to Steven's house, she thought—for the first time, strangely enough. It would have to be sold. And its contents? The bed? The chair on which she'd draped her clothing? She realized she didn't even have a picture of him. She'd have to make do with her memories.

A woman spoke to her. "You're Mirjam?"

"Yes. How did you know?"

"I'm Anneli, Steven's sister."

Mirjam hadn't even known there *was* a sister. They shook hands.

"He told me about you, a few weeks ago," said Anneli. "My New Love, with capital letters, that's what he called you."

Don't cry, Mirjam warned herself. *No tears!*

She bowed her head, looked away, cleared her throat, brushed a strand of hair off her eye. "Yes, that's what he was for me, too," she said, her voice pinched tight.

Anneli laid a gentle hand on her arm. "This must be so horrible for you."

Mirjam wanted to be left alone, yet she wished Anneli would hug her, put her arms around her and whisper soothing words in her ear and stroke her back. That would bring her a little closer to Steven this one last time before they put him in the ground and he was lost to her forever.

"I don't know what to do," she said. "Steven and I were going to—"

"He told me. You were going to get a divorce and move in with him."

A small knot of people came out of the chapel, attendees at the funeral of a belovéd someone else.

"My marriage is over. I can't just pick up the pieces and move on. I don't *want* to. I think David—that's my husband, David—I think he had something to do with it, with Steven's death."

"Your husband? You're not serious."

"I think—"

The chapel doors opened again, and the Veenstra mourners began to move inside.

"I'll call you," Anneli promised. She headed for the front row, which was reserved for the immediate family.

The chapel was too small to hold the gathered crowd. Mirjam stood in the back. A fat man was pressed up against her, breathing heavily. On her other side was a redhead in glasses, sniffling into a handkerchief. Mirjam thought she recognized her as one of the secretaries at Veenstra & Watzlawick.

She felt claustrophobic in the overcrowded space. She soaked up all the grief in the room. As if things weren't already bad enough, a mournful string quartet began to play.

She fled before the first speaker, Steven's father, could begin his eulogy. "Sorry," she said, "sorry," pushing her way toward the door.

She drifted around the cemetery for half an hour, reading the names of people she'd never known on the tombstones. The birth and death dates told her the ages of the dead, and she lingered by the children's graves.

Next to a freshly dug hole—Steven's?—she saw a portrait of a curly-haired child of two etched into a small headstone. The girl looked a little like Romy.

"Sweet dreams," said Mirjam softly. "Sweet dreams."

∽

Hein thrived on speed, and it all happened swiftly. The negotiations for the building were concluded. They registered the deed with the same notary who'd served Hein as middleman previously, when he'd bought several properties in David's name and immediately turned around and sold them at a good profit.

David had jumped aboard just in time to catch the train, and his life was now steaming ahead at a faster clip than he felt he could handle.

Before their meeting with the notary, Hein had taken him to Oger Amsterdam, an exclusive menswear shop in the P.C. Hooftstraat. "That suit," he'd frowned. "What did you do, pick it off the rack at C&A with your eyes closed?"

"It's Hugo Boss," David had protested, and Hein shook his head and said, "Yeah, that's C&A for guys with more balls than money."

With Hein's approval—and bank card—David had picked out a suit by Corneliani. It fit him perfectly. "Now I don't have to be embarrassed to be seen with you," Hein said.

When they left the notary's office, Hein asked in passing for one of the three sets of keys to David's new offices. David said he couldn't possibly hand them over.

"What, you don't trust me?"

"That's not the point," David replied.

"You bought the place with my money. You haven't forgotten that, have you?"

David swore he hadn't, but explained that, if he'd taken out a mortgage instead, the bank wouldn't have asked for a set of keys. Hein seemed to accept that argument, but he didn't look happy about it.

He made an appointment to meet with Starrebeek Senior the following week. Once that was taken care of, all he had to do was register with the bar association, which would cost a few hundred Euros, and with the Chamber of Commerce, and he'd be all set. It surprised even him how simple it was to hang up a shingle as an independent attorney. Why hadn't he done it years ago? Apparently he'd needed Hein to give him a push.

David was wearing his new suit when he got home at 6 PM, but Mirjam didn't notice. Nothing had changed, these last weeks. On a scale of one to ten, their situation had stabilized—frozen, really—somewhere below zero. He couldn't expect anything more, since she still harbored suspicions against him. They talked only when absolutely necessary, and then only about the practical matters of running the family and the household. Mirjam limited most of her communication to notes, texts, and e-mails. Sometimes he wanted to ask her to come out and *tell* him what she thought he'd done, but he always managed to bite back the words.

Biesterbos had spoken with him a second time, but it was clear that the police investigation into the Steven Veenstra murder had hit a brick wall. Naturally, David kept his own suspicions to himself. Eventually, official interest in the case would die out, he thought. *Die out.* The exact opposite of what had happened to Mir's lover, who had died *in* his own apartment.

Last night, he'd gone out for a couple of drinks with Hein, who'd convinced him that, sooner or later, things would get better with Mirjam. "Don't rush her. You know what they say, my friend: 'Softly, softly, catchee monkey.' She'll come around. She needs you. She knows you're a good dad for her kids, a good provider, a good partner. She just needs time to kick the Veenstra habit."

It sounded like he'd had personal experience with a similar situation, but David realized he knew very little about Hein's private life.

They discussed David's new practice. Hein had used his connections to furnish the office inexpensively. Inexpensively, but not crappily. He'd arranged for stylish desks, bookshelves, filing cabinets, tables, chairs, lamps. Under Hein's approving eye, David had signed the various purchase orders.

"You need a plaque for out front," Hein suggested. "'D Square, Attorneys,' and under that 'Mr. David Driessen and Partners.' Not so formal if you use your first name."

"Good idea."

"Instead of spelling out 'Squared,' you could use one of those little uppy twos."

"Superscript," David supplied.

"Whatever."

"I don't know. Everybody'll think it says 'D Two.'"

"Yeah, you're right, just spell it out."

After their second whiskeys, something annoying happened. A man with a camera appeared out of nowhere and took a photo of the two of them.

Hein shot to his feet and grabbed the camera. "What the fuck you think you're doing?" he demanded.

The man asked for his camera back.

"Sell my picture to the fucking tabloids? Shit." He flipped open a little plastic hatch on the side of the camera and removed the SD card. "I'll hold on to this." He returned the camera.

"Hey, there's like fifty other pictures on that card!"

Hein raised a hand, not even remotely threatening, and the man took off.

Now David was in his office at Starrebeek & Starrebeek. He'd looked through a couple of file folders and filled Joost in on a new client, a twenty-one-year-old who'd abused and threatened his own mother. As was so often the case, money was at the root of it. The son had refused to go on paying for room and board.

Room and board. David was paying for that himself. He had a hell of a lot of money going out, but there was never enough coming in. He fantasized about the sums his new practice would generate. Major clients, lucrative assignments, business travel, stimulating company.

He kept putting off the conversation he knew he had to have with Starrebeek Senior, to tell the old man he was leaving, quitting, cashing in his chips. The sooner they talked, the better, so he could write off this disappointing chapter of his career and move on to the exciting next one.

First, though, he opened up the safe and took out Hein's envelope and the second envelope with the copies he'd made. Better now to keep those at home.

Then he called Arnold Verhagen, a recent law school graduate who'd done a summer internship at S&S. He got voicemail and left his name and number and a message asking Arnold to call him back. He'd been impressed by the young man's acuity, insight, and initiative. He'd make an ideal second attorney in the new firm. Would Hein agree?

The moment he had the thought, he shook it off. This was *his* practice, not Hein's. He'd choose his own employees and colleagues. He'd need a secretary right away, maybe part-time for starters.

Hanna buzzed him. There was a young man out front who said he had to speak with David.

"Who is it?"

"Lucas Groothuis."

"Tell him I'm busy. I don't have time for him—not now, and not ever."

A minute later, there was a commotion out in the hall. "Get off me!" someone cried.

"Stop it! You can't go in there!"

David headed for his door, but it flew open before he could reach it, and there was Lucas Groothuis. Hanna was clutching at his arm, trying to pull him away.

"I just want to talk to him," said Groothuis, his eyes wild. "That's all. Let go of me!"

David took his other arm. "We've already talked, Lucas. There's nothing more to say."

By now, Hein would have grabbed his jacket collar and thrown him down the stairs.

"There's plenty to say. You need to know what's happened."

Joost came out of his own office and wanted to know what was going on.

"Kid's upset," David explained, "but it's really got nothing to do with us."

"All right, you. Let's go." Hanna stepped back, and Joost took her place on Lucas' other side.

"Fine," the boy snarled. "I'm going."

When he was gone, David took a few deep breaths and headed for Starrebeek Senior's lair.

☙

David said hello, but Mirjam didn't react. He made another attempt to get through to her. "You like this suit?" he asked. "It's new. I needed a new suit."

She didn't even turn her head.

Although he'd promised himself to behave, he couldn't hold it in any longer. "Goddammit, you could at least *look*. We live in the same house, we've got two kids together."

She remained stubbornly silent. It was like she was *trying* to piss him off.

His meeting with Starrebeek the Elder had been enough of a trial. Naturally he'd accepted David's resignation, even allowing him to leave in a month though his employment agreement required him to give two months' notice.

But then came the lecture. As if he had nothing better to do, Starrebeek seemed to feel it was incumbent on him to give David the benefit of his wisdom, an interminable guided tour of the pitfalls and pratfalls that would plague him as he embarked on this new adventure. "Relationships with clients can be particularly delicate if you don't have the support of a large and reputable firm," he said, and then launched into a long saga David had heard at least twice before about a bad faith client. At the end of the story, of course, Starrebeek came out smelling of roses. "And they thought they could put one over on me," he concluded—the exact same words he'd used to wrap up both previous tellings of the tale.

And now Mirjam, whose silence was even more infuriating than Starrebeek's yammer. It was haughty, condescending, as if he was beneath her contempt, some random peasant good for nothing more than money. He could pay for her clothes, sure, her vacations, her luxuries. He did everything for her, dammit, everything to provide their family with a decent standard of living, to make their lives comfortable and easy. And what did he get? Not one ounce of consideration, no respect, and forget about affection.

She was in the kitchen, slicing tomatoes. He grabbed her arm. "Why are you treating me like this? How long are you going to keep it up?"

Her only response was to slice away more determinedly.

David tightened his grip. "I'm asking you something."

She turned toward him, the knife in her hand, but still refused to speak, her lips pressed tightly together. Her eyes said it all. Rage, hatred, maybe even fear.

"We can't go on like this," said David.

She shrugged.

He grasped her other arm and shook her. The knife fell out of her hands. "I can't take any more of this, do you understand? We're married, we have kids, we live in the same house, but you act like I don't even exist, like I'm nobody."

"You're hurting me," she said dully. "Let me go."

He shook her even harder. "*Talk* to me, goddammit. Are you trying to get me to give up and move out? Is that the plan?"

"Steven," she whispered. "You killed him. Why don't you admit it?"

"Me? Mirjam, that's fucking insane. If the kids hear you say shit like that, how are they supposed to deal with it?"

"Or you hired somebody else to do it," she said, louder now.

"You are *nuts*!"

She tried to pull free of him, but he held her tightly. Her nails raked his face.

"You had him killed!" she screamed. "I know you did! I know it!"

Desperate to stop the yelling, he let go of one of her arms and covered her mouth with his hand. She bit him, hard enough to draw blood. He pulled back his other hand and slapped her.

☙

There was no D. Driessen in the online Amsterdam phone book. Just to be sure, Lucas checked the surrounding towns: Amstelveen, Bussum, Naarden. He finally struck pay dirt in Hilversum. He dialed the number.

"Hello?" said a woman's voice.

"Is this D. Driessen?"

"That's my husband. Who's calling?"

"I'm looking for the D. Driessen who's with Starrebeek & Starrebeek."

"No," said the woman. "My husband works at the AVRO."

"I'm sorry to bother you."

Shit, he was never going to find the bastard's home address.

☙

Mirjam stared at him, almost as astonished as he was. He stammered an apology, tried to take her in his arms, but she pushed him away so forcefully that he stumbled and almost fell. She snatched up the knife from the floor.

He took a step toward her.

She thrust out the knife, the point stopping an inch from his stomach.

"Get away from me, David! Get away!"

❧

He'd been in his study for hours, trying to work his way through a thin sheaf of case files, losing himself in the accusations, witness statements, and transcripts. Whatever he read, Mirjam loomed between his eyes and the page, staring at him in absolute shock after the slap he'd given her. There was no way to wash the image out of his mind. Her last words echoed in his ears: *Get away!*

He wished he had a few of Hein's paper packets to make the world a little rosier. If he went downstairs, would Mirjam be waiting for him with that knife in her hand? He'd better keep his distance.

The world of online gambling was a temptation. He knew that it could chew you up and spit you out, but at last he gave in and went to a roulette site. He needed the distraction, and it was all Mirjam's fault.

His Visa card was maxed out, but he figured he could squeeze five hundred Euros from his MasterCard. He had a right to a little relaxation. Certainly today, to take his mind off all the swirling emotions. And his luck had to change eventually, he was convinced of that.

Mirjam's image slowly faded.

He began with small wagers and hedged his bets. He won a little, and then a little more. Yes, this was his lucky night. It was about time the pendulum swung his way. He was careful to bet no more than he'd already won, so he couldn't slip into the red.

Until the turning point. He saw it coming, but refused to take it seriously. A voice in his head told him *come on, you can do it, go for it!* This was his lucky night, remember? He had to keep playing, had to win enough to set things right with Mirjam. There was no other way. Lady Justice was blind, but Dame Fortune could see him clearly. She winked at him, she was on his side. He hesitated only long enough to slip downstairs and fetch a bottle of whiskey from the kitchen cabinet. He could hear the television playing in the living room.

With a drink in his hand, things went better for a few minutes, but then quickly spiraled downward. Still, every loss called him to carry on, to recover, to make good. He gulped the dregs from his glass and refilled it. In the same way that he couldn't believe the criminals who denied their crimes, he couldn't believe he could possibly continue losing. Some miracle was bound to save him. He just hadn't figured out yet how to make the magic happen.

There was no magic. Not tonight, anyway.

He lay down on the bed that had been set up in his study a few days earlier. Mirjam had apparently ordered it, without consulting him. He'd have to pay for it, of course.

He willed himself to be optimistic, but the idea of a divorce and alimony and child support threw him off balance. He poured another glass of whiskey and settled back in at his desk.

He found a piece of paper and began scribbling figures. The numbers in the left column, the credits, were limited. The right column, the debits, kept growing, like a metastasized tumor. Every entry led to another, larger sum. The low-interest loan Hein had given him to invest in the Papaya Resort was coming due. And then the thousands of Euros he'd gambled away at Café Schemer!

He never should have bought the shares in the resort, but it had sounded so attractive. Hopefully Hein would grant him some respite, maybe even give him another loan, so he could make a good start with the new practice.

Hein was his savior. He was convinced of that.

Chapter 23

"Doesn't it look great?" Hein made a sweeping gesture. "It's all yours, D Squared. You're gonna make it big here, I know it."

As they had agreed, a plaque beside the front door read "D Squared" in big bronze letters and, beneath that, "Mr. David Driessen and Partners," though there weren't any partners as yet. Arnold Verhagen was taking David's offer under advisement. Apparently he had other irons in the fire.

David went inside. This was it, his future.

For the last few weeks, he'd been putting his affairs in order at Starrebeek with as much cheerfulness as he could muster. No slacking off, just keep on working till the end, everything above-board and by the book.

But it got harder and harder to ignore Starrebeek Junior's snide comments. "So, you're opening up a one-man show," he'd say, nodding his head in mock pity. "Good luck with that."

Joost seemed to have already written him off. Starrebeek Senior walked right past him in the hall one afternoon, paying no more attention to him than if he been a bit of fluff drifting in the breeze. And Junior put him through an unpleasant lecture about poaching clients. David decided not to say anything about Hein.

Nothing had changed at home, at least not in Mirjam's attitude or behavior. She showed no interest whatsoever in David or his concerns. One morning, he found a note on his desk. Scrawled in big letters were the words, "Why don't you confess?" Two days later, another note: "Coward."

Before much longer, they'd have to start making arrangements for the holidays: Sinterklaas, Christmas, New Year's. He'd already tried once to raise the subject, but her only response had been a withering glare. He hadn't bothered to try to talk about presents for Bas and Romy. She seemed determined to freeze him out of the house.

☙

"This is your office," said Hein. "The big chief's tepee."

David spun around in the large, airy space. Yes, the big chief, that would be him. Now all he needed was a tribe.

He would never be anybody else's Indian again. He might have to suck up more of the usual minor cases at first, but he'd work his way ahead, certainly with the sort of clientele Hein would bring in.

It seemed at last the right moment to ask the question he'd been holding back for months. "And what exactly do you expect from me, Hein? What do you want me doing for you?"

Hein pulled his head back and frowned. "For me?"

"Sure. Business, transactions, deals, you know. What's my role? I probably ought to know."

"Patience, my lad, patience." Hein patted the air. "All will be clear. Trust me."

"But I," David began, uncomfortable in the dark.

"*Do* you trust me?"

"Of course I do. But if I'm going to be handling… things for you, I need to know what they're going to *be*."

"When we get to that point, you'll know everything you need to know. You're not having second thoughts, are you?" Hein walked around the big desk, moved the computer monitor back an inch, tapped out a quick drumbeat on the desktop. "Nice stuff, huh? It all looks perfect. You don't even notice it's secondhand."

David knew he should be grateful that Hein had been able to furnish the place so inexpensively. He settled in behind the desk and opened and closed a couple of the drawers. There wasn't much in them, but that would change. The smooth way they slid in and out on their rollers cheered him up. It was a metaphor for how the practice itself would run. The bookshelves, empty now except for the leather-bound volumes of the Criminal Code, would overflow with case files.

"Come on," said Hein, "let's get a drink to celebrate and then grab a bite to eat. Vinkeveen later? That little cutie you liked? What was her name again?"

∽

"D. Driessen" was cut into a nameplate beside the door. About ten days ago, after a couple of failed attempts, Lucas had managed to follow Driessen home from Starrebeek & Starrebeek. Turned out lawyers sometimes travel by bike, just like normal people. But that was the only normal thing about this guy. He was a prick, a heartless shit.

Lucas didn't ring the bell. He crossed the street and picked out a vantage point from which to watch the house. Typical building for this upper-middle-class section of Amsterdam-South: four stories, two two-story apartments. It looked like Driessen and his family had the bottom half. He was probably married. Were there children? Where was he most vulnerable? Where would it easiest to hurt him?

He couldn't stop his thoughts from drifting back to Selma. He saw a montage of scenes in quick succession: Selma as a little girl, splashing in the sea. Selma sitting next to him in the second grade—the next year they were separated, because she'd become too dependent on him. Selma growing up, the problems, the knives, the razors that had to be hidden from her. Selma at the university. Selma's funeral.

Their parents had come down from Finland, of course. Their mother blamed herself, mostly, but Lucas, too. "We shouldn't have left you two here, at least not Selma. Why didn't she come to Finland this summer? She was lying about writing her thesis? Why didn't you tell us?"

That was why he'd been given some of the blame, because he hadn't told their parents what had happened to her. But Lucas knew that—now that Patrick was out of his reach—that left one and only one person responsible for Selma's death: Mr. D. Fucking Driessen.

In the chapel at the funeral, Lucas had wanted to speak, but he'd choked up after a single sentence. He sipped a glass of water, but it didn't help. He couldn't get out another word.

Now, the eulogy he'd prepared rang loudly in his head. His life with Selma, from the very beginning. "My other half is dead." That was the one sentence he'd been able to say aloud.

He recrossed the street and rang the bell. It took a while, but then the door was opened by a woman who looked him up and down in utter silence.

"I'd like to see Mr. Driessen."

"He's not here."

Lucas had expected this. Obviously Driessen wouldn't dare to face him.

"It's urgent. It's about a murder." The official police report had called it a suicide, but Lucas knew better. "I need to talk with him about it."

"I knew he had something to do with it," the woman said.

⁓

Half an hour later, Lucas was back on the street. He didn't understand much of what Driessen's wife had told him. She was skittish as a kitten, yet still she'd welcomed him, a complete stranger, into her home. And she'd confirmed that her husband—who it turned out really *wasn't* home—*was* involved in something shady. She'd talked about the murder of someone named Steven, but who he was and what role Driessen had played in his death was unclear.

He'd asked when he could speak with her husband. "I don't know," she'd said. "I don't know when he comes and goes." She'd also told him that Driessen no longer worked at Starrebeek & Starrebeek.

"Tired?" Lucas asked hopefully.

Apparently not. "Things got too hot for him there," she said, "so now he's working for himself." She nodded her head meaningfully, but then turned away. Lucas didn't know what she was implying. He asked for the new address, but she merely shrugged.

Anyway, at least he now had a first name: David.

He lingered outside the house for a few minutes. The woman wasn't quite all there, he thought. In fact, very little of her seemed to be "there." Was that Driessen's fault, too? Just how dirty *was* this guy?

He biked home, powered up his computer, and Googled the name David Driessen. There were five people by that name registered with LinkedIn and a few more on Facebook, but none of them was *his* David Driessen. According to an American website, there were four people by that name in the US. In The Netherlands, there was a David Driessen Courier Service in Spijkenisse. David Driessen, courier of death. Lucas found a couple of photos on Google Images, but none of them was Patrick Hamilton's attorney. He found nothing whatsoever about a new law practice. Maybe the moron didn't even have a company website. Tomorrow he would call Starrebeek and see if he could get an address for the bastard's new office.

೧

David found a note from Mirjam when he got back from Vinkeveen around 2 AM: "I'll be gone all weekend." That was all.

Gone? Gone where? And why?

It was probably a strategic move, designed to make him uncomfortable. As if things weren't difficult enough with his gleaming new spotless, nearly clientless office. Start all over, yes, he and Mirjam would have to do that, too. Throw the ballast of the past overboard.

She tried to avoid him again in the morning, but he found her in the kitchen and boxed her in when she tried to slip past him.

"Where are you going this weekend?"

"None of your business."

"It *is* my business."

"Get out of my way."

He stayed where he was. "When you tell me where you're going."

"I'll scream," she warned him. She opened her mouth wide.

He gave in and stepped aside. What else was he supposed to do? The kids were upstairs. He had to protect them from their mother's craziness. It was Friday morning, his turn to bring them to school. By the time he got home, she'd probably be gone.

When Bas and Romy were safely deposited—and promised that he'd be there at the end of their school day to fetch them—he drove to his new office. He stood before the building, admiring the plaque beside the door. "D Squared," he said aloud, enjoying the taste of the nickname in his mouth and the sight of it in raised bronze letters.

He knew he should be happier than he was, but something was nagging at him, a vague disquiet. He couldn't put his finger on it.

Or could he? As a criminal defense attorney, he always had to be thinking at least two moves ahead. He only asked questions to which he already knew the answers. But Hein, who had all the answers, was keeping them to himself.

A man with long unkempt hair straggled by, wearing two overcoats and a pair of knit gloves with the fingertips cut off. He held up a hand-rolled cigarette and asked for a match.

"Sorry," David said, "I don't smoke."

"Can you spare a Euro, then?"

Nicely played, David thought. He checked his pockets, but the smallest thing he had was a two-Euro coin.

The man was watching him closely. "I don't mind two," he said.

David gave him the coin and let himself into his office.

"Thanks, chief," the man called after him.

Chief.

He liked the sound of it.

Inside, everything was all so new that it didn't feel quite *real* yet. He listened to the sounds of his own breathing, his footsteps on the hardwood floors, the traffic passing by outside.

There wasn't exactly a mountain of work awaiting him. Under the law, suspects who can't afford or simply don't have legal representation are assigned counsel by the court, and David, as he had been at Starrebeek, was still listed as one of the attorneys who handled such cases. He had three of them on his plate now: a man accused of stealing a computer and printer from his workplace, a man accused of abusing his elderly father, and a woman who'd summarily evicted two student tenants from the rooms they were renting in her house.

Hein had promised him something much bigger, a case which, in the near future, ought to bring him a fat fee and some invaluable publicity. Ben Heuvelink's business practices were the subject of an upcoming investigation. Heuvelink was suspected of pressuring a major contractor into paying him hefty off-the-books commissions on several real estate deals, although he had in fact done no work entitling him to such compensation. To ensure the contractor's cooperation, Heuvelink had sent a couple of 'Stache's friends to pay the man a visit, a visit which had not been good for the contractor's health. Not only that, but a person or persons unknown had "coincidentally" forced the contractor's wife off the road when she was driving home from the grocery store. Hein had made it clear that David would be entrusted with Heuvelink's defense, but the prosecution service hadn't yet filed an indictment, so there wasn't yet anything to be done.

David knew the drill: patience, patience, and more patience. If he could simply bide his time, all would be well.

Yesterday, Joost had stopped by. David had shown him through the three rooms, only one of which was in use at this point. "Looks good," Joost had said. Had there been a note of jealousy in his voice? "I'd love to branch off on my own, but, yeah, I don't know where I'd get the start-up capital. How'd *you* manage it? An inheritance? Hit the lottery?"

He used to set up little office wagers at Starrebeek, with Joost and a few of the other attorneys. How many days would Hanna stay out when she called in sick, for example, or what color tie would Senior wear to work the next day? Always twenty Euros. When the other lawyers started saying no and he began to get a bit of a reputation as a gambler, he'd put a stop to it.

To Joost's question about the lottery, David mumbled something about an investment paying off big. He certainly wasn't going to tell his former colleague the truth.

The telephone rang.

"Driessen and Partners."

"Yeah, it's Simon. Simon Berghoek, you know me."

Simon Berghoek? David thought the voice sounded familiar, but he couldn't remember having heard the name before.

"I'm sorry," said David, "but I don't think I do."

"'Stache, remember? The trip to Zeebrugge? With that *madammeke* in that *cafeeke*?"

"Oh, sorry, I never knew your real name."

"Doesn't matter. I been pinched. Last night. Had a few pills in my car. They pulled me over for a traffic thing and found 'em. Can you come? I'm at the Havenstraat station."

↷

"It was a setup. They hooked me good."

"Were you drinking?"

"Two beers, absolutely no more."

"But you're here because of pills. How many?"

"Couple thousand. I got a great deal on 'em, and I know a couple guys who were gonna get 'em out on the street. I was delivering 'em to them. No problems, till the traffic stop."

David asked him what exactly had happened.

"There was two of 'em. Cops, I mean. Everything was cool, I blew in the whatchamacallit, the breath thing… no worries. I was bein' a good little boy, 'cause I had the pills in the trunk, you know, and I didn't want no trouble. The one cop says I can go, but then the other one wants to see in the trunk. That's when I knew I was fucked."

"He told you to open your trunk?"

"Well, he checked my license and registration, all that. He looked like he was tryin' to memorize 'em. But I had the idea I knew him from somewheres, couple years ago, when I was haulin' some stuff for Hein. An' he reckanized me, too."

"Were you convicted, that other time?"

"No. But this cop, see, he says I gotta open up my trunk. I says why, and he says, 'Don't argue wit' me, just open it.' It was like he already knew about the pills, you know? And now here I am."

"Not for long," said David.

'Stache cocked his head quizzically.

"Did he have a warrant to search your car? Your car's as entitled to privacy as your house."

A smile appeared on 'Stache's face.

"Without legitimate authorization, it's an illegal search and seizure," David continued. "This shouldn't take long to clear up. I'll have you out of here in no time."

༄

David collapsed onto the sofa, completely spent. Sally jumped up to his lap, purring.

He had resolved to keep Bas and Romy busy and happy all weekend, and he'd made it happen. Except for dropping Romy off at a girlfriend's while Bas had his fencing lesson on Saturday, the three of them had been together the whole time. He had damn well proven himself a devoted father. He'd planned it all out: a home-cooked breakfast, the zoo, a movie. He'd made pancakes, for God's sake. They'd played a dozen games of *Mens erger je niet*. David couldn't remember the last time he'd played the Parcheesi-like board game, but he remembered the picture of the angry guy in the dark suit on the box.

His cell phone rang.

"This is David Driessen, attorney."

Hein had impressed on him the importance of identifying himself as a lawyer when he answered his phone. That way, the police couldn't listen in, since attorney-client conversations are privileged.

"It's me, Hein."

David sat up. "Hi."

"Nice work you did for Simon. I'm paying, naturally."

"Did you have anything to do with those—?"

Hein talked over him. "Tomorrow afternoon, two o'clock. Pieter Hoogestijn is coming to your office. I'll be there to meet with him, and you're going to take a walk."

The name was familiar, if not exactly notorious. He'd been mentioned in the media lately—by first name and last initial, as was the custom when the Dutch press reported on people suspected of but not yet convicted of a crime. In certain circles, Hoogestijn was known as "the Bald Man," despite his full head of thick brown hair. Joost had told David once that the nickname dated back to some years ago, when Hoogestijn had been diagnosed with lung cancer and gone through a course of chemo, which had caused all his hair to fall out.

"Why?" asked David.

Hein repeated himself: "You're going to take a walk."

"You know I can't do that. If anybody finds out about it, I'm dead meat."

There was a silence on the line. David thought he could hear Hein sigh.

"You understand the consequences," Hein said slowly, "if you don't play nice?"

"What do you mean? What consequences?"

Hein hung up.

༄

David jolted awake when the front door closed. He got off the couch and went out to the foyer, where Mirjam was hanging up her jacket.

"Nice weekend?" he asked.

She didn't respond.

"You have any interest in how things went with Bas and Romy?"

She looked at him. "Well?"

"Great. On Saturday, we—"

But she was already halfway up the stairs.

Chapter 24

She felt like she could finally breathe again, like the air was finally clean.

She and Thera had spent Friday and Saturday nights at a hotel in Otterlo, at Thera's suggestion.

"Why Otterlo?" she'd asked.

"Why *not* Otterlo?" was Thera's response.

The hotel was close to the entrance to the Hoge Veluwe National Park. They'd walked, biked, swum in the hotel pool, eaten, sipped wine, and talked and talked and talked.

The talking was more important than anything else, after the long silent hours in the house with David. Many of the hotel's guests were seniors—"It's like a nursing home," Thera had said—so the place was quiet and peaceful. It was nice to be the youngest person in the room for a change.

But this morning it was back to business as usual. The question was how long David would be able to stick it out. If *she* raised the topic of divorce, he was bound to refuse. He had to see for himself that it was the only possible way for them to move forward with their lives.

She wrote a note and left it on his desk: "I need five hundred Euros for household expenses. M."

☙

David had invited the woman who'd evicted the college students to his office. She was about fifty, with dyed black hair, bright red lipstick, big tinkly earrings—on the street, you'd hear her coming from a mile off—and a patchwork jacket stitched from squares of red, blue, and purple fabric. Part leftover hippie, part gypsy.

She looked around the office and said, her voice coarsened by cigarettes and alcohol, "Pretty sterile."

"We're remodeling," he told her.

When she was seated in the client chair across from him, David asked her to tell her story. It was hard to follow, the thoughts jumbled chaotically and illustrated with florid gestures.

Putting the pieces together as linearly as he could, David concluded that she, out of pure loving-kindness, had decided to rent two unused rooms in her home to students. As things turned out, however, the tenants she'd selected were messy and noisy, came and went at all hours, played loud music late at night.

"If you can call it music," she said. "That's not what *I* call it. I call it just a lot of *boom*-a-lacka, *boom*-a-lacka, *boom*-a-lacka." She stomped her feet on the floor with every *boom*. "It was making me crazy, so I—you mind if I smoke?" She'd already fished a pack of Marlboros from her embroidered Indian handbag. The tips of her index and middle fingers were brown with nicotine.

David smiled apologetically. "Sorry, this is a smoke-free office. The smell hangs in the air, and some clients have a problem with that."

"I don't see any other clients."

"Of course not. I'm meeting with *you*. Please go on."

She sighed deeply and put the pack back in her bag. She'd told them they would have to leave, she said, but they'd refused to move out. Finally she'd had to take steps to get rid of them. A friend who did occasional odd jobs for her had moved their belongings out to the street in their absence and changed the locks. Now she had new renters. "Two lovely nurses. They're paying me more than the students were. And it's *my* house—I can rent to whoever I want, can't I?"

"That depends. Did the students have a lease?"

"No, just an oral agreement. I don't need all that paperwork." Apparently without thinking, she took out her pack of cigarettes again, put one between her lips, and dove back into her bag in search of a lighter.

David cleared his throat, but she paid no attention.

"I'm sorry, but no smoking in the office."

"Fuck," the woman said, "I forgot."

"How did they pay?" he asked.

The doorbell rang. David wondered who it could be. He didn't have any other appointments scheduled. "Let me just see who that is. My secretary called in sick today. Flu. It's going around, I guess."

It was Hein.

"I'm meeting with a client," said David.

"Congratulations." Hein lowered his voice. "I hope he pays well, for both our sakes."

Loud enough for the woman in his office to hear him, David said, "You can take a seat here. I'll call you in when I'm ready for you."

Hein gave him a thumbs-up. "Nice of you to let me stay."

Back behind his desk, David asked again about the rent payments.

"Cash, the fifteenth of every month." The woman played nervously with her unlit cigarette. "I don't like banks. Cash on the barrelhead, that's my style."

"Did you give them a receipt?"

"No, nothing."

David saw a possible line of defense. With encouraging words and a hint of caution—"You can't ever be a hundred percent sure how a judge will see things"—he brought the conversation to a close and ushered the woman out. The door hadn't clicked shut behind her before she was lighting a cigarette and sucking at it greedily, as if it were the elixir of life. Which, in her case, perhaps it was.

Hein was sitting behind the desk eventually intended for a secretary. "Case closed? A good client, somebody you can soak for some decent money?"

David shook his head. He went into his office with Hein right behind him.

Neither of them spoke. David saw it was ten minutes to two.

"You're not going to start being difficult, are you?" There was a hard glint in Hein's eyes. It was the same cold look David had seen that first time, from the public gallery in the courtroom.

David had been able to resist Hein over the phone, but it would be harder face to face. Hein wasn't just *in* the room. He *dominated* the room.

"I'm not being difficult. I just—"

"So you think you're being easy?"

"No, but—look, Hein, I guess you had some… expectations of me when you helped me set all this up, but, if they go too far, I'm going to have to disappoint you, no matter how much I wish I didn't."

Hein stood up and came around the desk and right up into David's face. David could smell his aftershave. "You're going to take a nice little walk," he said, "so I can meet with Pieter Hoogestijn. He'll be here in about five minutes. Did you forget that?"

"I can't turn my office over to third parties, Hein."

"Oh, I'm a 'third party' now?" Hein was indignant. "Some nobody? I thought we were friends, buddies. I thought we could trust each other. What happened to that, buddy? You flush it down the toilet?"

David bowed his head. It was time to set some limits. Now, with Hein standing right here in front of him. "Of course you're not a nobody. You're just about the most important somebody I know. I wouldn't be here if it wasn't for you."

As he said it, though, he thought how much simpler his life would be if it wasn't for Hein.

"So what are you moaning about?"

"If I start letting you use my office for your meetings, I could get in all kinds of trouble."

"You know when you're gonna find yourself in trouble, David?" Hein clamped a heavy hand onto his shoulder. His fingers dug in painfully. "Do you?"

"No," David whispered.

"I'll tell you, then. If you're not out of here in two minutes so I can meet with Mr. Hoogestijn someplace more appropriate than a shitty bar, that's when you'll be in all kinds of trouble. You understand me, D Squared?"

❧

She was trapped at the end of a dead-end street. David wasn't budging an inch.

Mirjam sat in Thera's kitchen, pouring her heart out. In a while, she had to pick the kids up from school.

"He doesn't even seem to realize I'm ignoring him. He just plows ahead like nothing's wrong."

"They deport undesirable aliens," said Thera. "Why can't we just deport undesirable husbands?"

"If only."

"You want some tea? I've got fresh mint."

"I'd rather have a glass of wine."

"Now? It's only 2:30. Isn't that a little early?"

"I know. It's just, I can't take much more of this, Theer. He's dug in, and I don't think he's going anywhere. He thinks I'm playing some kind of game." Mirjam knew she was repeating herself. She dropped her head theatrically to the tabletop.

"Why don't *you* move out?" Thera suggested carefully. "With the kids?"

"Me? Where would I go? Move the three of us in with my parents? Rent some dingy little apartment in the Bijlmer?"

Thera sighed. "Point taken."

"He has to go. I'm suffocating. I can't breathe around him."

Thera sipped her tea.

"What am I going to do? How in God's name am I supposed to get rid of him? I need him out of my life, forever."

"Get rid of him," Thera repeated thoughtfully.

Mirjam looked up from the table.

"No," said Thera. "You know that's not what I meant."

❦

David spooned the last taste of foam from the bottom of his cup. How long had he been sitting here? Half an hour, at least, with his cell phone right beside the saucer. Hein was supposed to call him as soon as, as he'd put it, the coast was clear.

It gave David a bad feeling, kicked out of his own office. Like a kid sent outside to play, so the grownups could talk.

He paged through the paper and found an article about a 45-year-old English woman who'd promised two men in a bar that she'd sleep with them if they murdered her husband. "At Nottingham Crown Court on Friday, Charlotte Collinge, 45, was sentenced to twenty-three years in prison. Steven Shreeves, 40, and Kelvin Dale, 27, were each sentenced to eighteen years for the brutal murder last October of Clifford Collinge, 61. The three defendants had met in a pub. Under the influence of beer and cocaine, the two men accompanied Mrs. Collinge to her home, where they beat her husband to death with a claw hammer, inflicting a total of forty-six wounds. The Collinges had been married for seventeen years."

Divide forty-six wounds by seventeen years, David calculated, that was almost three wounds per year.

"According to the judge, the victim was a gentle man who had tolerated his wife's manipulative and faithless conduct for years."

A claw hammer. That must have been a gruesome murder, the victim screaming in pain, bleeding from four dozen wounds, begging for mercy. But once they'd begun, the perpetrators had to see it through to the end.

That's the way of the world, David thought. *You start something, you have to see it through. There's no turning back.*

The two men had probably grabbed whatever was handy, and what was handy was a claw hammer. David could see the two sharp claws. They would do a hell of a lot of damage. *Had* the murderers gone to bed with the woman afterwards? Were they still even interested in sex? What mitigating circumstances had their attorney tried to establish? There were always mitigating circumstances, if you looked for them long and carefully enough.

The wife's "manipulative and faithless conduct." The phrase summed up Mirjam pretty damn completely. She was as eager to get him out of her hair as Charlotte Collinge had been. Well, not literally, but it came down to the same thing: she wanted him out of her life. She didn't need to hire anyone to take care of it for her with the promise of sex. She didn't need to hire anyone at all. She was determined to deal with the problem of David's existence all by herself, to silent treatment him out of the house, to silent treatment their marriage to death.

This morning, he'd tried yet again to talk with her about Sinterklaas, but he might as well have been talking to the wall. He'd actually said that, "It's like talking to the fucking wall," and for once that had actually produced a response. "Why don't you do that, then?"

His phone finally rang.

"Hoogestijn's gone," said Hein. "We got everything straightened out."

Five minutes later, David was back in the office. Hein was still there, sitting behind *his* desk now and showing no inclination to move. David took the client's chair, a visitor in his own workplace. The only thing missing was Hein offering him something to drink.

Hein was shuffling through some papers. "We need to take care of a few financial matters. Best bet is to funnel everything through your account. I'll transfer the money to you, you pass it on to a couple other accounts. I'll give you the numbers."

"I'm not sure that's such a good idea."

"It's the way we're gonna do it, D Squared." Hein's upper lip curled, more of a grimace than a smile.

David shifted uncomfortably in his seat. "Hein, that's exactly the kind of thing that could come back to bite me. If anybody looks at my accounts, if I have to show them my books, then—"

"Won't happen." Hein leaned across the desk. There was something threatening in his voice, something cold, as if the words were being pronounced by a machine. "I hope you're not gonna start in again. I'm getting really tired of it."

David nodded.

"I got you this fucking building, I paid for it, I furnished it. *You* had to piss away a small fortune you didn't have at the fucking roulette table and who paid for it, who'd you keep hitting up for more?"

David wasn't sure he was meant to answer the question.

"You," he said softly, just in case.

"You bet your ass me, Hein Wesseling. I was good enough for that." He got up, came around the desk, and planted himself in front of David. "And I did it, because I thought we were friends. I trusted you, I've told you that over and over. That's why I helped you. You couldn't hack it at Starrebeek, you had to have your own practice, you had to be the big boss. But, no, Mr. Driessen's all of a sudden scared somebody's gonna look at his books the second his best client and only friend—because, you know what, I think I'm the only friend you've got left—asks him for a little fucking favor."

David cleared his throat. "That's not the point. It's not that I don't want to. But it's illegal, Hein. I'd be running the risk of—"

"Jesus Christ, it's illegal? All of a sudden you're worried about legal? Don't make me laugh." Hein barked out a single ha. "You're forgetting something, my friend. You still remember the name Steven Veenstra?"

David nodded slowly, fear blossoming in the pit of his stomach.

"And you remember what happened to him, that shitheel who was fucking your wife?"

David didn't respond.

"Oh, *that* you forget? Well, let me remind you, he's fucking dead. You had a couple little chats with Tommy Biesterbos about it, but the cops can't touch you 'cause they couldn't find anything to connect you to the murder." Hein paused. He brushed an invisible piece of lint tenderly from David's shoulder. Then, softly, "That could change."

Hein stepped over to the blinds and pushed down one of the slats so he could look outside. He stood there, looking, as if there was something more interesting to see than parked cars, bikes chained to trees, pedestrians toting shopping bags, an old man pushing a walker, a mother with a baby in a stroller. David could imagine the scene. When he had nothing to do—and that was often the case—he stood in the same spot himself, peering through the same gap between two slats.

He didn't dare say a word, could barely breathe. The slightest sound could blow up his dream of a practice of his own.

What could change in the Veenstra investigation? How? He'd had absolutely nothing whatsoever to do with the murder. There was no way to tie him to the crime.

Hein came back to him, grabbed him by the lapels and pulled him to his feet. His face only inches from David's, he said, "You remember our little run down to Zeebrugge? With your new client, Simon Berghoek?"

David nodded.

"Look, here's a photo. Cool you can shoot pictures now with your phone."

Hein produced a picture of David and 'Stache outside the customs shed in the Zeebrugge harbor. It was taken from a distance and wasn't especially clear, but there was no doubt it was David and 'Stache in the shot.

"Well?" asked Hein.

"It's just a picture."

"Right, a lawyer and his client. What they were doing in Zeebrugge will remain a mystery."

Hein sounded suddenly cheerful. "And it's just a coincidence they're standing right in front of the customs office, correct?"

"I'd say so."

"Fine, then that's clear." Hein went to the door.

David wondered what exactly it was that was clear, but he didn't think it would be smart to ask.

Hein turned. "Oh, I keep forgetting. After that little pleasure trip to Belgium, I found a scarf in the back of my car. Was that yours?"

"Mirjam gave it to me. What—?"

"A gift from the loving spouse. I thought so. I've been meaning to give it back to you, but, hell, maybe I can use it for something."

❧

Hein had been gone for hours. What was it he really wanted? And what was the point of the photo? All that fury, just because David didn't want to launder money through his own bank accounts?

He'd clicked through to a new internet gambling site, but both of his credit cards were refused, so he couldn't play. He kept trying to distract himself, but his thoughts returned again and again to Hein. What was he planning to do with that picture? Were there more of them, shots of him and Jeanine or Juliette, of him gambling in the casino in Knokke? What good would they do Hein, and how could they be used to hurt David?

He couldn't believe that Hein's threats were idle, though. Hein wasn't the sort of man who made idle threats.

He opened the folder for a new case he'd been assigned by the court. Purse snatching. The idiot had knocked some woman to the ground, scooped up her shoulder bag, and "escaped" into a blind alley, where a platoon of good Samaritans had grabbed him and held him for the police. Not much there on which to base a defense, and the victim had broken a hip in her fall, which would add at least a couple of extra months to the sentence.

It was 5 PM. Time to head home.

"I'm the boss," he muttered, but he wasn't sure that was really true.

The doorbell rang while he was slipping on his jacket.

Hein, he thought, *maybe with reinforcements.*

He took a few deep breaths and went to the door. He probably ought to get a chain, so he could open up a crack in safety.

He planted his foot two inches from the closed door as a barricade but knew that wouldn't keep out one of Hein's bruisers.

It wasn't Hein or 'Stache or some muscle-bound hoodlum, though. It was Lucas Groothuis, the brother.

"What do you want?" he asked.

"I want to talk to you."

"Make an appointment."

"My sister, Selma, she—"

David cut him off. "There's nothing more to say. I told you, that case is closed."

Lucas Groothuis bounced his shoulder off the door. "Let me in!" he yelled.

David held fast. He couldn't think of anything else to say.

"She killed herself! She's dead!"

The boy rammed into the door again. It was like a scene from a slapstick movie, except there was nothing funny about it. Anyone passing by would get the wrong idea about his new practice. David considered letting the kid in but decided against it. Who knew what he might do, the state he was in?

"It's your fault," Lucas Groothuis screamed. "You got that fuck Patrick off."

"I did my job," David said between clenched teeth, holding the door closed with his foot and shoulder. Then something boiled over inside him, and he thought *the hell with it* and stepped away from the door. Lucas came stumbling into the office, and David pulled an umbrella from the umbrella stand and hoisted it over his head. "If *you* don't fuck off," he snarled, and left the rest of the sentence hanging.

The boy scrambled to his feet and stood there panting, glaring at David with unremitting hatred. "I'll get you," he said. "You wait and see."

℘

The house was dark. There was a note on the doormat: "Sinterklaas at my parents'. I bought presents. M."

It was the last day of November, so Sinterklaas was less than a week away. Should he get something for Mirjam? A piece of jewelry? And what about the poem? Like most Dutch families, they always celebrated the December 5 return to Holland of Saint Nicholas and his helpers, the Black Peters, from their summer home in Spain by composing a funny or sentimental rhyme to accompany each present.

> *If you remain so rough and reckless,*
> *You might choke on this gold necklace.*
> *But if you're done with causing pain,*
> *Then maybe we can start again,*
> *For Peter Black and Sint on horse*
> *Are both against divorce, of course.*

Not bad. Maybe *he* should have gone into advertising…

He prowled restlessly from room to room. Where the hell were they? This was probably part of her strategy, but he was not about to bend. If he could just tough it out, she'd be the one to cave.

He poured himself a glass of whiskey and turned on the television. This was his role, the husband who comes home from a hard day at the office and stretches out in front of the TV with a drink close at hand. So far, he was managing to carry it off. Used to be the drink was a glass of wine, but since he'd gotten to know Hein he'd switched to whiskey.

There was a story on the news about a man dressed as Sinterklaas who'd been mugged. His Black Peter stood by helplessly as the attackers ran off with his bag of presents.

The camera cut to the weatherman, and David's phone rang. Mirjam, calling to say she was on her way? No, the display showed a number he didn't recognize.

"David Driessen, attorney."

"At least you learned *that* much from me," said Hein.

David sighed. Right now, Hein was the last person he wanted to talk to.

"You and me have some business to transact," Hein went on.

"What business?"

"Come on, D Squared, don't play games with me. It's not good for you. Or for our ree-lay-shun-ship." He turned it into four separate words.

"You're talking about the money?"

"I'm always talking about money. You should know that by now."

David had no idea what he was supposed to say. He figured it would be best to let Hein move the conversation in whatever direction he wanted it to go.

"When do you plan on paying me back?" asked Hein.

"Paying you back?"

"Don't be naïve, counselor. You borrow, you gotta pay it back. Debt doesn't just vanish into thin air."

"But I thought we—"

Hein didn't let him finish. "Look, you want to be stupid enough to gamble away thousands of Euros, that's your business. I didn't lend you money because you're such a sweet little boy, I don't need to tell you that. The Papaya Resort, that building I got you… you think I can wait forever to get that money back?"

David understood. Now that he'd refused to let Hein use his personal bank accounts as a Laundromat, Hein was changing the rules of the game. There would be no more loans, and cash was going to have to start moving in the other direction.

Hein repeated his question.

"No," said David, "of course not."

"I don't mind staking you to a good meal and a glass of booze, but I'm not your ATM. I lend you money, you pay me back, that's the way it works. So when are you planning on getting started? I'd like to see some return on my investment before the end of the year."

"I—I'll try to free up some cash as soon as I can."

"And I'm talking about real money, okay? Don't insult me with some piddly-ass thousand Euros."

"I won't."

"Unless you want me to send 'Stache around to negotiate with you?"

Chapter 25

"I've got ten thousand Euros for you."

"Good," said Hein. "Somebody die? You hit the lottery? Don't tell me you finally had some luck playing roulette."

David didn't respond. The day before yesterday, he'd sold the Peugeot 308 for about sixteen thousand. Way under market price, but waiting around for a better offer had been out of the question. For five grand, he'd picked up a 2005 Peugeot 207, and—though he'd sworn he'd never show his face there again—he'd taken the remaining thousand to the casino on the Leidseplein. When he was down to his last thirty-five Euros, he'd had the presence of mind to leave the table and head for the bar.

"You still there?" asked Hein.

"How do you want me to get it to you?"

"I'll let you know."

David wanted to say something like "I await your further instructions," but he bit his tongue.

"Ten thousand's peanuts," Hein said.

"It's all I can get my hands on until after the first of the year. The holidays, you know? Extra expenses, and—"

"That's not my problem."

"I understand that," said David.

"Well, at least there's *something* you understand. Now understand this: I expect another ten grand next week."

"There's no way I can—"

"I don't give a shit how you get it," Hein cut him off. "Rob a bank."

༄

Her plan was to present David with a *fait accompli*. Over the Christmas break, she and Bas and Romy and Thera and her kids were going to a holiday park. They'd reserved a little bungalow for the six of them. The park's website boasted of its many attractions: a supermarket, cafés, a pancake house, a restaurant, a snack bar… and, most important, an indoor swimming pool, an enclosed playground with swings and slides and every exciting piece of equipment a child could want, even an archery range, which Bas would love.

This way, she'd have an excuse to bypass the usual Christmas dinners with her parents and her eventual ex-in-laws. She'd make it up to her Mom and Dad sometime soon. And, anyway, she'd just been there with Bas and Romy for Sinterklaas.

She heard David at the front door. He came into the kitchen, but he didn't say anything, just looked at her with somber eyes. Maybe he'd see how hopeless it was and finally give in. If that happened, she might cancel the trip with Thera.

"I called a therapist," he said.

She said nothing.

"I checked her out, and she's got a lot of experience in couples therapy. She's supposed to be great, she's helped a lot of people."

Mirjam refused to take the bait. They'd had this conversation before, more than once. Some things, when they break, it's possible to fix them. But some things get broken beyond repair. And their marriage was broken beyond repair. It was time to take it to the dump.

"Come on, Mir. We can't just keep on like this."

"Exactly. I'm glad you agree. When are you moving out? Can't you just put a bed in your new office?"

David swore. He threw open the fridge, grabbed a bottle of beer, twisted off the cap, and took a long swallow.

"Thera and I are taking the kids to a vacation park over the break. Two weeks. That'll give you time to find yourself someplace to live."

"Jesus Christ!" He flung the bottle—half empty, not half full—at the wall. Shards of glass and gobbets of foam flew everywhere.

☙

Lucas was ashamed. Not of what others thought about him, but of what he thought about himself. The bottom line was that he'd let himself down. Nobody knew, no one could see it, but it was the truth. He'd let that cocksucking lawyer intimidate him. He tried to make excuses for his cowardice, but who did he think he was fooling? He'd been tossed out the door like a bag of garbage.

His parents were flying in from Finland today. They were staying for ten days, so it would be ten long days of silent recrimination, ten days in which the first item on the conversational agenda would be Selma, Selma, Selma.

The semester was over, so there were no classes to escape to. The only thing on his plate was a make-up paper he had to write for his Urban Planning in the Twentieth Century class. For some reason he couldn't even remember, he'd chosen as his subject "The Socio-Economic Development of the Eastern Islands of Amsterdam in the First Half of the Twentieth Century." The Eastern Islands weren't actually islands at all, but a residential area just outside the city center, and basically his paper would be a study of the economic collapse of the neighborhood. Maybe he'd selected the topic because he knew a guy who rented a room in a student building near the Kattenburgerplein. He'd been over there, and the place was as chaotic as the house in which Patrick Hamilton had lived.

Patrick Hamilton.

Someday, Lucas would go to New Zealand and find that bastard.

He checked his watch. Had to leave for the train station in a bit. In two hours, his parents would be landing at Schiphol Airport. This would be the second time he'd be picking them up without Selma.

When they'd celebrated their twenty-fifth anniversary, he and his sister had turned an old bed sheet into a banner, painting "Congratulations on 25 Years Together!" on it in big black letters. They'd stood in the arrivals area with the banner stretched out between them, waiting for Mom and Dad to come through customs. It had probably looked pretty stupid, but he'd gone along with it. More for Selma's sake than their parents'.

✑

David sat at his desk. There was very little on it: a couple of case files, the morning paper. A front-page article caught his eye, something about American police officers conducting surveillances dressed up as Santa Claus. He'd seen something similar a couple of weeks ago about Black Peters here in Holland. "Sneaky Petes," they were called. Their job was to tip off the local police if they witnessed suspicious activity or spotted suspects wanted for questioning. They were not empowered to perform arrests themselves, though that would be something: *The suspect was taken into custody by Black Peter, who stuffed him in a sack and carried him off to Spain.*

He got up and opened the blinds enough to look outside. Wet snow was falling. It was a good day to be somewhere else, preferably some tropical island far to the south. The Papaya Resort. He found the brochure in a drawer of his desk. Too bad they'd never gone. If Mirjam would ever come around, maybe they still could. Somehow or other he had to get out from under the weight of that investment.

He googled "Papaya Resort." There seemed to be two of them, one in Thailand and one in the Philippines. He checked the brochure again. There was a URL in small print at the bottom of the second page: *www.*

papayaresortcuracao.com. With growing unease, he typed the address into his browser.

Sorry, the website www.papayaresortcuracao.com cannot be found.

That didn't make sense. Maybe they'd changed the URL. He tried several variations, added underscores here and there, but kept getting the same error message. He made himself a cup of coffee with the Senseo in the office's little kitchen. Hein had called it "the poor man's Nespresso." He drank the coffee standing up, hoping it would clear his head, but all it did was put pressure on his bladder. He went to the bathroom.

Back at his computer, he tried more variants, this time replacing the *.com* with *.org.* No luck.

Was there a Papaya Resort on Curaçao? The glossy brochure was beautifully done, the site map of the houses—"each with a lovely private garden"—seemed convincing, the photographs of the completed bungalows and swimming pool were attractive. But they were just photos. They could have been taken at any resort, anywhere in the world, and the shot of the sign at the entrance might have been taken in Thailand or the Philippines.

David examined the pictures more closely. There was a photo of a quaint little shop—the caption read: "Every morning, enjoy fresh bread from the Sun, the best bakery on the island!"—with a few houses visible in the background which looked totally different from the resort's bungalows, although the brochure's text suggested that there was only one basic model with slightly different floor plans.

He hardly dared admit it to himself, but the reality seemed unavoidable. Hein's words echoed in his head: *I trust you, and you trust me.*

He'd sunk a hundred thousand Euros into the project, every last cent borrowed from Hein, a hundred thousand Euros in what was beginning to look like a fantasy, a Caribbean mirage. According to Hein, the investment was a no-brainer, dirt cheap for a vacation home you could rent out when you weren't using it.

He pounded the desktop until his hands were numb. As numb as the rest of him.

He found an online travel agency specializing in vacation rentals on Curaçao, but there was nothing there about a Papaya Resort.

If it didn't exist in the digital world, odds were it didn't exist in the real world, either.

He loosened his tie. Sweat trickled down his back, though his hands and feet were ice cold. Who could he talk to about Curaçao? Old friends, acquaintances, colleagues, business contacts, neighbors?...

Eddie! Didn't he move out to the Antilles five years or so ago? They'd gone to law school together, another friend who'd fallen out of touch. Several generations back, there'd been some Curaçaoan ancestor in a high branch of his family tree, which accounted for his cappuccino complexion. Eddie'd sent him a change of address card, and now David remembered the cartoonish illustration: on the left, a family of four huddled under umbrellas in the rain, and then a thick arrow pointed to the same foursome on the right, lounging around a swimming pool beneath a palm tree, with a benevolent sun beaming down on them. Eddie had gotten a job with the Public Prosecution Service on Curaçao.

David checked his contacts on both computer and phone, but he hadn't recorded the new address. What was Eddie's last name again? Something directional. Noordeman? Oosterbroek? Westerveld?

It suddenly popped into his head: Westerveen, Eddie Westerveen, short for Eduard.

He was halfway through an e-mail to Curaçao when the doorbell rang. He peered through the blinds. 'Stache was at the door, bouncing from one foot to the other in the cold.

David hesitated.

The bell rang again, followed by polite knocking that quickly swelled to angry pounding. 'Stache bent down and yelled through the mail slot, "Mr. Driessen! It's me, Simon!" Then he rang the bell again.

David figured the man would stand there banging on the door until someone let him in, so why delay the inevitable?

Before he could say a word, 'Stache brushed him out of the way and bustled in. He went straight through to David's office.

"I was in the bathroom," said David. "Sorry."

"Look, here's the account number in Switzerland where you transfer the money. Just a number, no name. Do it right now, from your personal account, not the business account."

David didn't bother telling him there wasn't enough *in* the account to comply.

☙

On Christmas Day, David visited his parents. He had to take the train to Rhenen, because Mirjam had gone off in the car, without any explanation, as if she'd bought it herself. She hadn't said a word about the switch from the luxurious 308 to the penurious 207. Only Bas had remarked on the family's new "junkmobile."

It took forever to soothe the ruffled feathers caused by Mirjam's and the children's absence. No, of course they weren't splitting up. She just needed some breathing room, a sort of time out, a chance to get her ducks in a row. His mother hadn't understood the expression. *Ducks? Why does Mirjam have ducks?* He didn't know how to answer that one.

He called her, every day, and she kept their conversations—as expected—as short as possible. "I'll put Romy on," she said. Or Bas, whichever was within reach. When his son was able to tear himself away from his Xbox for a few seconds, he chattered about the level he was trying to beat, the cool sliding board in the pool, the archery.

He spent hours in the living room, cloistered in his armchair, surrounded by piles of newspapers. He kept the room dark, only turning on his trusty old desk lamp. Today, he hadn't even left the house. Around seven, he had a pizza delivered. He leafed through the papers, but nothing held his attention. His own life was just too enervating. He had nothing left over for the outside world.

The Public Prosecution Service in Curaçao had declined to send him Eddie's e-mail address but was willing to forward a message. It had taken a few days, but Eddie's response had removed all possible doubt. He'd made several phone calls, and ultimately learned that work had in fact begun on a proposed vacation park to be called the Papaya Resort, near but not in any way connected to the well-known Landhouse Papaya restaurant. About a year ago, all work on the project had been suspended; as far as Eddie could determine, the financing had dried up. Some foundations had been poured, construction had begun on several bungalows, an access road had been asphalted, "but the only thing it really accesses is bankruptcy court. If you're looking to book a vacation in Curaçao," Eddie wrote, "I can steer you to some places that actually exist! And you're always welcome at our place for beer and barbecue!"

A day in the sun, swimming and snorkeling in the crystal Caribbean waters, and then a grilled steak and a cold beer. It sounded wonderful. He could just see Eddie in a chef's apron and toque.

His cell phone rang.

"David Driessen."

"Attorney," said the voice at the other end of the line. "How many times do I have to tell you?"

David shuddered.

"You home? I'm coming over. We'll have a drink and figure out where we go from here. Nice and cozy around the Christmas tree. Convenient, with your wife and kiddies gone."

David wondered how Hein could possibly know that.

"I have to go out," he said. "I have a meeting."

"With who? Nicole from Vinkeveen?"

"No, somebody else."

"I'm kidding you, D Squared. Where's your sense of humor? I'll be there in half an hour."

◡◠

It was thirty-five minutes later, and Hein had not yet arrived. David had debated just leaving, but he knew that would only grant him a stay of execution.

A stay of execution, almost literally.

Or maybe Hein had just meant to scare him, and was sitting now in Café Schemer, laughing with 'Stache over that chickenshit D Squared.

D Squared. Once upon a time, the nickname had sounded almost endearing.

The documents David needed were spread out on the table, and he was studying them for the zillionth time. These were the pages he'd photocopied, back when his relationship with Hein was young and innocent. They were the records of a series of intricate money transfers; some of the people involved had surely been victimized, and the Fiscal Information and Investigation Service would be delighted to get a look at the paperwork.

Thirty-seven minutes.

Hein wasn't coming.

David went to the kitchen and got a beer.

And the doorbell rang. It sounded somehow threatening.

He opened the front door, and Hein was there.

"Is this a bad time?"

Without waiting for a response, he pushed past David into the foyer. "Sorry I'm late. Couldn't find a place to park, had to walk a few blocks. I guess you sold the car, huh? I don't see it out front."

"Mirjam took it."

Hein eyed him thoughtfully but let it pass.

"Have a seat." David gestured toward the couch.

"You got a beer for me?"

"Sure." He fetched one from the fridge. "Cheers."

Hein looked around the living room. "This is a nice place, D Squared."

"I'd rather you call me David."

"Really?" Hein seemed surprised. "Well, sure, if that's what you want. David. Mr. David Driessen, the noted attorney—who's saddled with a shitty marriage and enough debt to choke a horse. Pity. A pain in the ass for you. I don't need to say 'Your Honor' or 'Your Worship' or whatever, do I? No? That's downright neighborly of you, I appreciate it. At least there's a smidge of our old friendship left."

David didn't react. He'd once seen Sally playing with a mouse, and that's what he felt like now. He was the mouse, and Hein was the cat. He looked around to see if Sally was in the living room, but she was probably in the kitchen, hiding from the stranger. There was nothing wrong with *her* intuition.

"Yeah, nice place." Hein drank from his beer. "Shame if you have to sell it. Big mortgage?"

"It's manageable."

"Sell it, you can pay off some other debt."

"Mmm," said David. "That's a possibility."

"You think there's another way out of the hole you dug yourself?"

"Maybe." The room was charged with electricity. One wrong move, and the whole thing could short circuit, his whole life could implode. But he had to do *something*. He couldn't just give in without putting up *some* resistance.

The silence was the loudest thing he'd ever heard.

Hein rapped his beer on the end table and David jumped at the sound. "All right, enough bullshit, when do I get the second installment? It better be soon."

David tried to concentrate on navigating the minefield successfully, but he found himself distracted by the language Hein had used.

Installment? Why *installment*? As if that word gave the situation some sort of legal status, turned it into an honest business transaction.

"Well?" said Hein. "Let's hear it."

Chapter 26

Lucas sat in the tram, his gym bag in his lap. The grip end of his baseball bat stuck out a few inches, and a woman sitting across from him eyed it with suspicion. At the next stop, she got up and moved to the front of the car.

It was a pleasure to get away from his parents for the evening. The practice session had done him good, although not many of his teammates were around over the holidays. And winter training was kind of lame. Baseball was a summer sport. Still, it didn't hurt to get out of the cold and get in an hour of strength and conditioning time. He and the others had done some jogging around the track, run some sprints, hit the ground for sit-ups and push-ups, and then taken batting practice from the automatic pitching machine, which threw a mean curve.

After BP, he'd taken a long hot shower. And burning off calories had given him new determination. He was ready to take on the world, and definitely ready to take another run at that scumbag attorney. Why not? And that would stall off the next round of parental recrimination by another hour or two, an added bonus.

☙

"Yeah, and if you were stupid enough to walk right in with your eyes wide open, it's not my problem. You got nobody to blame but yourself for that one." Hein was smiling broadly, as if they were talking about a silly little goof that had cost David no more than a hundred Euros.

"The Papaya Resort doesn't exist," said David. "No bungalows, no swimming pools, nothing."

"Right. So now you know. You got another beer? I'm dying of thirst."

"No."

"Not hospitable, *David.*" He put exaggerated stress on David's name, turning it into an insult. "I'll get it," he said, standing up. "You want one?"

David sat perfectly still.

"Suit yourself."

Hein came back with a bottle in his hand. "Kind of a pigsty in the kitchen. You need to clean up in there, D Square. Hey, I'm a poet and I don't—"

David cut him off. "I told you not to call me that anymore."

"Aw, and it's such a nice little pet name. But, fine, if you're tired of it, out it goes. No problem."

David sat silently.

"But we have other problems to resolve, Mr. Driessen, i.e. the money you owe me. That's a pretty significant problem. Dangerously significant, you might say." He took a piece of paper from his inside jacket pocket, unfolded it, and laid it on the table. "Check this out. You signed it, in Knokke, right before you went upstairs with that hooker."

Yes, it was his signature. Shaky, drunken, but undeniably his. Above it, columns of figures, a lot of figures. He had a good idea what they added up to: complete ruination.

It was time to play his trump card. "I've got some papers, too," he said. He pushed the stack of photocopied transactions over to Hein.

Hein gave them a cursory glance. "Interesting. What do you think you're going to do with these?"

David tried to keep his voice from shaking. "I'd rather not do anything with them, but the FIIS might like to get a look at them."

"Is that your game? So now the claws come out, eh?"

David picked his words carefully. "You're forcing me into it, Hein. I don't have any other choice. There's no way I can pay you what you want."

"Come on, everything was going just fine."

"For *you*, sure."

Hein went on unperturbed. "Everything was fine until you started making trouble. First you won't give me a key to the office, then you don't want me meeting Hoogestijn there, and then I ask you to move a little money around for me, and what does the High and Mighty David Driessen say? 'Noooo, I'm not plaaaying anymore.' I can't let you get away with shit like that, don't you understand? I can't let some dipshit lawyer fuck with me."

David held his tongue.

"So you opened up the envelope and made some copies." Hein sipped his beer. "Not exactly playing by the rules, counselor." The edge had gone out of his voice. He seemed almost friendly, as if he was ready to come to terms. But then he turned hard again. "I figured you'd pull some shit like this. What do you think the bigwigs will say about you copying a client's confidential documents?"

"Don't you talk to me about playing by the rules!" David exploded.

Hein spread his hands helplessly. "I don't understand it," he sighed. "First we're friends, we go out, we have fun—you even try to look more like me, with that short haircut and the contacts. No, don't tell me you never thought of it that way. But then, boom, that's all history and you start kicking up a fuss, just because I want to get back some of my money. I mean, what's wrong with that? It's not like I'm your personal cash machine."

"Let me make this clear." David pointed at the papers he'd passed across to Hein. "Those are copies of copies. You can have them. The originals are somewhere else, somewhere you can't get at them."

"The man's prepared," said Hein. "So, what do you want?"

This was the moment David had been preparing *for*. His plan was to propose a deal that would benefit them both—though him perhaps more than Hein. He knew he was playing for the highest possible stakes, but he couldn't see any alternative.

"I want us to reset a couple of things," he said. "I'll give you all the copies of those documents—*all* of them, I won't keep a set for myself—and you wipe out the Papaya Resort loan. The rest of what I owe you, we'll work out a payment schedule, something I can actually handle, and I won't say a word about the Papaya fraud to anyone. And then we go our separate ways, Hein, we don't have anything more to do with each other. I think that's best for both of us."

Hein nodded thoughtfully and set his beer bottle down on the table.

Good, David thought, *he's thinking about it.*

The room remained quiet for more than a minute.

And then Hein sprang to his feet, grabbed David, and flung him to the floor. The desk lamp fell over, and its bulb shattered.

David's head smashed against the table leg. He felt a searing pain. He touched the side of his head, and his hand came away damp and sticky with blood. Hein loomed over him.

"I'm about this close to kicking the shit out of you, *David*, you understand that?"

Fighting against the pain, David weighed his chances. If he rolled into Hein's feet, maybe he could knock him down. Was there anything he could use to knock him out? The beer bottle? Probably not big enough to do any real damage. He remembered the way Hein had crippled that hulking guy at the gas station.

"There's not gonna be any deal," Hein said. "You're gonna hand over all those copies, you're gonna keep your fucking mouth shut about Papaya, and you're gonna pay me every cent you owe me. *That's* the deal. Do you understand?"

David felt his head again. It was still bleeding.

Hein kicked him in the ribs.

David gasped in pain. He touched his side gingerly. He didn't think anything was broken.

Hein reached into his jacket pocket. David couldn't see what he took out, but he feared the worst. He lost control of his bladder. His crotch became warm and wet.

"I asked you a question, you dumb fuck. You gonna answer me, or you want this fishhook in your face? I'd love to see you yank it out." Hein waved a wicked looking knife in front of David's eyes and laughed raucously, as if he'd heard a truly world class joke. "Think you got more nerves in your lip than a fucking fish?"

❡❡

A gentle rain was falling. Lucas tipped his head back and let the heavens sprinkle his face. It was wonderfully refreshing and filled him with energy.

He knew where Driessen's house was. When he was about fifty feet away, the light in the front window went out. Was Driessen already going to bed? No, probably not, it was only 10:15. Maybe he was on his way out. Lucas could catch him in the street, on neutral ground, where the lawyer wouldn't automatically be his superior, as he would be on his own turf.

He waited. The door opened, and Driessen came out. He looked a little taller than Lucas remembered. The streetlight was out, so he didn't have a clear view.

Lucas trotted after him. "Hey, wait up," he called.

Driessen spat "Fuck off!" over his shoulder and walked on.

Again, again that arrogant, holier-than-thou attitude, as if he was king of the hill, as if nobody and nothing but himself mattered worth a damn.

Lucas followed him. He slid the bat from his gym bag. "Hey, I want to talk to you!"

Without slackening his pace, Driessen said, "Get the fuck away from me."

Lucas swung the bat at his arm, not hard, but hard enough to hurt. Driessen clutched his shoulder, swearing.

"How 'bout now?" Lucas said. "You think you might have a minute for me?"

"Who sent you?" asked Driessen. "Ben? Some of John's old pals?"

"What are you talking about?"

They stood facing each other, a few feet apart.

Driessen pulled a knife from his pocket. The blade glinted in the pale moonlight.

Lucas thought, *What's a lawyer doing with a switchblade?*

He took his best home-run swing.

や

After Hein slammed the door behind him, David dragged himself upstairs. He examined his head in the mirror above the bathroom sink. He rinsed off the blood and bandaged the wound. Then he pulled on fresh boxers and trousers and went down to clean up the living room.

His desk lamp was shattered beyond repair. That was the last remnant of his student days.

Hein had taken all the papers, even the brochure for the Papaya Resort.

David lay on the couch. There was half a bottle of whiskey in the armoire in his study. He really wanted a drink but was too beat to tackle the stairs again.

Hein would be back. Next time, he'd probably bring 'Stache, and they'd finish the job. Hein wasn't one to leave things half done, that was now unavoidably clear.

He heard a police siren outside, then it was quiet again. The patrol car must have stopped here in the street. Groaning with pain, David struggled to his feet. He pulled the curtains aside, but all he could see was rotating blue roof lights in the distance.

He opened the front door. Across the street, other residents were coming out of their houses. The police car was parked in the middle of the road, a couple hundred feet away.

David's upstairs neighbor came over. "Any idea what's going on?"

"No, I—"

A second police siren and the wail of an ambulance drowned him out.

"I'm going to have a look," said the neighbor. "You coming?"

"Let me get a jacket and my keys."

A crowd had gathered, maybe thirty people. Several uniformed officers were holding them back. A man was lying in the gutter. Even from ten feet off, you could see blood streaming from his head. Two EMTs were kneeling beside him.

David's legs felt rubbery, his vision blurred. He wanted to say something, but he had no voice. He thought he might have to vomit.

"What's the matter?" asked his neighbor. "You're white as a ghost."

A woman complained loudly that they weren't even safe in their own street anymore.

The EMTs slid a collapsible gurney from the back of the ambulance.

"Is it someone from the block?"

"I can't see."

David knew who it was.

৩

Lucas stood on a bridge over a canal, leaning against the railing, gasping for breath.

He'd been running for at least half a mile. He'd dropped the gym bag at some point, but the bat was still clenched in his right hand. Should he go back for his bag? No, too dangerous. Were those sirens he heard?

A man came up to him. "You okay? You need some help?"

Lucas shook his head.

"Should I call somebody? Are you sick?"

"I'll be all right." Lucas stood up straight, wondering if the blood on the bat was visible in this light. "Thanks."

The man eyed him closely, not completely satisfied. "You sure?"

"I'm sure. Thanks again."

The man moved off, then paused and turned back. *Keep going*, Lucas thought. *Get out of here!*

When the man was out of sight, he considered throwing the bat into the canal, but he wasn't sure if it would sink or float. He walked on, putting more distance between himself and Driessen's house.

Up ahead, there was a dumpster standing before a building that was apparently undergoing renovation. He thrust the bat beneath some old boards and piled trash over it, hiding it from view.

❦

Mirjam's phone rang. She set down her book.

Thera smiled at her. "David again?"

No, there was a number she didn't recognize on the screen.

"Mirjam Zighorst."

"Hi, it's Anneli. Steven's sister?"

"Oh, hi."

"How are you?"

"Coping, I guess." These last days, she sometimes found herself getting through a whole hour without thinking of Steven. Now that she heard his sister's voice, though, images of their time together flooded through her mind. *Steven.* She had the urge to say his name aloud.

"I'm sorry to bother you," said Anneli, "but it's important."

Mirjam wondered what could possibly be important now. Had they caught the killer? Her heart pounded with excitement.

"We've sold Steven's house. It all happened really suddenly, and we have to close on December 31. It's crazy timing, but there's nothing we can do about it. I think the buyer needs to close before New Year's for tax reasons."

Mirjam's pulse slowed to normal.

"So we have to empty the place out as fast as we can," Anneli continued.

"I understand."

"And I thought you might like to have something of Steven's. I don't know, something to remember him by. So that's why I'm calling."

"That's very thoughtful, but—"

"Just think about it. You've got my number. Can you call me tomorrow?"

❦

David stayed up all night, clicking restlessly through Dutch news sites. The first story was posted a little after 6 AM:

"At around 11 o'clock last night, real-estate magnate Hein W. was murdered. He was found lying in a residential street in Amsterdam-South, bleeding from a wound inflicted by an unidentified blunt object. The police have released no further information as yet, but usually reliable sources within the department have told us that there are no suspects at this time. The victim was well known in real estate circles, and his name has been mentioned in connection with several criminal matters, including the murder of John van B. several months ago. The police are apparently looking into the possibility that the killing of Hein W. may be a case of gangland retribution."

David swore. So Hein steps out of his house, and minutes later he gets sent off to the happy hunting grounds. Maybe Hein himself was no longer a threat, but what would Simon Berghoek and the rest of Hein's underworld buddies think? Various scenarios danced around in his head. Depending on how much they knew about the David-Hein relationship, they might figure he'd dispatched him himself. Or maybe they'd suspect he'd ratted Hein out to some competitor. There was no way they'd miss the fact that Hein had been killed practically outside his front door.

Within half an hour, other sites had picked up the story. Slightly different words, but the same basic information. David took a shower and let the water caress him for almost half an hour as he thought his way through the question of what to tell the police if they showed up asking whether or not Hein had been to see him last night. It would be stupid to deny it. Hein had stuffed all those documents in his pocket, including the brochure from the fake Caribbean resort. David couldn't remember if his name was on any of the pages.

He made coffee. There wasn't any bread. Later, he'd go out and pick up some croissants. Would it make good strategic sense to check in with the authorities, rather than waiting for them to come to him?

∾

It felt strange to ring this doorbell again. Of course, she could have used her own key—she still carried it in her purse—but that didn't seem right. She should probably return the key to Anneli.

"Who is it?"

"Mirjam."

The door clicked open. Anneli was at the top of the stairs,

Mirjam climbed up, her steps heavy. She'd been thinking about what she might like to have from Steven's apartment. Maybe that watercolor of a dreamy riverine landscape that hung in his bedroom. How many times had she lay in his arms, in his bed, gazing at that picture? Perhaps someone else from the family had already laid claim to it, but she couldn't think of anything else she wanted.

Anneli hugged her. "I know this is hard."

Mirjam swallowed. "Yes, it is."

"For us, too."

"Of course."

Once the apartment was empty, Steven would be truly gone. His name would live on at Veenstra & Watzlawick, but that was just a name.

They were in the living room. The plants in the window niches were all dead. The TV and stereo were already gone.

"The movers are coming tomorrow. I think the buyer's going to remodel, knock out a couple of walls, upgrade the bathroom."

Mirjam looked around. That etching beside the door? The blow-up poster of a box of laundry soap? No. The framed photo of a cat cleaning its face with a delicate paw? Steven had joked that the picture was a pet he didn't have to feed or clean up after. It was cute, but it didn't really touch her. Maybe because she'd already made up her mind.

"I've always liked this one." Anneli picked up a picture of a gang of children jumping off a bridge into a canal. There was a thin girl standing off to one side, watching. You could see she was shivering with cold.

"It's nice."

Anneli put the picture down and went into the bedroom. Mirjam followed her. She looked around, pretending—she couldn't have said why— as if she weren't sure.

She went over to the watercolor. There were tears at the corners of her eyes, and she tried not to let them fall. "This," she said. "Would you mind?"

"No, that's fine. You can take it with you." Anneli leaned over the bed. "Here."

They were back in the foyer. Mirjam looked around, one final time, the framed watercolor clasped to her breasts. This was the last time she would ever see this apartment, and she tried to absorb it into her bloodstream so it would be part of her forever. Later, she could add herself into the scenes, add the two of them together, side by side.

Then she saw it.

A scarf, draped casually on the coatrack.

She recognized it immediately. She'd bought it herself, about a year ago. She remembered having trouble writing the Sinterklaas poem. The best she'd been able to come up with was a weak reference to the Ricky Gervais series she and David sometimes watched after the kids were in bed, something like *when you're wearing this scarf, you'll be having a larf.*

Silly.

ɕↄ

"David Driessen, attorney."

"Biesterbos here. Can you come down to the station today?"

"Let me check my calendar." There was no calendar. "I've got some time around four tomorrow afternoon."

"Today, please," said Biesterbos.

David understood. Hein's body was still warm, so to speak, so they had to move the investigation forward as quickly as they could. If a murder wasn't solved within two or three days, the chance that it ever would be declined precipitously.

He tapped a few random keys on his computer. "Well, if I shift some things around, I can make it around 4:45 today."

Biesterbos would notice the bandage on his forehead, but he'd make up some story to explain it away.

"Fine, a quarter to five. We appreciate your cooperation."

ɕↄ

David got to Biesterbos' office at 4:55 PM. He'd resolved to acknowledge right off that Hein Wesseling had visited him at home the previous evening. Wesseling was a client, and they'd discussed several business matters. He could list a few names that had come up in their meeting: John van Bremen, Ben Heuvelink, Simon Berghoek…

Yes, after his client's departure, he'd heard sirens in the street, but he'd had no idea that Wesseling had been attacked until he'd heard it on the news. There was nothing in their conversation that seemed in any way relevant to the investigation.

David knocked on the door.

"Come."

He went in.

The detective was sitting behind his desk, all smiles. "Ten minutes late, but at least you're here. Have a seat." He waved at a chair.

Then David saw it. His scarf, in a plastic bag on Biesterbos' desk, the scarf Mirjam had given him. He'd left it in Hein's car, and Hein had mentioned it several times. But what did it have to do with Hein's murder?

"I can see," said Biesterbos, "that you recognize it."

"I used to have one just like it. I lost it, a few months ago. Is there some connection to Hein Wesseling's murder?"

"Hein Wesseling?" Biesterbos looked at him strangely. "That's not my case. I'm still working on Steven Veenstra."

"Veenstra?"

"Can you explain the fact that your scarf was found in Mr. Veenstra's apartment, although you told me repeatedly that you'd never been there?"

The walls collapsed, the windows shattered, and the floor opened beneath him.

Acknowledgments

I'd like to thank the following people, who provided information and advice as I worked on this book: an attorney who prefers to remain anonymous, Ton Anbeek, Elsa den Boer, Frank Bovenkerk, Christine Degenaar, Harry Lensink, Anne Coos Vuurmans, and Kanta van Zonneveld.

Invaluable resources included Marian Husken and Harry Lensink's *Handboek Holleeder* (Uitgeverij Balans, 2007) and Coen Verbraak's *Strafpleiters: Kijken in de Ziel* (Uitgeverij Thomas Rap, 2011).